PORTIA MACINTOSH ⸺ long as she can remember ⸺ ⸺ blaming her siblings for that broke⸺ ⸺ was growing up, blagging her way backstage d⸺ ⸺ her rock chick phase or, most recently, whatever justification she can fabricate to explain away those lunchtime cocktails, Portia just loves telling tales.

After years working as a music journalist, Portia decided it was time to use her powers for good and started writing novels instead.

Bestseller Portia writes hilarious romcoms, drawing on her real life experiences to show what it's really like being a woman today – especially one who doesn't quite have her life together yet.

Visit Portia at portiamacintosh.com

Also by Portia MacIntosh

Love and Lies at the Village Christmas Shop

PORTIA MACINTOSH

ONE PLACE. MANY STORIES

HQ
An imprint of HarperCollins*Publishers* Ltd
1 London Bridge Street
London SE1 9GF

This paperback edition 2018
3

First published in Great Britain by
HQ, an imprint of HarperCollins*Publishers* Ltd 2018

A catalogue record for this book is
available from the British Library.

ISBN: 9780008310134

MIX
Paper from
responsible sources
FSC
www.fsc.org   FSC™ C007454

This book is produced from independently certified FSC™ paper

to ensure responsible forest management.

For more information visit: www.harpercollins.co.uk/green

Printed and bound by
CPI Group (UK) Ltd, Croydon, CR0 4YY

For
J K J A J P
B T D

Prologue – 1998

'Holly Jones, what have you done?' I hear my mum ask through gritted teeth, with enough volume to show that she's angry, but not so much that the shop full of customers can hear her.

I remove my nose from my copy of *Harry Potter and the Philosopher's Stone* to see what exactly my sister has done now. I wouldn't usually jump to conclusions, but this is Holly, and Holly will do anything if it has enough shock value.

We went our separate ways at the school gates no more than a couple of hours ago. Holly wanted to go into town with her mates for a while before tea, but I wanted to come here and read my book, sitting on my stool behind the counter of my mum's Christmas shop. I always enjoy spending time here but now that it's December – and actually Christmas time – the place feels all the more magical.

This afternoon the shop is overflowing with tourists, who have travelled from all over to check out Marram Bay's open-year-round Christmas shop. Christmas Every Day is so much more than just a shop though, it's like a magical Santa's work-shop, with wall-to-wall Christmas decorations and gifts, with glitter and twinkly lights everywhere you look. Mariah Carey's 'All I Want For Christmas Is You' is pumping out through speakers around the shop. It's such an infectious song, which you can't help but love and sing along to. I'm not even sure I can name another Mariah Carey song, but this one is a Christmas classic.

Despite the trees in the shop being artificial (they do have to stay up all year round, after all), my mum has these special pine air fresheners which, combined with the locally made gingerbread she's selling at the counter at the moment, give the place a real, irresistible Christmassy smell that I can't get enough of. Perhaps my favourite part of all – and a favourite feature of many of the customers who visit the shop – is the steam train that runs on a track around the shop, over bridges, through tunnels and even around the shop Christmas tree that stays up all year.

From the second you walk through the door there's just this magical feeling in the air. That warm, hopeful, festive feeling you only get at Christmas time. It makes you want to eat gingerbread, sing carols and be happy with your loved ones – and I get to experience it all year round.

But while I might share my mum's love and passion for all things festive, my twin sister Holly absolutely does not. In fact, she has such a strong dislike for the most wonderful time of year that she always acts up around the holidays. And now, here she is, like clockwork, on 1st December, with a drastic new hairstyle that my mum did not sign off on.

Holly's previously shoulder-length blonde hair, along with her hairline and most of her neck, is now bright red.

'It's just like Lisa Scott-Lee's,' my sister says, running both (stained red) hands through her hair, by way of an explanation. I think it's safe to say that her obsession with Steps has reached its peak.

'You're my 14-year-old daughter, you're not Lisa Scott-Lee,' my mum reminds her as she serves a customer. When the shop is so busy, my mum is forced to parent around working – or work around parenting, whichever needs to take priority at the time.

I laugh quietly to myself, although not quietly enough.

'Oh, should I want to be a wizard when I grow up, like Ivy does?' she says mockingly.

I clutch my book to my chest self-consciously.

The customer my mum is serving laughs as she watches our little family drama play out in front of her.

'Sisters, huh?' she says to my mum politely, like perhaps she has daughters of her own, and she knows exactly how tricky they can be.

'Would you believe they're twins?' my mum replies. 'Non-identical, in both appearance and interests. Fascinating really. Can I get you anything else?'

'No, that's great, thanks.'

'Have a very merry Christmas,' my mum says brightly as she hands over a receipt, before turning her attention back to Holly. 'Who did that for you?'

'I did it myself,' she says proudly. 'Only 99p from Boots.'

'Will it come out?'

'Yeah, well, in three washes,' she admits.

'Can you go and get started on the first wash now then, please,' my mum asks gently.

'I thought you'd like it,' Holly persists. 'Red is festive.'

My mum laughs wildly. 'You're not going to convince me you did this in tribute to Christmas – you hate Christmas.' We all know Holly hates Christmas; she's not exactly shy about it.

Right on cue, Wizzard's 'I Wish It Could Be Christmas Every Day' starts playing. Holly rolls her eyes.

'OK, fine,' she whines.

'Oh, Holly,' my mum calls after her. 'Ivy was looking for her boot-cut jeans. Have you taken them?'

'No, burglars broke in, and only stole Ivy's jeans,' she replies sarcastically as she disappears up the stairs.

'Never have teenagers,' my mum tells me once Holly has stormed upstairs. I blink at her. 'You don't count; you're not like a teenager. You're an angel.'

I smile.

'Holly doesn't think Christmas is cool,' I tell her. It's not a very good explanation, but it's all I have.

'Not cool like Steps.' My mum laughs. 'She's going to be mortified, when she's in her thirties and someone reminds her she used to wear a cowboy hat.'

With a moment of calm at the till between customers, my mum takes my natural long blonde hair in her hands, combing it with her fingers.

'It's no surprise your sister is sick of Christmas,' my mum reasons. 'She does live in a Christmas shop that's open all year round. You're lucky you love it as much as I do. For her, it must be torture.'

I replace my bookmark and close my book, setting it down to one side.

'Have you always loved Christmas?' I ask, because I realise I haven't actually asked her that question before.

'I have,' my mum says with a smile. 'This shop is my dream come true. Like now, in December, it's so wonderful to see people coming in, all excited for the holidays, looking for quirky decorations to hang on their trees, or unique little gifts to give their loved ones. I love it in the summer too, though, when tourists come in from the baking-hot sun, usually after a day catching rays on the beach – they literally step into Christmas and that pleasantly baffled look on their faces is one I never grow tired of.'

'I can't wait to work here,' I tell her. Ever since I was little, all I've wanted to do is help out in the shop. My mum sometimes gives me little jobs to do, so that I think I'm working here, but now that I'm a teenager, I'm hoping she'll let me work here properly one day soon.

'And I can't wait for you to help out, but you need to finish school first,' my mum insists.

I smile as I watch a dad lifting up a little girl so she can choose a bauble from the tree. She delicately removes a glass bauble with a white feather inside – a great choice; I've always loved that one. We have the exact same one on our tree in the living room upstairs.

I feel my smile drop as I think about my own dad. It doesn't matter how many Christmases go by since he passed away, I still miss him now more than ever. They say these things get easier with time but every time I see something that belonged to him, someone mentions his name, or I see a happy child playing with their dad, it gets me. I miss him so much.

'You know, apart from you and your sister, this shop is the thing I'm the most proud of. It's practically like one of my kids.' She laughs. 'It's taken a lot more raising than you – probably less than Holly, but don't tell her that.'

I giggle.

'I like to think about when you and Holly are grown up, happily married, with kids of your own. I imagine you bringing them here and then, after I'm gone, I don't know... I imagine the shop being in the family for years, generation after generation. That's silly, isn't it?'

'That's not silly,' I reassure her.

'You're a sweetheart, Ivy Jones, but you know I'd never expect either of you to work here. I'm sure you've got your own big ideas for the future.'

'Mum, I mean it. We'll keep the shop going forever.'

'That's my girl,' she says, squeezing my hand before turning to serve yet another smiling customer, delighted by the armful of Christmas decorations they have selected.

I'm not sure whether or not she believes me, or if she's just humouring me, but I'm serious. I know how much this shop means to my mum. I'll always be here to help.

I hear thudding on the floor upstairs – most likely Holly working on her routine to '5, 6, 7, 8'. Holly might not care about Christmas or the shop, but I do. I know how important this shop is to my mum and I'll always do whatever it takes to keep it going.

Chapter 1

I sit up in my bed and stare straight ahead, as though that might make my ears more efficient. Did I just hear something or was I dreaming?

After a few seconds I hear the noise that woke me again and realise it's a knock at the door.

I grab my phone from next to me and look at the time. Uh-oh, it is 8.45, which means I've overslept – I never oversleep.

I grab my brown reindeer dressing gown (complete with antlers on the hood) and throw it on over my nightshirt before dashing downstairs to answer the door, combing my hair with my fingers and wiping sleep from my eyes as I hurry down the stairs.

As I approach the shop front door, I can just about see Pete, the postman, on the other side of the glass, which, now that I think about it, I maybe went a little too heavy on with the spray snow. The white, frosty edges frame his face, giving him this angelic white glow. I don't suppose I look so festive from where he's standing; all he'll be able to see is me hurrying across the shop floor undressed, with my bed head hair, fumbling with my keys.

He waves at me, all smiles, as I unlock and open the door.

'Hello, Ivy, sorry, did I wake you?' he apologises as he clocks my dressing gown.

'Hey, Pete. I'm glad you did,' I admit. 'I need to open the shop in 15 minutes.'

'It's not like you to sleep in,' he says, handing me a parcel. 'Is everything OK?'

'Everything is fine,' I assure him. I don't tell him that I was up late looking over my finances, worrying a few years' worth of wrinkles onto my face until I finally dropped off some time after 3 a.m. 'I was up late reading.'

'Now that I believe.' He laughs. 'Is that what's in there?'

Is there not some kind of law that prohibits postmen from asking you what's in your parcel? There could be anything in this box – what if I'd ordered some super sexy lacy underwear or something? I mean, it *is* from Amazon, and it is book-shaped, but still. I'm not always so predictable (I am).

'Yep, another book,' I tell him. 'Something to read while I'm working.'

'Business still quiet?' Pete asks.

'Yeah,' I say with a sigh. 'It's December 1st though, so things should pick up a little.'

'I'll be in for a few bits,' he assures me.

'Thank you.'

'I'm sure I had something to tell you,' he says, hovering outside the door. I appreciate that it must be uncomfortable, talking about my difficult livelihood – especially for the man who delivers my bills. I usually enjoy his friendly small talk, but today I just want to get back inside and get some clothes on.

Pete furrows his brow for a second, visibly racking his brain until he has a thought. The second it hits him his face relaxes again.

'Oh, some gossip for you,' he starts, setting his bag down on the floor and taking his phone from his pocket. 'I saw a man in town today.'

'A man?' I gasp, faking shock.

Pete laughs. 'No, like…a mysterious man. He isn't a local, and

8

he doesn't look like a tourist. He's walking around, wearing a suit, carrying a briefcase. Seems like he's scoping the place out.'

'Hmm. For what, I wonder.'

'Indeed,' Pete replies. 'I snapped a photo of him, put it in the Facebook group. Just in case he's one of those white-collar criminals – you know, in case he steals something or what have you.'

'I don't think a white-collar criminal is just a criminal in a suit,' I point out with a laugh.

'See,' Pete says, holding up his phone to show me a photo of a man in a suit, eyeing up a building on Main Street. 'He's weird.'

He's gorgeous – but I don't say this out loud. I study the photo for a moment, as my head fills with fiction-worthy reasons why this mysterious man might be hanging around town. The eligible bachelors in this town are few and far between. All the good ones are taken. This guy is definitely not from round here – take it from a single girl who knows.

'Weird,' I say in agreement, pushing all fantasies of handsome, mysterious strangers from my mind. 'Well, I'd better get on with opening up the shop.'

'Yes, I suppose the post won't deliver itself,' he says. 'Not yet, anyway.'

I don't have the heart to point out that emails are pretty much that.

'Same time tomorrow,' he says as he walks off down the path.

'Yeah, if I don't sleep in,' I joke. 'Have a good day.'

I watch Pete head for his van before he drives off. My lonely little shop is his only stop here. The shop sits alone, on a quiet country road, outside the town. It's an old, stone cottage, which used to be a big house, sitting smack bang in the middle of a massive, beautiful garden. Just like a house, it has a little gate at the bottom of the garden, and a cute little pathway that leads up to the shop doorway.

When my mum took on the place, she converted the downstairs of the cottage into the shop, with a kitchen at the back, and the upstairs became our living space. It was strange, growing up above a shop when all my friends lived in big houses, but come summer time, when I had this massive garden to play in, I didn't think twice about how cramped things were indoors.

I notice a bill, hiding under my package. I shove it in my dressing gown pocket, to be worried about at a later date – probably tonight, when I should be sleeping.

I unlock the fire exit at the back of the shop before flicking the switch that turns on every fairy light, every musical statue and snow machine. The things that make the shop seem alive, even when there's no real people in it.

I check the shop floor to see if anything is out of place, or if any rubbish is lying around, before turning the sign around on the door to say that we're open…for all the good it will do. I don't tend to see any customers until the afternoon mid-week – usually tourists in the middle of a hike, or, at this time of year, the occasional local in need of some new decorations or wrapping paper.

I was only standing in the doorway chatting for ten minutes and I'm positively freezing. I'm almost always freezing, sometimes even in the heat of summer. I don't know how long it has been since my last summer holiday, but I'm pretty sure it's a double-digit number of years now. I don't like to think about it; it makes me feel old.

What I need right now is a steaming-hot cinnamon latte, with a generous dollop of whipped cream and a sprinkling of tiny golden white chocolate stars, to make it extra festive. I'll make myself a drink, warm up a little and then head upstairs to throw some clothes on before the lunchtime rush which, yesterday, was a whopping four people.

I plonk myself down on the stool behind the counter and fire up the usual Christmas playlist. The dulcet tones of Mud drift from the speakers, with 'Lonely This Christmas' – not exactly the vibe I need this morning.

I take my phone from my dressing gown pocket and load up

the Marram Bay residents' group on Facebook. It's a private group, strictly for locals and businesses in Marram Bay and over on Hope Island, mostly used for selling things, announcements and a good old gossip. People in small towns just love to talk – mostly about each other.

Today's gossip du jour is the 'mysterious man' Pete was telling me about. I see Pete's paparazzi-style photo of a man wearing a suit, and carrying a briefcase, and otherwise not doing anything at all unusual other than being uncharacteristically good-looking. A glance at the comments tells me more about the man. He's been spotted all over town this morning, driving around in his convertible Porsche – some reckon he's a professional athlete buying one of the mansions that sits just outside town, someone else swore blind it was Henry Cavill, while someone else has corrected them that, no, it was in fact Jamie Dornan.

It's only now that I'm thinking about it that I realise Henry and Jamie do actually look quite similar and the thought of this man being a hybrid of the two is, coincidentally, exactly what I asked Santa for this year – well, it would be, if I were remotely interested in having a man in my life.

Hmm, no, he's definitely not a famous actor. I suppose he could be a sportsman. He's got the build for it, but I don't know nearly enough about sports to recognise anyone other than David Beckham.

Perhaps he's a prince, visiting from a sexy European country, looking for a woman to be his queen, or maybe he's a spy, deep under cover in Marram Bay for some Secret Service operation… Perhaps I've just read too many books.

Speaking of which, I unwrap my latest Amazon package to find a copy of *Little White Lies*, the latest Mia Valentina romcom. I do feel guilty, buying books when money isn't exactly great, but the day I begrudge myself a £3.99 book (when reading is my favourite thing to do) is the day I really need to think about selling a kidney.

You can't beat a good book, can you? The way it just drags you in, taking you into someone else's life, into their home, their relationship – into their everything. It's a sneak peek into something you don't usually get to see, and I think that's why I love it so much. Whether I'm walking through the streets in King's Landing in *A Game of Thrones* or being a fly on the wall in Nick and Amy's house in *Gone Girl*, people are living a million lives far more interesting than mine, and with books, I get to live them too.

I have my coffee, I have my book, I'm all snuggly and warm in my dressing gown. I know that I won't have any customers until after lunch at least, because I never do, so there's no harm in starting my book and enjoying my drink before I head back upstairs to get ready. One chapter turns into two, and before I know it my cup is empty and I'm almost four chapters deep. I'll finish this one and then I'll get back to reality.

'Hello,' I hear a man's voice say in an attempt to get my attention.

I glance up from my book to see *him* standing in front of me – the mystery man, the athlete, the Henry Cavill-Jamie Dornan hybrid, (almost) all I want for Christmas.

'I'm so sorry,' I say. 'Have you been here long? I used to do the exact same thing when I was younger, just sit here behind the counter, lost in a book while my mum did all the hard work.'

'Am I in your living room?' he asks with a laugh.

I pull a puzzled face as I close my book and place it down in front of me. It's only as I do that I notice the brown sleeves of my reindeer dressing gown and I remember what I'm wearing.

'Oh, God, no, sorry,' I babble. 'It's a long story. This is a shop and we're open. I run the place. I'm Ivy.'

I hope down from my stool and walk around the counter to shake his hand.

'Nice to meet you, Ivy. I'm Seb.'

Seb holds my hand for a few seconds as he peers over my shoulder.

'Are...are those antlers and a red nose on your hood?' he asks with an impossibly cheeky smile.

I feel my cheeks flush the same colour as the nose on my dressing gown. 'Yes,' I reply with an awkward laugh. 'I wasn't expecting any customers yet and it was cold...'

'No, I like it,' he replies. 'It's cute.'

If it's even possible, my blushing intensifies.

'So, business is quiet?' he asks, walking across the shop, picking up a snow globe from the shelf before shaking it up and watching the flakes fall.

I can't help but stare at him – not watch him, really stare at him. Taking him in. Seb must be over 6 feet tall, and he's so muscular that I feel like an elf next to him, my petite, 5'3" frame resulting in me not even coming up to his shoulders.

He has perfectly neat, swept back dark hair, and a thick but short beard – combined with his sexy blue eyes, his chiselled cheekbones and those gorgeous dimples when he smiles are probably the reasons why people so easily mistook him for a Hollywood actor.

'It's picking up for Christmas,' I assure him.

'It's a strange thing, a Christmas shop that's open all year round,' he muses as he strolls around.

'It's not that,' I insist, following him closely. 'My mum opened the place up when I was a kid and it was always heaving back then. I took over, after she died, and we were busy for a while. It's since satnavs became popular. This road used to be the main way into town, so tourists would always pass the shop on their way in or their way out. These days, satnavs lead everyone along the new road, so no one even knows we're here. We get hikers, and other shops let tourists know we're here, and they usually remember to stop by.'

'Hmm,' Seb says thoughtfully. 'So, is it just you working here?'

'You ask a lot of questions,' I point out.

'I do,' he replies. 'It's been said before.'

'What do you do for work?' I ask.

'At the moment, nothing,' he replies.

I raise my eyebrows.

'What?' Seb laughs, and there are those dimples again.

I suddenly remember what I'm wearing and tighten the belt of my dressing gown self-consciously.

'You do nothing?'

'Nope.'

'How does a man who does nothing afford a suit like that? And drive around in a Porsche?' I ask suspiciously.

'You've got me, I'm a drug dealer,' he says sarcastically. 'No, I'm just between jobs at the moment. Does this train work?'

Seb runs his hand along the track until he reaches the miniature steam train that used to run all around the shop.

'Not anymore,' I admit. 'It needs repairing.'

'Shame,' he says. 'I like it.'

'So, you're just taking a break in Marram Bay then?' I ask.

'Just having a look around.'

'Well, if you need someone to show you the sights,' I start, before my brain has chance to catch up with my mouth and reality hits me. What am I saying? This isn't me; I don't talk to men. Well, I do talk to men, most days in fact, but this isn't Pete the postman, this is a *man* man. I don't know what on earth I was thinking, saying that. There's just something about Seb that is drawing me in. I quickly backtrack. 'I'm sure you don't…'

'I might just take you up on that, Ivy,' he replies with a big smile. 'Do all your customers get this kind of special treatment?'

'What customers?' I joke.

Seb takes the snow globe from the shelf and brings it over to the counter. 'Is this Marram Bay, inside?'

'It is. There's a local guy who makes them – I buy them from him.'

'I'll take it.' He grins, placing it down in front of me.

I can't help but wonder if he actually wants the snow globe, or if he's only buying it because he feels sorry for me, for seemingly having no customers. I can appreciate that, to an outsider, a Christmas shop that is always open might not seem like the kind of place that would get much custom, but things *will* pick up in the run-up to Christmas. Either way, I appreciate him buying something. Along with his cheeky smile, Seb has a glimmer of kindness in his eyes, a glimmer that I can't help but notice twinkling when I look at him.

'That's £9.99, please. Would you like me to wrap it up for you?'

'That's OK, I'm going straight to my car,' he says, before furrowing his brow. 'How did you know I drove a Porsche?'

'What?'

'You know what kind of car I drive…'

'Oh, just a guess.'

Seb laughs. 'Is that your party trick? Guessing what kind of car people drive?' he asks.

'Is it even possible for anyone to be able to do that?' I reply.

'Sure,' he tells me. 'Hold out your hand.'

I place my hand out in front me, which Seb takes in his hands, examining my palm. It's amazing, just how warm his hands are compared to mine.

'Let's see…you drive…a Honda HR-V,' he says.

Spooked, I snatch my hand back.

'A gold one,' he adds with a smug grin.

'Ahh, you saw it outside,' I say, suddenly self-conscious that he's seen my 1998 plate Honda. It might be old, but it's an amazing car that never lets me down. It's no convertible Porsche though, that's for sure.

'How could I miss it?' He laughs. 'It's the only car for miles.'

I step out from behind the counter and walk Seb towards the door. He stops in his tracks to say something to me, stopping when he notices the mistletoe hanging above us.

'How seriously do you take Christmas tradition?' he asks with an awkward laugh.

'Pretty seriously,' I say cautiously. 'I pretty much live Christmas every day…'

'Hmm,' he replies.

There's an awkward silence between us, but only for a few seconds. I glance around the room awkwardly until I notice Seb's face just inches from mine. He plants a quick peck on my lips, immediately seeming surprised at himself for doing so. Maybe, as cool and as confident as he seems, he doesn't do this sort of thing often. I guarantee this sort of thing happens to me even less.

'OK, well,' he says, a little flustered, but with a smile on his face. 'See you around, Ivy.'

'Bye,' I call after him, running my fingertips over my lips, where Seb's lips touched them even if it was only for a second. As I sit back down behind the counter, I look at my book. For the first time – maybe ever – something happened to me in real life that was fresh out of a romcom, and I can't quite believe it.

He said 'see you around' when he left – it would be great to see him around, but what are the chances I'll ever see him again? He's not about to need another snow globe anytime soon, is he? He's got a posh, southern accent, and we don't have too many men like that in Marram Bay. We have farmers, fishermen – we even have a guy who makes snow globes, but no well-spoken southern men in flashy suits.

Nope, I don't think I'll ever see him again. But if I do, I really hope I'm not dressed as a reindeer.

Chapter 2

'I need a 110-millimetre hex head bolt,' I say.

'What did I give you?'

'A 35-millimetre hex head bolt.'

'What's the difference?' she asks.

'Exactly 75 millimetres,' I joke. 'Are you OK?'

My sister, Holly, doesn't seem herself today. She never really seems herself around Christmas time – more so now than ever. Growing up in a Christmas shop, with a Christmas-crazy mum, Holly quickly became sick of all things festive. My sister and I are best friends, but around this time of year, she becomes insufferably miserable. She's antisocial, short-tempered and goes into her shell until New Year's Eve, when she's as far away from the festivities as she's ever going to be, when she can draw a line under the year and start afresh. At least I know this though – that fun-loving Holly will be back by January, and it makes it easier to endure, knowing that there's light at the end of the tunnel. I just need to give her the space she needs, and take over the festive duties, and everything will be fine.

My mum's passion for the holidays is one that predates my sister and me – either that, or it's just a huge coincidence that we were named Holly and Ivy. She opened Christmas Every Day so that it could feel like Christmas every day, and as a result we've lived our lives in a snow globe. I think it's more than that these days though. I don't think Holly is just sick of Christmas still; I think it reminds her of Mum. I always miss her so much more at this time of year too.

'I'm fine,' she assures me, brushing the longer side of her freshly cut asymmetrical bob behind her ear.

With Holly's latest short, brown hairstyle, we couldn't look less alike. I still have the long, blonde hairstyle I've had my whole life – I don't like change, or rather, I'm too scared to pull the trigger.

Despite the fact that now, more than ever, Holly and I look absolutely nothing like sisters let alone twins, I think it really suits her. It's her annual 'it's December, I should do something reckless' stunt out of the way, at least.

My sister hands me the bolt I think I need.

'Erm…'

I hesitate, only for a second, and the two pieces I'm trying to connect fall to the floor.

'Ergh, just leave it,' my sister snaps.

'Hey, are you sure you're OK?' I ask, putting down the bolt, taking my sister's hand.

'I'm fine, I'm fine.' She mellows a little. 'It's just – and I would hate for Chloe to hear me say this – but I think we need a man.'

'Can't you do it?' Chloe asks from the doorway.

Holly jumps. 'She's always sneaking up on me, listening to everything.'

'Don't worry,' I reassure her. 'She's too young to think her mum is a bad feminist.'

Chloe, my 7-year-old niece, joins us and sits on my lap. 'Do we need Daddy?' she asks.

'I think we do,' Holly replies, before turning to me. 'It's times like this that I miss Lee.'

'Only times like this?' I laugh.

'I miss him all the time, of course,' she clarifies. 'But, I mean, it's when we need man's work doing that I really feel him not being here.'

'Man's work,' I repeat back to her, grimacing. 'You're letting the patriarchy win.'

She laughs. 'I think I'm just missing Lee; that's why I'm so stressed. I could do with him here to do this. We were crazy to think we could build bunk beds. And don't give me that patriarchy rubbish – it's just genetics. We're both small, with zero upper body strength.'

'When is Lee back?'

'Christmas Eve,' she says with a roll of her eyes. 'Which is not helpful at all.'

Lee, Holly's husband, works in the oil industry. He's a drilling engineer, in Qatar. He works for six weeks, then he's home for three weeks, so Holly has to look after the house and two little kids while he's away, which is probably why she's stressed out so often – especially when there is flat-pack furniture to contend with.

'It's OK, Mum,' Chloe reassures her.

'We could put the Christmas tree up. Would you like that?' I ask.

'Yes,' Chloe squeaks, her eyes lighting up. 'I'll go get Harry.'

Harry, my nephew, is 5 years old, and like his sister, he loves Christmas. With their mum not being much of a fan, I've always stepped up to make Christmas amazing for them, going through all the Christmassy motions, just like my mum used to do for me.

'Thanks,' Holly says. 'I really can't face it.'

'You know I enjoy it,' I tell her. 'And there's no man required.'

We stand up and head downstairs.

'You know, this is why you need a man,' my sister says as we walk downstairs. She's always pointing this out. Holly found a man, got married, had kids and now she's this perfect little housewife. She looks at me, her twin sister, a hardworking spinster, and she wonders where it's all gone wrong for me, why I just can't seem to find a man.

'I need a man because you need a man?' I laugh. 'To build your bunk beds.'

'That and, well, I just don't like to see you alone,' she says softly.

'I'm not alone, I have you and the kids.'

Holly just smiles.

I probably won't tell her that a stranger kissed me yesterday. I don't think that's what she has in mind for me. Anyway, that kind of thing just doesn't happen to girls like me – I doubt she'd believe me anyway.

'Oh, I need a favour,' Holly starts. 'You remember when you played Mary in the school nativity.'

'Most years,' I reply with a chuckle.

My sister rolls her eyes. 'Well, Chloe has been chosen for the part this year and I'm supposed to make her costume. I'd be surprised if you didn't have at least one in all the junk you hoard in your loft. If you do, can Chloe borrow it please?'

'Of course,' I reply. I'm sure I could take a little offence at that if I wanted to, but I won't. I'm pretty sure I'll have every costume I've ever worn up there. I like to hang on to things – especially things that remind me of certain times or events.

As Holly cooks dinner, the kids and I put up the tree. I've never been able to persuade Holly to have a real tree, hard as I've tried. Obviously in the shop I have artificial trees, because I need to keep them up all year round, but I have a real tree in the flat, which, teamed with the fresh popcorn I painstakingly string each year to drape around it, makes the place smell incredible. Holly doesn't want the hassle, though, so we've taken out her good, old artificial tree, and the box of decorations that I've been adding to each year.

If I had the space Holly did – a whole house, instead of a tiny flat above a shop – I'd do so much with my Christmas décor. I used to have a house – although I can't claim it was as big as this one. Still, I would go all-out at Christmas time, decking the halls inside and out. When my mum died Holly wanted to sell the shop, but I wanted to keep it. I wound up selling my house to buy Holly's half, but even though business isn't as good as it used to be, I have no regrets. It would be nice to have more space sometimes though.

I love spending time with my niece and nephew, especially at Christmas time, because there's something all the more magical about seeing Christmas through the eyes of a child. As much as I love it, when you're grown up, Christmas is stripped down, just a little. You can see the commercial side of it, you know there's no Santa Claus, you know that it's a lot of hype and pressure to get everything perfect for just one day of the year. But for the kids, it's still just pure magic. They don't have to go to school, the whole family get together, they get presents and chocolate and watch festive movies all day. Holly might not be a fan of the festivities but the silver lining is that I get to go through all the motions with her kids.

'OK, who wants to put the star on top?' I ask.

'I do, I do,' Harry sings.

'Let him do it,' Chloe says with a casual bat of her hand. She's such a little diva, for a 7-year-old.

I carefully hand Harry the gold star before lifting him up in the air so he can place it at the top of the tree. After a lot of wriggling I lower him back down.

'There we go,' I say. 'I think it looks even better than last year – what do you think?'

'It's amazing,' Chloe says as she admires our handiwork.

'That was some great teamwork,' I tell them. 'Good job.'

Holly walks into the room with a tray of drinks.

'What do you think, Hol?' I ask.

'It's…a tree,' she replies, feigning enthusiasm.

21

'It is a tree,' I reply. 'Do you like it?'

My sister forces a smile. 'It's great,' she eventually says. 'I'd better go check on the chicken.'

My sister hurries back into the kitchen so I leave the kids admiring their handiwork and follow her.

'Are you sure you're OK?' I ask her.

'You know I don't really like Christmas all that much.'

'I know, but you're worse this year,' I point out.

'How's the shop doing?' she asks, changing the subject.

'Meh,' I reply. 'I'm hoping it picks up now it's December. It's just so hard, because no one knows we're there, now that cars don't really drive past anymore.'

'You not fancy going back to plan A?' she asks.

'The shop has always been plan A,' I remind her. 'What you're talking about is just something I did because Mum wanted us to do something different and come back to the shop if we wanted to. And I wanted to.'

Our mum was always adamant we do our own thing; she didn't want us to feel pressured into joining the family business. So, after school, as well as working part-time in the shop, I pursued a career in catering, eventually training in patisserie and confectionery before getting a job at Walters, a shop on Main Street that makes and sells chocolate and sweets. It turned out that cooking was something that came naturally to me, and while I knew the shop was safe in my mum's hands, it was something I was more than happy doing full-time. But then, when my mum died, my priorities changed. I knew that stepping up to take over the shop was the right thing to do.

'That reminds me,' I say, grabbing a bag from under the kitchen table. 'I brought the kids advent calendars from Walters.'

'Oh, I already got them ones.' Holly points to two, not-very-exciting-looking advent calendars.

'Where are they from?' I ask.

'Buy one get one free at the petrol station.'

'These are the ones Mum used to get us,' I say, showing her. 'They deserve special ones.'

'So mine aren't good enough, but amazing Auntie Ivy comes along with her fancy ones and—'

'Hey, I'm not trying to steal your thunder, I just thought they'd love these. I won't say they're from me, just say they're from you.'

'Can I pay you for them?' she asks.

'No, you're my sister, you cannot pay me for them. Just take them.'

With a shake of her head, Holly takes the bag from me.

'Are you sure you're OK?' I ask again. 'I'll stop asking if you want but you just don't seem OK.'

'Ivy, I'm fine,' she says slowly.

'OK,' I say, because what else can I say? But for some reason, I'm just not convinced.

Chapter 3

Today I did not sleep in, nor did I forgo getting dressed before opening up the shop so, despite the usual lack of custom, I'm already having a great day.

I have adjusted the countdown to Christmas (it's 23 days, in case you were wondering), turned up the Christmas music (we're kicking things off with Michael Bublé's cover of 'It's Beginning to Look a Lot Like Christmas', which is much better for morale than yesterday's offering), made myself a cinnamon latte and I'm currently reading my book and tucking into a slice of pistachio panettone that I bought from the deli in town. As mornings go, this isn't a bad start.

I'm not so deep in my book that I don't notice a customer walk in today. As I hear the door, I snap my book shut and place it on the counter.

'Good morning,' I say brightly, snapping into professional mode.

As I look up I realise that it isn't just any customer, it's Seb, here again. He's wearing a grey suit with a long black coat and a black scarf. He's a snappy dresser, with a really stylish, cosmopolitan look that I appreciate.

'Good morning,' the man replies. 'Oh, you're dressed today.'

'I am,' I reply. 'And you're here again – twice in two days – are you after another a snow globe?'

He laughs. 'I am not.'

What is he after then? If he's not here to buy something...is he here for me? He's not...he's not here to ask me out, is he? I mean, I'm flattered, he's obviously good-looking, rich and successful, but I'm not after a fleeting encounter with a tourist.

'I'm just having another look around,' he says. 'Don't let me distract you from your book.'

'Oh, it's fine,' I assure him.

'You a big romance fan?' he asks, eyeballing the cover.

'I'm not just into romance, I'm into a bit of everything,' I reply.

As I watch Seb's eyebrows shoot up I realise that what I just said didn't sound exactly as I intended it.

'I mean as far as reading goes,' I clarify.

'I see.' He laughs again. 'I dated a girl who was obsessed with the *Fifty Shades* books. I didn't see the fascination with those.'

An awkward silence follows.

'Do you read?' I ask him.

'I don't,' he replies. 'But I'm hoping that will change. I've always been so busy so, now, I'm looking for somewhere to settle down, run a small, easy business, where I'll have more free time.'

'That sounds like a good idea,' I reply. 'Where are you thinking of moving?'

'Here,' he replies.

'Oh really?' I reply.

Suddenly, Seb isn't just a tourist. The fact that he might be moving to Marram Bay changes everything. I've always thought I was too busy for relationships but there's just something about Seb... Maybe he's worth breaking my self-imposed man ban for. Business is pretty quiet at the moment, and other than hanging out with my sister's kids, I have almost nothing going on in my life. Maybe I should go on a date with him and see what happens...

even though it's been so long since I went on a date, I don't really remember what's supposed to happen on them. As far as I remember, you just make awkward conversation before feeling largely disappointed, and going home alone. I'm pretty sure that's right.

Seb's phone rings, interrupting our conversation.

'I'm sorry, I really need to take this,' he tells me. 'Maybe I'll pop back in and see you later?'

'I'd like that,' I call after him.

'Great,' he replies. 'There's something I want to talk to you about.'

That sounds ominous… Then again, I did offer to show him the sights, so perhaps he just wants the benefit of my local knowledge.

I try not to think about it – although my mind is racing – busying myself with a few little jobs before grabbing my book again while it's quiet. Just as the story starts to pick up, I hear the door again. It's another familiar face: my landlord.

'Ivy, hello,' he says. 'Are you OK?'

'Sorry, I was miles away,' I say, coming back down to earth as I wonder how long I've been lost in a combination of my thoughts and my book. 'How are you, Mr Andrews?'

'Can't complain,' he says before clearing his throat. 'I need to talk to you.'

'Oh?' is about all I can reply. Suddenly, I'm terrified, racking my brains to figure out when the last time I sent him a rent cheque was, and if it might have bounced.

My mum may have owned the business, but she has always rented the shop and the flat above it from Mr Andrews. So, when my mum died, I didn't just take over the shop, I took over paying the rent too.

'You know Sean, my son?'

I nod.

'Well, he and his family live in Australia and, my wife and I,

26

we're getting on a bit now and, well, we want to join them over there for our retirement.'

'That's lovely,' I reply.

The idea of packing up and starting again in another country is an idea that I can get on board with. Just wiping the slate clean and starting again in a new place with new adventures to be had, rather than spending day after day in the same small village, where one day blurs into the next because nothing ever really happens.

'To do this, though, we need money, so we'll be selling this place.'

'Oh,' I reply. 'So, will I be getting a new landlord?'

'That's what I need to talk to you about,' Mr Andrews replies. 'You know how the shop is in quite a large plot, and, I don't know if you know this, but planning permission is already approved here.'

'Right,' I reply.

'So, that actually makes this place quite valuable to me, but less so with a tenant. Most people who want to buy the place want to knock it down and build something new. I mean, this place has seen better days, hasn't it?'

I feel hurt on behalf of my shop and my home. Sure, the windows maybe need replacing, because as soon as there's a bit of wind they whistle and let cold air in, and maybe the place is a bit tatty, but in a shabby chic, country cottage kind of way.

'OK.'

'I've found a buyer for the place, Ivy, and…well, someone has made me an offer I'd be crazy to refuse, but the offer is on the understanding that I sell the place without a tenant.'

'You want me to leave?' I squeak.

'I don't *want* you to leave, I *need* you to leave,' he clarifies. 'Believe me, if there was some other way, I'd take it. You and your mum have both been excellent tenants. You've always paid on time, never caused me any problems.'

'I don't want to leave,' I tell him firmly. 'I won't leave, in fact. I have rights, you can't just kick me out.'

'Actually, I can,' he replies. 'Your mum's tenancy agreement ran out a long time ago and, well, it's a small place, we all trust each other. We just had a handshake deal. We never renewed anything. I always intended to, and then she passed away and you took over and…it was just an oversight.'

'So, you're telling me I have no rights? And that you're just going to kick me out?'

'Ivy, it sounds awful when you put it like that. But this is the only way I can move closer to my family,' he stresses. 'You're close with your family, you must understand.'

I do, but I don't. How can he do this to me?

'So who is buying the place?' I ask. 'And what are they going to do with it?'

'Perhaps you should have a meeting with the buyer?' he suggests. 'The plans really are something special, and they do have the town in mind.'

'The town, bar one,' I point out.

'Ivy, I'm sorry, but I really need the money if I'm going to emigrate,' Mr Andrews insists. He does sound apologetic, but that doesn't change anything.

'Can't you sell it to me?'

'Can you afford it?' he asks.

'How much is it?'

Mr Andrews takes a folded-up piece of paper from his pocket and hands it to me.

'This is the offer the buyer just made.'

I raise my eyebrows as I look at the astronomically high number.

'How long have I got?' I ask.

'Until you have to leave?'

I was going to say to raise the money, but I suppose the answer to both questions is the same.

'The buyer has a few checks he wants to make but I'm ready to sell when they are ready to buy. I'm going to Australia tomorrow, to look at some houses.'

'What if you held off, until you got back?' I suggest. 'Maybe I can sort something out and you can sell it to me instead.'

'You know I'd rather sell it to you,' Mr Andrews says. He scratches his head. 'Look, I need someone to assist the buyer while I'm away. If you do that, I won't sell until I'm back. If you have the money, I'll sell to you, OK?'

There's something about Mr Andrews' voice – I don't think he thinks I'll be able to get the money together, but he doesn't want to quash my hope. But it doesn't matter if he believes me or not; all that matters is that he agrees. Maybe it's a long shot, but maybe I can get the money together in time. If I can increase business, get a mortgage… There must be lots of options.

'So, assisting the buyer,' I start.

'Just, make them feel welcome, help them take measurements, or do whatever is needed. Answer questions. I'll be back before Christmas. Can you do that?'

'Of course,' I reply. 'I'm a professional.'

'Your mum would be proud of you,' Mr Andrews says. 'I'll give him your number, and tell him that you'll be here, so he can come and talk to you about his plans.'

'OK,' I reply, with faux positivity. 'Have a nice time in Australia.'

Once Mr Andrews is gone, I sit down on my stool and place my hands over my face. I take a few, calming deep breaths. Conscious breathing – that's what Holly calls it. Holly is a big fan of conscious breathing, and always recommends it to me when I'm feeling stressed. Further proof that my sister and I are polar opposites: the reason Holly likes it is the reason I don't. Focusing on your breathing is supposed to remind you that you are breathing, that you're alive. It only reminds me how fragile we are though. I watched my mum take her final breath and then she was gone. I don't like to think about how life hinges on our ability to take a breath. It fills me with panic.

Over the years, this shop has become as important to me as breathing. It's my reason for getting up in the morning, it's my livelihood, it's my way of making sure my mum lives on. And, what, some man in a suit is just going to come in and knock it down? I'll be jobless, homeless... He must not know that, otherwise I'm sure he wouldn't be going through with it. Maybe, if I explain to this buyer, he'll go find somewhere else and, if not, well, I suppose I have until Christmas to try and get the money together. Otherwise...I don't know what I'll do.

Chapter 4

After a long day of few customers and lots on my mind, it's a relief when I finally walk towards the shop door, to turn the open sign to closed. As I approach the door, I see Seb walk up the pathway, and seeing his face instantly perks me up. It's been a tough day, but seeing a friendly face – even a new one – is suddenly making all the difference. For the first time today, I smile.

'Hello,' I say brightly.

'Hey,' he replies.

'You said you would be back,' I say.

He smiles. 'I did.'

'And that you wanted to talk,' I remind him.

'I do.'

'Well, come in, I'll make us a couple of coffees. I made some fruit mince tarts, topped with meringue. You can try one, tell me if they're any good.'

'That would be great,' he says, loosening up a little.

It surprises me that someone so cool, with so much confidence, could be so awkward after one little peck.

I show him into the kitchen and place a coffee and a tart down in front of him.

31

'Wow, you made these? They look amazing,' he says.

'I was a chef in a past life,' I admit.

'I'm happy to see you're still dabbling,' he says, taking a bite. 'Wow, they're incredible.'

'Thanks,' I reply, with a weak smile.

'How are things?' he asks.

'Not ideal,' I tell him honestly. 'I spoke to my landlord today.'

I pause for a second, unsure whether or not someone who is pretty much a stranger is the right person to tell this to. And not only is he someone that I don't know very well, but he's also someone I don't want to scare away by banging on about my problems.

'Do you want to talk about it?' he asks.

'No, it's fine,' I reply.

'You're taking this better than I thought. It's a huge relief,' he says, picking up a second tart.

I stare at him blankly.

'I was worried about telling you,' he clarifies.

'Telling me what?'

'That I'm buying the shop,' he says.

I don't know what I do with my face, but my reaction is all Seb needs to realise that I didn't know *he* was buying the shop.

'Wait, I thought you knew? I thought your landlord had spoken to you?' he asks, suddenly looking even more worried than when he arrived earlier.

I shake my head.

'Oh, Ivy, I'm so sorry,' he says. 'This wasn't how I wanted you to find out. I thought Mr Andrews would have said.'

'He just told me that someone was buying the place, not who or why.'

'Oh…well, me,' he replies, cringing at his own delivery. 'My plan is to knock the place down and build holiday homes.'

'So do that someplace else,' I say angrily, the idea of the shop being knocked down suddenly seeming so much worse than someone else simply buying the place.

'This place is perfect,' he tells me. 'It's the only spot I can find that is big enough, which already has planning permission. There's huge demand for holiday homes in Marram Bay – you can't keep up with the increasing number of tourists. And, well, speaking from a strictly business point of view, there's not much demand for a Christmas shop that's open 12 months of the year.'

I place my hand on my chest. Ouch.

'I just mean from a business point of view,' he says. 'There are other things you—'

'Seb, just stop,' I say. 'We don't need to talk about it.'

'Ivy—'

'I've told Mr Andrews that I'll be here to help, if you need anything,' I remind him. 'For now I think it might be best if you leave.'

'OK, sure,' he replies.

Seb opens his mouth, as though he's about to say something. His words are on the tip of his tongue before he obviously thinks better of saying them. Well, what can he say? He gives me a half-smile before heading for the door, like I asked him to.

I can tell that he feels bad about the way I've found out but, again, what good does pity do me?

I am angry and I'm upset, but I'm not going to show it. Instead, I'm going to do everything I can to make sure I can buy this place first. He might have money and charm, but I have roots here. I believe that Mr Andrews will sell to me over Seb if I can make the money first. I just need to figure out how on earth I can do that...

Chapter 5

I have come to a shocking and saddening realisation. It has occurred to me, in light of recent circumstances, that I don't have a life. I suppose I already knew it, at the back of mind – maybe not even the back of my mind, perhaps it was obvious – that I didn't have much going on other than my work. A love life, a social life, a family... These are all things that have taken a back seat to business. Sure, I have a best friend in my sister, but if I think too hard about it, I feel like that's maybe just by default. We shared a womb, *of course* we're best friends. Taking joint second place on my list of friends are my niece and nephew and then, I suppose, Pete the postman takes the bronze.

That's sad, isn't it? I don't get invited anywhere, apart from my sister's, and I don't really do anything but work, read, or watch TV. If I lose the shop I'll lose my home, my income, my mum's legacy and my reason to get up of a morning all at once, in an instant, gone before the New Year.

The first thing I need to do is increase the number of customers, and the amount of stock they are buying. That's why I've spent the past two hours making glitter-covered signs letting people know that we've got a big, pre-Christmas sale on. I've also been going around with a pad of little white stickers too, reducing the price of almost everything.

I'm not crazy, I know that knocking a couple of quid off snow globes isn't going to save the shop, but if I can improve things just a little, maybe it will help me secure a mortgage. With the way business is at the moment, the banks aren't exactly going to be fighting over me.

I examine the sparkly 'sale now on' sign I made to place in the window before securing it in place. As I do this, I notice a couple of men outside, standing at the end of the front garden.

'Can I help you?' I ask them, the similarity between myself and Tubbs from *League of Gentlemen* making me feel both uneasy and amused.

'Don't worry, Ivy, they're with me,' I hear a familiar voice say.

That's when I notice Seb is with them, and that they're spraying paint all over the ground.

'What are they doing?' I ask.

It looks a little like they're holding a handheld vacuum cleaner, like my mum used to have.

'They're checking for unexploded bombs underground,' Seb replies.

I feel my eyebrows shoot up around the same time I hear the men sniggering quietly. A joke. Wonderful.

'They're tracing the utilities in the road, so we can work out where to connect services to the new buildings.'

'You've not even bought the place yet,' I point out.

'I know.' He laughs. 'But I will. I'm just making sure everything is right first.'

I glance down at the spray paint on the ground.

'Don't worry, it washes off,' he says with a smile.

I bite my lip, the way I always do when I'm thinking.

'Nice hands,' he says and laughs again. 'Very festive.'

I glance down at my hands, which are covered in glitter.

'I've been making signs,' I explain. 'Don't worry, it washes off. Do you want to come in for a drink?' I ask, quickly clarifying what I mean. 'A tea or a coffee.'

'That would be great, thank you,' he says. 'Boys, tea break.'

Oh, I actually meant just Seb, and I'm not being nice, I'm on a fishing expedition. If I know what his plans are, maybe I can work out a way to put a stop to this.

'OK,' I say, gesturing towards the door.

The three men follow me inside the shop. I take drinks orders before popping into the kitchen and making them. I place the drinks on a tray, along with a few of my homemade gingerbread men – why am I snapping into hostess mode?

'Here we are,' I say, setting the tray down on the counter where Seb is waiting.

'Does the train work?' one of the men calls over.

'It doesn't,' I reply. 'It needs repairing.'

'I've got a screwdriver in the van,' he starts, but I stop him.

'That's very kind of you, thank you, but it requires some kind of vintage model train expert, and an expensive repair. It was my mum's so, when I've got some spare money, I'll get it done.'

'No worries,' he calls back.

'I know a train guy,' Seb tells me. 'He's pretty cool, actually. He's famous for making the smallest running train sets you can get.'

'Doesn't sound cool.' The workman laughs, grabbing a gingerbread man before biting his head off.

'This is Barry and Paul,' Seb tells me. 'Do not, under any circumstances, make a Chuckle Brothers joke, because they will not laugh.' Seb's cheeks dimple at his own joke. 'Boys, this is Ivy.'

'Your name is Ivy and you run a Christmas shop,' Barry points out.

'My sister is called Holly,' I tell him. 'My mum loved Christmas – that's why she opened this shop.'

'Why are you selling it?' he asks.

'I, erm, I'm not,' I tell him. 'My landlord is. I'm being kicked out.'

'You're kicking her out of her family's business before Christmas?' Barry asks, shocked.

'And my home,' I tell him. 'I live upstairs.'

'Mate,' Barry says.

Seb raises his eyebrows at him, I'd imagine to subtly remind Barry who he works for.

'So, when are you hoping to knock this place down?' I ask, trying to work out how much time I have.

'You said in the New Year, did you, gaffer?' Paul offers, helpfully.

'Yes,' Seb replies, seeming ever so slightly annoyed that Paul has answered. 'It's not set in stone – we'll see.'

'And then you'll start on the new building?'

'Buildings,' Paul points out.

'Oh, there's going to be more than one building then?'

'Paul, thank you,' Seb says. 'Why don't you lads go finish up if you've finished your drinks?'

'Sure, gaffer,' Barry says, taking the hint.

'I like them,' I say, once we're alone. 'They're chatty.'

'Too chatty,' Seb replies with a smile.

'Tell me a bit about you,' I say, hugging my mug with my hands to keep warm. I'm wondering what kind of person can happily move to a new town and kick someone out of their home.

'About me?' he replies, sounding surprised. 'OK. Well, I'm from Oxford.'

That explains the accent. Seb has a very BBC newsreader kind of way with words and it makes me feel a little self-conscious about my Yorkshire accent.

'How did you get into this line of work?' I ask. What I really mean is, how did he get into knocking down people's childhood homes, but I'm too polite to say that.

'I was all set to play professional cricket,' he tells me. 'And life just…I don't know, it did its own thing. I went from one business venture to the next – I've been living in Dublin for the past four years.'

Well, I suppose I can relate to that. I was a chef, before life changed my plans. 'So, what, you just decided you wanted to move to the Yorkshire coast?'

'I decided I wanted to move out of the city,' he says. 'And I knew I'd need to make a living.'

I nod thoughtfully.

'I'm sorry for the way this is playing out,' he says. 'I'm a little surprised you're not fighting it…'

I am fighting it; he just doesn't know it yet.

'And I appreciate you telling Mr Andrews you'd look after me while he's away,' he adds.

I didn't, well, not really. Not by choice.

I just smile. I'm not taking it well at all, but I'm not taking it lying down either. Sure, let Seb come here with his workmen and do his tests. It will all be for nothing when I swoop in and buy the shop first.

'I suppose I just expected a little more resistance, when I realised you were being made to leave against your will,' he persists.

'It's the rest of the locals you need to worry about,' I tell him. 'You're not the first southerner to come here and try to open up a business.'

'Oh?'

'A few things the people of Marram Bay don't take too kindly to: outsiders, big businesses, any threat to local business – I imagine your venture is an unwelcome mix of all three.'

'It sounds like it.' He laughs.

Seb laughs so much, he's just so easy-going. It's like nothing worries him – perhaps that's an easy confidence that comes with having a lot of money. Whoever said money can't buy happiness obviously never had a failing business and impending homelessness hanging over them.

'I have a meeting with the board,' he tells me.

'The Nation of Shopkeepers?'

'That's the one. I'm told that if I can sway them, I'm a shoo-in.'

'I'd say that was about right,' I reply.

'Your accent amuses me.' He laughs. 'Say that again.'

'No.'

'Nooo,' he repeats, in what I'd imagine is his attempt at a strong Yorkshire accent.

Unimpressed, I furrow my brow.

'So, what happened with the last southerner who tried to start a business here? Did they let her open it?'

'They did,' I admit.

'There we go then. I'll see you tonight,' he says, taking the last gingerbread man from the plate.

'You will,' I reply.

'Wish me luck,' he says as he heads for the door.

'Good luck,' I call after him.

He's going to need it.

Chapter 6

In the Marram Bay Town Hall, the Nation of Shopkeepers gathers every other month to discuss all of the big issues affecting business in the town.

'And that's why anyone who has opted for blue fairy lights, instead of the traditional white lights, needs to take them down,' George Price, chairman of the group and owner of Frutopia jam shop concludes.

Yes, this is one of today's biggest issues: that someone has gone rogue with their fairy lights.

Mary-Ann – who runs the local dairy farm – raises a hand as she uses her other one to play with one of her brown plaits.

'I think the blue lights look nice,' she says softly, once she is given permission to speak.

'Well, you'd be wrong,' George says confidently. 'Now, our final order of business. Waiting outside we have Sebastian Stone. He's a property developer looking to knock down Christmas Every Day, and build holiday homes for tourists. Before we invite him in for his pitch, Ivy, would you like to say a few words?'

I stand up from my place on the U-shaped table. 'I, erm... Closing down Christmas Every Day is not a decision I've been a party to,' I say, pausing to anxiously nibble a fingernail. 'I'm not saying Seb shouldn't be allowed to start a business here, I just wish it weren't at the cost of an already established one.'

An echo of 'hear hears' bounces around the room.

'Does anyone else have anything to say on the matter?'

'After everything I went through to open a business here, I don't see why this guy should have it easy,' Lily, who runs the Apple Blossom Deli, says with a laugh. When she tried to open the deli earlier this year almost everyone was against it, and now here she is, a fully-fledged member of the community.

'It wouldn't be right, to push out a long-established business with deep roots in the community, in favour of something new,' Tommy, who owns the local bookshop, adds.

'Well, I think we're all in agreement there. Let's bring him in,' George says, gesturing at the person nearest the door so that they can get Seb.

Seconds later Seb walks in, in yet another one of his expensive suits. I feel like they're symbolic of his wealth, his attention to detail, his attitude towards business – all things that look good, when you're standing up in front of the people who will decide your future. Seb looks the part, from his suit, to the large iPad in his hands, to the confident smile on his face.

'Hello, everyone, my name is Sebastian Stone, and this evening I'd like to share with you my proposal for new holiday homes on the current Christmas Every Day site.'

Seb taps on his iPad a few times before his proposal appears on the big screen behind him.

I notice a couple of gaps around the room.

'Bloody hell, we've never been able to get that to work,' George tells him.

Geroge is a living, breathing example of exactly what you'd expect a Yorkshire man to look like. He's a big, broad fifty-something man, with dark hair that's slowly being consumed by grey, starting with the sideburns. He knows what he likes and he likes what he knows, and for that reason, you can't tell him

41

anything. That's why, at times like this, he's the perfect chairman of the Nation of Shopkeepers, because he'll take one look at an outsider like Seb and see everything that he hates about 'this bloody country' – consumerism, cutthroat businessmen, the *bourgeoisie*.

'Ooh, he's doing a keynote speech, just like Steve Jobs,' Adam, who owns the Treasure Island arcade on the seafront, leans over to me to whisper.

Adam is quite the hipster, so I'm not surprised he's impressed. His arcade isn't really an arcade, it's a speakeasy hidden behind an area where parents can ditch their kids while they get drunk.

'Marram Bay is a popular tourist hotspot that, unfortunately, doesn't have enough accommodation to meet demand during peak seasons. This results in fewer visitors, less footfall, less business for everyone,' Seb explains.

He changes the slide to reveal a beautiful artist's impression of the modern townhouses with dark cladding and grassy roofs. It's so colourful, surrounded by blooming gardens and smiley people – if I didn't know what I was looking at, I wouldn't have recognised it as the spot where my shop currently stands.

Seb cycles through a few slides, talking everyone through how his presence will increase business for everyone.

'And through my proposed collaboration with holiday accommodation booking site Let's Go, we'll attract even more tourism. The last coastal town to work with them won the prestigious Staycation of the Year award.'

I glance around the room, trying to read the audience. He has their attention, that's for sure.

'The project will also meet passive house standards, which reduces the building's ecological footprint. The result will be ultra-low-energy buildings that require little energy for space heating or cooling. Each building will have a green roof, which will provide further insulation – it will also keep the houses cool when they need to be, provide space for birds, and, well, I just think it looks cool.'

Seb gives his audience a wink and, as I look around, I notice that his charm offensive is working. All eyes are on him. From his tech skills to his innovative business ideas, to his good looks and his eloquence. The audience is his, with everyone fully captivated, so impressed by everything he has to offer. I'd go as far as to say a few of the women are swooning – maybe even a couple of the men too.

'If that's not enough, the development will be entirely self-sufficient thanks to renewable energy sources. We'll combine the use of wind and solar power, which, actually, will create a surplus of electricity, which we'll be donating to your local school.'

'How would that work?' George asks.

'All the energy that we create, that we don't use, will go back to the grid and the net profit will be deducted from the school's energy bill.'

As Seb continues to share his plans with his spellbound audience, I tune out a little. His plans are perfect and, if they were anywhere else, I'd want to get behind them too. It's just…it's my home, and my business, and if he could find somewhere else, everything would be fine.

'You've given us a lot to think about,' George says, pulling me from my thoughts, bringing me back into the room. I'd say his poker face was firmly on, were it not for the strong handshake he gives Seb. 'We appreciate you running your plans by us.'

'And I appreciate you taking the time to listen,' Seb replies. 'Your blessing is important to me, as is your local MP's. I'll be talking with her tomorrow afternoon.' He starts collecting his things, getting ready to leave. 'See you, Ivy,' Seb says to me directly. I give him a half wave and as much of a smile as I can muster.

'Ooh, Ivy, get you,' Lily from the deli teases, as soon as Seb has gone. 'So, that's what I needed to do to get accepted quicker, hmm? Have better tech skills and look good in a suit.'

'OK, thank you, Lily, we're judging him on his proposal,' George reminds her. 'So, let's go around the room and find out what people think.'

I notice George glancing around, making awkward eye contact with me before purposefully picking someone from the other side of the room.

'Rob,' he prompts, calling upon the local butcher first.

'He was very persuasive, wasn't he?' Rob says cautiously, testing the waters.

George nods thoughtfully.

'The thing he was saying about the electricity – I didn't know that was a thing; that's pretty cool,' Lily says.

'Yeah, free electricity for the school...' George says.

'The stuff about the booking website, and the Staycation of the Year award,' Arcade Adam starts. 'Is that legit?'

'It is,' Tommy from the bookshop chimes in. 'Just Googled it, Portmeirion won last year.'

'It does sound like it will be good for everyone...' George says slowly.

I can hear the excitement in their voices building as they talk about Seb's proposal. The love hearts in their eyes have turned to pound signs now.

'Ivy?' George finally says. 'What do you think?'

'It's a good idea,' I admit. 'But at the cost of my shop and my childhood home...'

As my voice trails off, an awkward silence follows. I feel like everyone in the room is looking at me, just waiting for me to take one for the team, to put the town before myself. They've all been charmed by Seb, with his flashy suit and his big ideas and his cheeky smile.

'Yes, it would be a shame to lose your shop,' George says. 'What about an anonymous ballot?'

'We don't normally do things anonymously,' I say.

'I know,' he replies. 'But, with this affecting a member of the panel, we need to make sure people feel free to vote for what they want.'

'OK, sure,' I reply.

Pieces of paper and pens are handed out, for each of us to write down whether we are for or against Seb's proposal, but as I write my objection down, I can feel that this isn't going to go my way.

George collects the pieces of paper, then takes them back to his seat to count them.

'Based on these votes, the majority would like to support Seb in his business venture,' George announces.

'How many people were against?' I ask curiously.

'Now, Ivy, if I told you that, it wouldn't be an anonymous vote, would it?' he replies, which can only lead me to believe that I was the only person to vote against it.

I don't think there's anything I can say that will convince people my shop is worth saving, so I'm just going to have to do it myself. How, I'm not exactly sure.

Chapter 7

To the best of my memory, I've only really been in trouble once in my life – nearly 20 years ago.

Holly and I were in different ability groups for every subject, apart from art class. This not only meant that we got to sit together for something, but I also got to see my sister in all her rebellious glory.

My mum was always getting letters about my sister, then phone calls, before she was finally was called in for a meeting. In Holly's defence, she wasn't bad, she was just...disruptive, and while the rest of the class found her cheeky antics funny, things had got to a point where Holly was on her last warning – one more major disruption, and she would be excluded.

On this particular day, my sister was more preoccupied with flirting with Lee Blake than she was with the silhouettes we were supposed to be painting.

I never liked Lee. I always found him to be really smug and entitled. Like he thought just because he was the 'coolest' boy in our year then everyone else should bow down to him. My sister was not only willing to take the knee, but she wanted to be his queen.

I was just sitting and rolling my eyes as they flirted, ignoring the task at hand, until their playful flirting escalated into flicking black paint at each other, which also escalated into black paint being flung across the table, with yours truly being caught in the crossfire.

Ms Evergreen caught wind and came charging over, ready to reprimand the suspects. She had seen Lee throwing paint so he was banged to rights, but his opponent was still unknown.

'Holly Jones, aren't you on your final warning?' she asked angrily.

'It wasn't me, Miss,' Holly insisted, unsuccessfully trying to hide her grin.

'No? Then who was it?'

I didn't actually think about what I said, before I said it. It just felt right. 'It was me, Miss,' I confessed.

'You, Ivy?' she gasped in disbelief. I remember her glancing down at the painting of a willow tree I'd been working so hard on, and looking back up at me. Now that I think about it, it was obvious I'd been working hard all lesson and that Holly, whose paper was suspiciously blank, apart from a few abstract splashes, had not.

'It was me,' I said again confidently. This was my first taste of trouble, and while it didn't feel good, it did feel right, to help out my sister. We're two halves of the same thing. Her problems are my problems.

I don't think Ms Evergreen believed me, but she had no choice but to send Lee and me to Isolation (a room where kids were put for extended periods of time to keep them from disrupting lessons). There, we chatted and I guess taking the fall for my sister went a long way to impressing him because from that day on, he thought I was OK. Predictably, being on the receiving end of attention from a cool, good-looking guy resulted in me developing a silly, schoolgirl crush on him. My sister went on to marry him, so all is well that ends well. I'd be mortified if either of them knew that, and it's safe to say that, post GCSEs, my crush soon died.

The point is, other than that occasion, I've never really been in trouble because I've never really done anything wrong. I'm just not very good at it – even a harmless little white lie fills me with guilt. That's why I've been staring at my phone for half an hour now, thinking about whether I should do what I'm planning on doing. It feels wrong, but…when Seb first came into the shop, I felt just like I did at school – flattered that someone out of my league was giving me attention, and I don't ever want to feel like that again. Being so easily flattered doesn't make for a very good feminist, does it?

Speaking of good feminists, I pick up the phone and dial and, after a few seconds, I am connected with Prue Honeywell, our local MP.

Prue is exactly the kind of person you want speaking for your town, because she really cares about everyone – especially women. And, look, my plan isn't to lie to her, it's just to tell her about the kind of man Seb Stone really is.

'Hello, Ivy,' she says brightly. 'How are you?'

Prue and I have spoken on many occasions. I'm one of the first people to help out when it comes to all of her charitable causes for the town.

'I'm not too bad, thank you. How are you?'

'Oh, you know,' she says. 'Stressed but blessed. What can I do for you today?'

'It's about Seb Stone, the man who is hoping to buy the land my shop stands on, to build holiday homes,' I start. 'I just…I don't think he's right for the town, and I know you have a meeting with him today.'

'Tell me more,' she says curiously.

'Well, he's been quite underhanded about it all. He came in to scope the place out, without telling me why – and now he's buying it from under me. He's obviously a big, important busi-nessman—' it's hard to hide the sarcasm from my tone '—and it just seems like he has no respect for the place. He's going to build these modern-looking homes and he thinks he can just do whatever he wants, so long as he smiles and winks while he's doing it.'

'He sounds dreadful, based on that character reference,' Prue agrees. 'Ivy, if you know one thing about me, it's that I want what's best for this town, and I take care of us without taking any stick from men. Let me meet with him this afternoon and, if he's not right, I'll make sure he knows it, and I'll put a stop to this, OK?'

'OK, great,' I reply, a wave of relief washing over me.

'Why don't you meet me in the deli afterwards, say 3 p.m.? And we can discuss any concerns you still have.'

'Thank you so much,' I say, emotion prickling my throat. It's just nice to feel like someone has my back.

After the call, I shut up shop for the day, which is fine because, until I figure out how I'm going to draw in more customers, it's not like people will be beating the door down to buy baubles.

With Holly resisting all things festive more defiantly than usual this year, I am trying extra hard to make things special for Chloe and Harry. They don't have school today because, thanks to a dusting of snow last night, someone skidded off the road and crashed into one of those green boxes that are something to do with the phone lines.

Holly sounded especially stressed to be entertaining the kids today, so I have offered to take them to see Santa Claus – the only Santa in town, at Wilson's garden centre.

'Thanks for doing this,' Holly says, as she fastens the kids into the back of my car.

'I should be thanking you,' I say enthusiastically, mostly for Chloe and Harry's benefit. 'I'm more excited than the kids.'

'I'll get my jobs done while you're gone, hopefully. Let me know when you're on your way back.'

'Will do, sis,' I reply, lowering my voice. 'Are you OK?'

'Yes, why?'

'You just seem a little flustered.'

'I'm fine,' she says firmly, although not entirely convincingly.

I know my car is old, but it's safe. She seems even more worried than usual to be sending her precious cargo off with me.

'Well, we're going to have more fun than your mum is, tidying up all day,' I say as we make the short journey to the garden centre.

'Mummy is going out,' Chloe informs me.

'Is she?'

'Yep, I heard her on the phone,' she says. 'She was saying she would see someone.'

'Are you sure?' I ask. It's not like my sister to lie to me.

'Yep,' Chloe says confidently.

Could she be right? Holly did say Chloe had been paying more attention to things lately, hanging around, listening to the adults. And Holly has been acting a little odd recently.

'We're here,' I say, pushing any thoughts of my sister being up to something from my mind. She's probably just organising their Christmas presents or something. No matter how Holly feels about what she calls the so-called most wonderful time of the year, she always buys her kids presents.

I hurry to keep up with the kids as they charge through the various departments of the garden centre, before we finally reach Santa's grotto, a small log cabin surrounded by sparkly fake snow, stuffed reindeer and plastic elves – none of which lend well to the legitimacy of this Santa Claus. Well, it's 2018, and our children have Google. They watch Marvel movies and read Harry Potter books, and know exactly what is real and what isn't, so if we want them to buy into this Santa character, we need to do a much better job of selling it. Fake snow, stuffed animals and plastic people aren't going to cut it, although perhaps that's just my cynical, grown-up point of view because Chloe and Harry are happily caught up in the excitement, glee-fully unwrapping their candy canes as we join the queue. They're not worrying about the aesthetics and *I really* miss that about being young.

'Ho, ho, ho,' Santa bellows, as Chloe and Harry cautiously make their way towards him. I suppose, to them, he's a superstar. It would be like me queuing up to sit on Henry Cavill's lap.

I suck on my candy cane as I glance around Santa's grotto. It's not up to much this year, but it is the only one in town so I suppose it will do.

'And how is Mummy doing today?' Santa Claus asks.

I quickly turn to face him, widening my eyes. 'Sorry?'

'She's not our mummy,' Chloe informs him. 'She's our auntie.'

'Your auntie, huh? And is she on the nice list or the naughty list?' Santa enquires.

'The naughty list, for sure,' Chloe says emphatically. 'Because she didn't build our bunk beds, like she said she would.'

I feel my jaw drop a little, as my sweet little niece throws me under the bus.

'Well, that's OK, Santa doesn't mind a naughty auntie,' he tells her. 'So, what do you two want for Christmas?'

Santa is well hidden, under his suit, hat, and fake beard, but I can see his blue eyes clearly. I can tell that he's young, and that there's a cheeky glimmer of something behind them.

'Well, other than my bunk beds,' Chloe starts, and as she reels off a list of all the toys she wants, I can't help but feel like Santa is undressing me with his eyes.

'And what about you, young man?' he asks Harry.

Harry thinks for a moment. 'A bike,' he says excitedly.

'Well, if you're both good kids – which I'm sure you are – then I'm sure you'll get everything you want. But you have to be good between now and Christmas. Can you promise me you'll be good?'

The kids nod. As I begin to usher them away, Santa places a piece of paper in my hand.

'I think I could be really good for you,' he whispers. 'Call me.'

I can't work out if he's the best or the worst Santa Claus I've ever encountered. He's great with the kids, but giving me his phone number is a majorly creepy move.

'Go play on that swing,' I instruct them, eyeballing the shop's manager.

'Excuse me,' I say politely. 'I, erm, I just took my niece and nephew to see Santa and, well…'

'Was there a problem?' he asks.

'Yes…' I reply. 'He was hitting on me. In fact, he slipped me his phone number in front of the kids.'

The manager takes the piece of paper from my hand and cross-references it with the number he has saved in his phone.

'I don't want to get him in trouble,' I say, although I'm not sure why. If he's being inappropriate, he should be reprimanded.

'Don't worry,' the manager insists. 'In fact, to say sorry, allow me to buy you and your family hot chocolates in our café.'

'That's so kind of you,' I reply. 'I'm sure the kids would love that.'

The manager escorts us into the cute little café area and instructs the employee there to make us our drinks, on the house.

'This is the best day, ever,' Chloe says, before delicately blowing her hot chocolate to try and cool it quicker.

'You having fun, Harry?' I ask.

Harry, a man of few words, gives me a strong nod.

The three of us catch up, talking about school, Christmas, and how Holly has told Chloe she's too young for a Kardashian lip kit – at 7 years of age. I can't even imagine how she knows what one is.

It occurs to me to tell them about the shop, although I'm not sure if they're old enough to understand, and I wouldn't want to upset them. They both love coming over and hanging out while I work, just like I used to love doing when I was their age and my mum was running the place.

'Oi,' I hear an angry voice call out. I turn around to see a twenty-something man in a pair of grey trackies and a white

T-shirt. His arms are covered with tattoos, the most obvious of which is the name Gaz in that gothic lettering you often see used in tattoos. He's not very tall, although still much taller than me, with dirty blond hair and piercing blue eyes. He's got one of those scruffy designer beards that I acknowledge are a stylish choice, but it just makes him look like he needs a shave.

'Hello?' I reply, glancing around the busy café to make sure it is actually me he's talking to. 'Me?'

'Yeah, you,' he replies angrily. 'You got me sacked.'

'I got you sacked?' I ask, puzzled.

'Yes,' he replies.

'Oh,' I say as it occurs to me who he is. 'Oh! Can we just… talk about it…over here,' I say as I scramble up from my seat. I really don't want the kids realising this man is the Santa Claus they just saw.

I usher the horny Santa away from the children.

'I…I didn't mean to get you sacked,' I explain weakly. 'I just felt so uncomfortable with you giving me your number in front of the kids, and if you're doing that with other aunties, or mums, or grandmas…'

'I'm not handing out my number with the candy canes; I only gave my number to you.'

'I'm flattered…but…'

'No, not like that,' he interrupts. 'You're the lass from the Christmas shop, right? I thought you might want a Santa Claus, maybe on the days when I'm not here. Didn't think I could just come out with it, so I slipped you my number.'

Oh God, what is it with me lately, thinking every man who talks to me is trying to ask me out? With Seb, he was there about the shop. Now, with Santa, he's just trying to get a job. I feel my cheeks flush.

'Oh,' is about all I can say.

'So, now, not only am I without a job, but Marram Bay is without a Santa Claus. That's on you,' he says.

I feel so guilty. I didn't want to get him sacked; I just didn't want him being inappropriate in front of the kids. I feel like such an idiot.

'I can't believe I thought you were hitting on me,' I say, embarrassed.

'You could hire me,' he suggests.

I think for a moment. That might be a good idea. Now that Marram Bay doesn't have a Santa Claus, it would give people a reason to visit the shop.

'I'm not sure,' I say, trying to work out whether I can afford to hire him. If he makes money, then it will be worth it; it's just a gamble.

'I'm pretty well known,' he says. 'Do you know Hugh Jackman?'

'Of course I do. Do you know him?'

'No, but I played Wolverine at the Milton Keynes Comic Con. I perform at all the big holidays – Easter Bunny at Easter, a leprechaun for St Patrick's Day – and I'm free as bird now, until I play Cupid on Valentine's Day.'

'I don't know,' I say cautiously.

'I'm a single dad,' he admits. 'Little Timmy's dad losing his job before Christmas – isn't that just the saddest thing?'

His words tug on my heartstrings. I already felt guilty for losing him his job, but now I know that he's a single dad I feel even worse.

'I'm not going to regret this, am I?' I ask him, although it does occur to me that he may not be the best person to ask.

'I'm gonna change your life,' he says confidently.

I pull an unsure face. 'Well, OK then, can you start tomorrow?'

'I can,' he says.

I look back at the kids. Chloe is watching me like a hawk.

'OK, sure, give me your number again and we'll figure it out,' I tell him.

'Really?'

'Really.'

'Ah, love, you're not going to regret this,' he insists. 'Give us your phone.'

I reluctantly unlock and hand over my phone. When he passes it back, I glance at the screen.

'Your name is Gaz?' I ask.

'That's me.'

'You have a tattoo of your own name?' I blurt.

'Yeah,' he replies. 'What's your name, love?'

'Ivy,' I reply. 'No tattoo though.'

He laughs. 'Well, boss, I'll be hearing from you.' Gaz points at me as he says this.

'You will?' I reply, which sounds more like a question than an answer.

'For the record,' he starts, before he leaves, 'I would've given you my number anyway, just not while I was working.'

He flashes me a cheeky smile and then he's off.

I sit back down to see that the kids have drained their mugs. I sip my own, but its contents have gone cold while I was chatting.

'Who was *that*?' Chloe asks.

'That's Gaz,' I tell her. 'He's going to be working at the shop with me sometimes.'

I feel safe telling her this because, along with playing Santa Claus, I'm hoping Gaz will help out with other shop duties too – especially if, by some miracle, we get busy.

'He has a lot of tattoos,' she observes. 'I want a tattoo when I grow up.'

'Oh, do you?' I laugh. 'Would you want to wear the same dress every day?'

'No,' she replies, as if I've just asked a stupid question.

'Well, if you get a tattoo, you'll have to wear the same one every day, so you need to be sure it's what you want.'

Chloe pulls a face. I've clearly given her something to think about. I'm not sure I can think of anything that I'd want to 'wear' every day – I could always go for something timeless, like my own name, like Gaz has. Gosh, I really hope I haven't made a mistake, hiring him. I suppose he can't exactly make things any worse – I can't have minus customers – but it still feels like a risk. What if he causes trouble? But what if I'm the reason his son has a rubbish Christmas? I really don't want that on my conscience, and I definitely can't afford any bad karma at the moment.

I swear, I didn't intend for things to play out this way, but if Wilson's was the only place in town with a Santa – and now they don't have one – it feels like a really good time to invest in one. I'll have the only Santa in town, and that's got to be good for business.

Santa Claus might not have wanted me to sit on his lap, but maybe him falling into mine is a blessing in disguise...

Chapter 8

After dropping the kids off at my sister's, I head straight into town, to the Apple Blossom Deli, to meet up with Prue and find out what she made of Seb. On the drive over, I fantasise about what she might have said to him. Prue is a bizarre combination of a very modern woman, with very old-fashioned values. Neither charming men, nor outsiders, do much for her. She works hard for Marram Bay – mostly to protect it and to preserve it. Seb riding into town, in his diesel-guzzling car, bragging about his modern, hi-tech holiday homes isn't going to do anything for her at all. If I'm lucky, she'll single-handedly put a stop to his plans, giving me time to work out how I can buy the shop and the land as well.

I approach the deli excitedly, ready for the good news that is going to turn this whole situation around for me, only to spot Prue and Seb through the white-framed arch window, still chatting away, getting on famously, it seems.

I watch them for a second, Seb saying something obviously charming, Prue placing a hand on his forearm.

I feel my face being to scrunch up in annoyance, when I catch Seb's eye. I quickly try to look away before 'casually' glancing back and waving, trying desperately not to look like I was looking, even though I was.

Seb beckons me inside. 'Ivy, hello,' he says as I walk in.

'Hi,' I reply cautiously. 'Hello, Prue.'

'Ivy, lovely to see you,' she says, in what you'd probably call a posh North Yorkshire accent. 'Sit with us, we're having a lovely chat.'

I pause for a second.

'Actually, I've got to go,' Seb says. 'I've got dinner plans over on the Island, I need to set off because the causeway closes.'

I wonder who he could possibly have dinner plans with, and it annoys me that it's even crossing my mind. What do I care, if he's got dinner plans?!

'Well, it was lovely to meet you, Sebastian,' Prue coos.

Seb extends her a hand to shake and, as she takes his, he uses his other hand to encase hers tenderly.

'And it was a real honour to meet you,' he replies. 'See you around, Ivy.'

'Yeah, bye,' I say, mustering up as much enthusiasm as possible.

I take a seat opposite Prue. I'm just about to grill her when Viv, one of the ladies who works here, comes over to ask if she can get me anything.

'I can't stay long, unfortunately,' Prue informs me.

'In that case, I'm fine, thank you, Viv.'

Viv smiles, leaving us to chat.

'Ivy, thank you for raising your concerns with me earlier,' Prue says, and I just know that I'm not going to like what's coming. 'I know that you were worried that he might be doing things in an underhanded way, or that he might not have the town's best intentions in mind, but I can assure you that Sebastian is a lovely man.'

Brilliant, he's charmed her too.

'Oh,' is about all I can reply.

'He's told me all about his plans and they sound well thought out and like they have the town, the country and the world, in

58

fact, in mind. His environmental efforts are incredible. We need more conscientious business developers in this world. He's also told me of his plans to make the location more accessible for all, by proposing alterations to current bus routes, which we shouldn't have a problem approving. He makes a lot of sense.'

'Well, that's great,' I lie. What else can I say? I can't argue with his perfect facts and statistics. I'd be lying if I said that his plans weren't great; they are. I just wish they didn't impact on me. If they didn't, I'd be just as excited as the rest of the town. More tourist accommodation is exactly what we need, especially in this part of the town – I know I'd benefit from it.

'Sorry I can't stop longer,' Prue says. 'That Sebastian can talk.'

'He can indeed,' I reply.

'Oh, I can count on your support at the Christmas charity drive this year, can't I?'

Every year I volunteer at the Marram Bay Christmas Charity Drive, where the town all come together to raise money for a variety of good causes. This year, for the first time in a long time, I wasn't going to volunteer, because I just have too much to do. But, now that she's put me on the spot like this, I can't exactly say no.

'Count me in,' I reply.

'We'll have another catch-up soon,' she assures me, before grabbing her bag and dashing off.

'You sure I can't get you anything?' Viv calls over.

'Maybe a cannoli to go,' I call back. 'I think I've earned it.'

Prue hating Seb and putting an end to his plans might not have worked out, but it has given me another idea…

Chapter 9

'Your train is broken,' Gaz points out.

I glance over at him, to see him holding the model steam train in his hands, turning it upside down to examine it for faults. The garment bag containing his Santa suit, which was previously wedged between his body and his arm, slips to the floor.

I hurry over to him and take it from him, carefully placing it back down.

'I know, but please don't pick it up,' I say. 'It's worth a lot of money.'

'Even broken?'

'Even broken,' I reply. 'I'm going to get it fixed, it's just expensive.'

'It's a catch-33, innit?' he says.

'What do you mean?' I laugh, not getting the joke.

'I mean that, if you sell the train, you'll have enough money to repair it,' he unhelpfully points out.

'Cheers, Gaz,' I reply sarcastically, certain he means 'catch-22'. 'Anyway, if the shop floor is all clean and everything is in its place and switched on, we're ready to open up, so we can unlock the door.'

Gaz walks over to the door and unlocks it, exaggerating every movement.

'I am a classically trained actor,' he points out.

A classically trained actor who plays Santa Claus; wow.

'So?'

'I thought I was just going to play Santa Claus. I'm too skilled to be working in a shop.'

I roll my eyes.

'Take it or leave it, Gaz,' I tell him. 'You want to work here, I'm going to need you to help out with everything. We don't need a Santa if we don't have any customers.'

'Another catch-33,' Gaz points out.

'That really isn't helpful,' I tell him.

Gaz walks over to the counter, taking a candy cane from the jar that sits on top of it.

'Want one?' he asks.

'No thanks,' I reply.

'So, how do we get more customers?' Gaz asks, crunching a chunk of peppermint candy as he speaks.

'The problem is that since satnavs started taking people along a different road the tourists just don't know we're here,' I tell him. 'So, I've hired a vehicle that will do round trips each day, picking people up in the tourist hot spots and dropping them here before heading back into town.'

'That's mint,' he replies. 'Like a minibus?'

'Not like a minibus.' I laugh. 'It's due to arrive any minute – you can see for yourself.'

'Exciting,' Gaz replies, through more crunching. 'So, we get more customers, I get to be Santa again?'

'Yes,' I reply. 'Obviously I'm having to pay for the train, so I want to make sure that's worth its money first, but if it is, then I'll be able to afford to build a little grotto here – even better than the one you were in before.'

'I do deserve a better grotto,' he replies thoughtfully.

I kind of like Gaz. Sure, he's a little rough around the edges, but that's part of his charm.

'We just need to get busy,' I say.

'Now who is flirting?' Gaz laughs.

It takes me a few seconds get Gaz's joke. 'Gaz.' I laugh. 'That was not flirting.'

'Sorry, boss,' he says. 'You could go for a drink with me though. Try the flirting thing out.'

'Sorry, we have a very strict policy on workplace relationships here,' I inform him.

Gaz frowns.

Our conversation is interrupted by a loud whistle.

'What the hell was that?' Gaz asks, jumping out of his skin.

'Ahh, that's my transport,' I say excitedly, hurrying for the door. Gaz follows close behind me.

Parked up outside the shop is the miniature road-going steam train that I've hired to make trips into town and back, picking up tourists and bringing them to the shop, before giving them a lift back into town. Not only is it free, but it's just a fun thing to do, which hopefully people will jump at the chance to experience, whether they want to come to the shop or not. Then ideally, once I've got them here, they'll be happy to stay, and when they're inside the shop will speak for itself.

'Whoa, this is awesome,' Gaz says, running towards the train like an excited kid. 'Can I sit in it?'

'Hello there,' the driver says cheerily as he climbs out. 'Ivy?'

'Yes, hello,' I say, making my way towards him.

'This is just awesome, so awesome,' I hear Gaz's muffled voice coming out from one of the two carriages.

'I'm Mick, I'll be driving the train. Would you like to come on the first run?'

'Yes, please,' I say. 'Gaz, are you OK to mind the shop while

I'm gone? You shouldn't have anything to do, just don't touch anything.'

'Really?' Gaz replies, disappointed. 'OK, fine.'

I take a seat in the first carriage and wait excitedly for Mick to set off. It's bizarre, to see a steam train with tyres, and I feel that weird nervous excitement you get before a rollercoaster sets off. Hopefully it will be a smoother ride than Thunder Mountain though.

As we set off, it's nice to take the journey into town at a slower pace than when you're driving, and you certainly take in a lot more of the scenery – something Marram Bay is rich in.

Driving along the road that runs alongside the coastline, I look out to sea, admiring Hope Island, Marram Bay's tidal island. Depending on the time of day you visit, Hope Island is either isolated by the North Sea, or connected to Marram Bay by a mile-long road. Twice a day, the tide comes in and fully covers the road, so you have to check the causeway times if you're planning on visiting or leaving Hope Island. It might feel like a slow process, like the tide creeps in, but at high tide the water can reach 6 feet deep.

It's a fascinating phenomenon, which I suppose I've gotten used to, living here all my life. Visitors don't always take it seriously though, expecting the water to not be very deep, just like a big puddle that they can drive through. That's why, at least once a month, some chancer will think they can race the tide, only to get stuck in the middle. I remember, when I was learning to drive here, my instructor told me that a sea rescue cost £2,000, whereas an air rescue cost over £4,000. After learning those numbers, I could never, in good conscience, take my chances crossing outside the safe times that are clearly posted on the noticeboards at each end of the causeway.

We arrive at the bottom of Main Street, on the seafront, which is abuzz with people.

'This is the pick-up point we decided on,' Mick tells me, after parking up, getting out of the locomotive and opening the carriage door for me. 'And we've made this sign, with approximate pick-up times.'

I step out and take a good look at both the sign, and the train.

'This is a brand-new logo,' Mick tells me.

You can really tell. It's cherry red, with gold lettering on it. Although it isn't intended to be, it's festive-looking, which is perfect for what I need it for.

'Shall I get people's attention, encourage them to get on board?' Mick suggests.

I nod.

'Ladies and gentlemen, step right up,' Mick, a stout, grey-haired man in his sixties calls out. Mick would make a much more authentic Santa Claus than Gaz, although I don't suppose that would be much of a compliment if I were to tell him so. 'We're offering free train rides to the cutest little Christmas shop in the UK, if not the world. Enjoy a scenic, leisurely ride, before a pleasant stroll around the stunningly decorated shop.'

Mick also has more of a stage presence than Gaz, the supposedly classically trained actor.

Amazingly, Mick's patter works, as he catches the attention of all kinds of people, who make their way towards the train, intrigued by the weird little engine.

'Ivy,' I hear a familiar voice say.

'Seb,' I reply. 'Hello.'

Seb, who is wearing a grey suit and a long black smart coat, rubs his hands together as he smiles at the train.

'What is this?'

'Oh, it's just a cute little thing to take people to the shop and back,' I tell him. 'Being so out of the way, no one knows we're there.'

'That's a really good idea,' he says. 'You know, I'm actually planning something similar, for when the holiday homes are up.'

'Oh really?' I reply, doing my best to feign ignorance.

'Yeah,' he replies. 'Potentially reworking the bus routes, or adding a new one in. It's a woefully neglected side of the town.'

I know that all too well.

'Hey, can I get a lift?' he asks. 'It would be great to experience the route as a passenger.'

'Sure,' I reply reluctantly. Well, it's a free train. I can't exactly stop him, can I?

It's amazing, to see the train carriages packed with people. I just wish I didn't have to sit with Seb on the journey back.

For the first minute or two we enjoy the silence between us, before Seb breaks it.

'Prue is lovely, isn't she?'

I ponder for a second whether his proper, Queen's English way of speaking might be put on – then again, I'm not sure he could keep up the act.

'She is,' I reply.

'Everyone is lovely, really,' he continues. 'They told me, don't waste your time in Marram Bay, they're closed-minded, they don't like outsiders, they won't give you a fair shot.'

As Seb badmouths my hometown, I only feel my anger increase.

'But everyone has been great, and I feel like I have everyone's blessing. That's so important.'

'Yes,' I lie, because he doesn't have my blessing at all. It suddenly occurs to me that I've been timidly hinting that I'm not happy about how things are playing out, but at no point have I gone all out, speaking my mind, shouting at the top of my lungs about how important the shop is to me. I haven't actually told anyone that I'm devastated to be losing the shop that my mum built up from nothing. I haven't said that I'm terrified of losing my livelihood and my home. Instead, I just hoped that nature would take its course and the locals would reject Seb and his plans. Now, everyone has accepted him and given the project their blessing, I feel like it's too late for me to say anything.

'Is there anything I need to know about the town?' he asks.

'Like what?' I reply, gazing out of the window. The last thing I want to be doing at the moment is hand-holding Seb.

'The kind of things that an estate agent would never tell me.' He laughs. 'Any dark secrets? Flooding issues? Weird cults?'

'No, nothing like that,' I tell him. 'It's quite boring here, really. If you're used to living in big cities, it's going to be a shock to the system.'

I don't know why I'm wasting my breath, trying to put him off moving here.

While moving from a big city to a coastal town like Marram Bay may be a shock to the system, life here is in no way boring. Being a tourist hotspot, there's almost always something unique and fun going on. At this time of year, we have our Winter Wonderland Festival, down by the beach, with stalls, rides, games, and entertainment. In the summer, we have our annual Forties weekend where, to raise money for charity and remember the war, everyone dresses up in fashion from the era, we put tape on our windows, and we rid the streets of all things modern. Union Jack flags fly everywhere, on streets crawling with army vehicles and personnel, and people take it really seriously – it's fascinating. If that's not weird and wonderful enough, we even have our own hot air balloon festival, which sees over 100 hot air balloons gathering here. It's simply amazing, to see them all dotted around in the sky. Oh, and don't even get me started on the food festivals.

When you throw in the eclectic cast of characters who live here, and their often dramatic day-to-day lives, it's never a dull moment. Even for someone like me, with a painfully boring life, things aren't all that boring really, because there's so much to see and so much to do – even watching the tide come in is a blast here, watching the sea slowly consuming the road, isolating Hope Island from the rest of the country, leaving it out there alone in the North Sea, to fend for itself. Apparently the Vikings raided the island, once upon a time, and if they could survive that, I'm sure they can survive anything.

'Hmm,' he replies. 'Well, maybe that's just what I need.'

We fall silent again. Surely Seb can tell that I don't really want to talk to him? Maybe that's why he's persisting, to toy with me.

'So, business is picking up?' he asks.

'It is,' I reply.

'And, you have a train full of customers,' he points out.

'Did you have to go to business school for many years, to make such intelligent observations?' I ask sarcastically.

Seb laughs. 'I actually had a business idea for you,' he starts.

I turn to face him, suddenly interested. Well, all Seb's business ideas do seem to be genuinely brilliant ideas.

'Oh really?'

'Yeah,' he says with a smile. 'You've got all that stock, you just need people to sell it to, and there is one place that has even more people than the town centre does.'

I raise my eyebrows, waiting for answer.

'The internet,' he says proudly.

'The internet?'

'Yeah, what you need is an eBay Store,' he says. 'You can list all your things on there and people all over the country can buy them – people all over the world, even. You just list things online, wait for the orders and then post them out. You'll significantly increase your customer base, and your profits, obviously.'

I think for a second. Wow, that's actually a really good idea. I can't believe I'd never thought of it myself. I do have so much stock, and if half my problem is visibility, then selling online is just what I need. Best of all, I'm tech savvy enough to execute it – this could be just what I need to boost my profits, which will go some of the way to helping me save the shop.

'That's actually a great idea,' I tell him with a smile. 'Thank you.'

'I am not good at many things, but I'm good at this. Don't sound so surprised.'

'I guess I'm just surprised because you're helping me – why would you help me increase business at a shop you're closing down?'

'That's exactly why I'm helping,' he admits. 'I do feel for you, Ivy.'

I give Seb a half-smile. I'm still not exactly sure why he's helping me.

'I don't want to see you stuck,' he continues. 'Changing your business to an online only one is the perfect way for you to keep going, without premises.'

My heart sinks, so low I can feel it knocking around in my Ugg boot. Seb isn't helping me with the shop at all; he's helping me deal with the aftermath of losing it. I suppose that's good of him, he doesn't have to help me pick myself back up...but, given that he's the one knocking me down, it's hard to be grateful.

'I'll give that a go,' I tell him honestly, because I will, but I have no intention of rolling over just yet. Perhaps Seb's idea, along with my other efforts, will go a long way to helping me get a mortgage. That reminds me, I need to arrange a meeting at the bank, to see what my options are.

'Please don't think I don't realise that my plans will impact on you. But it's business, not personal, and if it isn't me buying the place, it's going to be someone else – someone who might not do as good a job.'

I can see sympathy in his eyes, like he knows what he's doing is going to ruin my life, but if he were that sorry, he wouldn't be doing it, would he?

'I do have another suggestion, to make the transition easier for you,' he starts.

I detect a hint of apprehension in his words.

'Oh?'

'Yes, well, once we're up and running, there are going to be lots of jobs going around the accommodation, and you're being so helpful, I could do with someone like you during the planning and building stages.'

'Are you offering me a job?' I ask in disbelief.

'Yes,' he replies. 'Just until you figure things out, or long term, if you'd like.'

'So, let me get this straight, you're knocking down my business and my family home in one fell swoop of a bulldozer, and now you're asking me to work for you as a glorified skivvy, running around after you until the holiday homes are built, and then you'll let me clean the toilets?'

'Ivy, I didn't mean it like that,' he says softly. 'I just thought it might help you.'

'I'm fine, thank you,' I stress. 'I don't need any help from you.'

We make the rest of the journey in silence.

I can't seem to figure Seb out. He's either a really good person, or doing a really good job at pretending to be one. Ruthless businessmen don't have consciences, do they? They don't destroy people's livelihoods but then offer them jobs, do they? Or drive around in diesel-guzzling cars, constructing buildings in the beautiful countryside, only to go all out with their environmental efforts, trying to make the world a better place? It has to be an act, and it's annoying me that everyone but me seems to be falling for it.

My bad mood lifts a little, at the sight of a crowd of people all walking up the pathway to my little shop. I watch, as people marvel at the Christmas decorations outside. I am delighted to see that the slushy remains of the snowfall has caused Seb's spray-painted markings on the road to almost disappear, leaving behind nothing but running colours on the wet road which, although they still look out of place, are less conspicuous.

I follow the crowd into the shop and spot a panic-stricken Gaz behind the counter, because he hasn't been trained on how to deal with customers yet. When he notices me, I watch as his panic turns into relief.

'Don't worry, I'm here,' I tell him, joining him behind the counter. 'I can show you the ropes with real customers, rather than hypothetical ones.'

As customers step up to the counter with their purchases, I begin taking Gaz through the motions of how to serve them.

Gaz's natural charm shines through with the customers and, to his credit, he manages to be charming without flirting, even when he serves a woman in an especially low-cut top. I would've thought that would trigger the horny Santa in him, but he is the model employee.

'This isn't so bad,' he says. 'It's a good laugh.'

I smile. It's hard not to be taken with the atmosphere here when it's busy. Seeing everyone so happy, so full of festive cheer, so in awe of all the decorations – it's nice.

As Gaz serves customers, I rearrange things behind the counter, making it an easier space for Gaz to work in. It may be organised chaos back here, but it's my chaos. Only I know where everything is.

'This place is different when it has customers,' I hear Seb's voice from behind me.

'It is,' I reply. 'You see, Christmas shops are popular, people just need to know where they are.'

He gives me a very business-like nod. 'I just had a few questions about the place,' Seb says. 'When you have time?'

'How about now?' I suggest, just wanting to get it out of the way. 'You can handle things, right, Gaz?'

'Oh, you know me, I can handle anything,' he says with a wink.

I ponder for a second whether or not he's flirting with me. I don't think he is. I think a flirtatious tone and winking just come naturally to him. I imagine he's always like this, whether he's buying milk or asking for directions.

'Come through to the kitchen,' I instruct Seb.

As he steps behind the counter to follow me, I notice Gaz look him up and down, giving him an intimidating glare. Well, as intimidating as he can be with a man who is 6 inches taller than him.

We take a seat at the kitchen table.

'What are these?' Seb asks, looking at the plate on the table.

'Christmas chocolates for my niece and nephew,' I tell him. 'They're milk chocolate, with crushed-up candy canes and popping candy – feel free to try one. The kids love them. I make them every year.'

Seb pops one of the chocolates in his mouth.

'Ivy, these are amazing,' he says through a mouthful. 'You made these?'

'I was a confectioner,' I tell him. 'I used to make chocolates, sweets – all kinds of treats really – at one of the shops in town.'

'So you actually were a chef in a past life,' he says. 'I thought maybe you were just being cute. Can I…'

'Help yourself,' I say with a slight laugh. 'I can always make more.'

Seb gleefully takes another chocolate. 'So, I only have a few questions that you can hopefully help me with,' he starts, before placing the chocolate in his mouth.

'Sure, go for it,' I say.

'Does the traffic ever get noisy, on the road outside?'

'There is almost no traffic at all out there,' I say. 'I told you, satnavs don't bring people this way.'

'That's great,' he says. I suppose it is great for him. His customers will have booked; they won't be coming in from the street.

'Is it not a bit creepy here, just you, no other buildings, people, traffic…'

'I'm not a teenage girl in a horror movie.' I laugh. 'I've lived here my whole life. I'm used to it.'

'I'm used to living in apartments, with lots of neighbours, in cities with lots of sirens and drunk people shouting throughout the night.'

'Well, you won't need to worry about that here,' I tell him. 'There's virtually no noise here. Just foxes, the distant mooing of cows, bats…'

'Are there bats in here?' he asks, suddenly adopting a more formal tone.

'In the shop? No.' I laugh again.

'What about in the trees outside?'

'Unsurprisingly, I haven't climbed them recently,' I tell him. 'Why?'

'Well, we're not getting rid of the trees, but you're not allowed to disturb nesting bats, so that could be a problem,' Seb says, fully snapped back into business mode.

Oh, how I'm praying for a problem. Perhaps I could get some bats from somewhere, put them up in the shop somewhere, then he'll have to leave the place alone. Although not only would I not know where to find bats, I'm also weirdly terrified of them. I think I essentially view them as very large moths with teeth – a concept that is truly terrifying.

'Anything else?' I ask.

'That's it for now,' he replies. 'Can I take one for the road?'

He gestures towards the plate, and I nod.

'Hey, who is the guy out there?'

'Santa Claus,' I reply, straight-faced.

'He's shorter than I expected.' Seb laughs.

'Shorter? Not thinner, younger, or more covered with tattoos?' I reply, in Gaz's defence, for some reason.

'He didn't give me the warmest of looks,' Seb points out. 'I must be on his naughty list.'

'Sounds about right.'

'So, is he new here? Mr Andrews said you worked here alone.'

What does Seb care? It's none of his business.

'He is new,' I reply. 'He used to play Santa at the garden centre. Now he's going to do it here, and he's helping out with shop duties.'

'Are you old friends or something? He seems very protective of you,' Seb observes.

'Something like that,' I reply. I don't mention that we haven't even celebrated our 48-hour anniversary yet.

'He kind of seemed like he was flirting with you…'

'Are these business questions?' I ask. 'Are they going to help you with the sale?'

Seb smiles.

'That's just the way he is. He flirts with everyone,' I explain, although I don't know why I'm telling Seb this. 'He's harmless; it's not like he's planting kisses on me under false pretences.'

He must think I'm stupid, that maybe if he gives me a bit of attention, I'll do whatever he wants, because I'm a desperate female and he knows the power he has over women – well, not this one.

'Ivy, that's not what that was,' Seb explains. 'I wasn't trying to get one over on you. We were under the mistletoe, we were getting along… It just felt right, didn't it?'

'It didn't,' I say firmly. 'Do you know how many strangers I kiss under the mistletoe, what with it being there all year round?'

The answer is zero – I kiss zero people under that mistletoe. Well, I suppose my total is one now, since Seb.

'I'll get going then,' he says, but his eyes aren't on me, they're on the chocolates.

'Take one,' I insist.

He flashes that cheeky, dimpled smile of his at me, the one that, when I first saw it, sent me all googly-eyed. Now, it just makes him seem kind of smug.

'Probably see you tomorrow,' he says as he heads for the door.

Oh, I *can't wait*!

Chapter 10

It's true what they say: men are like buses. And, no, I don't mean they're dirty, unreliable, and will let just about anyone ride them. I mean you go from having none in your life, only for two to come along at once. That's me, the girl who has no men present in her day-to-day life – unless you count the postman – and now I'm spending my morning with two: Gaz and Seb.

I've gotten so used to spending my workdays alone but here I am, splitting my time between helping Gaz get to grips with things on the now much busier shop floor, and chatting with Seb in the kitchen, who seems to have an infinite list of questions for me.

I've noticed that Seb has a major sweet tooth and can't resist any of the homemade festive treats I place down in front him. There's something really attractive about watching him eat, which I hate to admit, even if it's only to myself. It just reminds me that, the first day I met him, I felt such an attraction towards him – I let him kiss me, for crying out loud, even if it was just a peck – and now it makes me feel sick, because he's the enemy.

'What's this key for?' Gaz asks me, taking a small, silver key out from inside the till.

'You see that ornament, over there?' I gesture towards a bauble, locked inside a box behind a glass door. 'That's an antique. My mum bought it at an auction.'

'How much is it for sale for?'

'It's £150,' I tell him. Gaz sucks air through his teeth. 'It's real gold. Don't worry, it's mostly just for show – no one will ever buy it.'

I remember my mum buying lots of antique decorations at this auction like it was yesterday. She picked up a few pieces, but this hammered gold sphere of festive ivy was her favourite. She said it was artisanal craftsmanship at its finest. Still, very few people want to own a £150 Christmas decoration, so it's more of an exhibit than an item I'm expecting to sell.

'Busy again today,' Gaz says, as he glances across the shop floor.

I smile. We might not be as heaving as we were back when my mum was running things, but this is such a vast improvement. When I go for my meeting with the bank later this week, the numbers I show them are going to be a lot better. It's a shame that it took potentially losing the shop to give me the drive to make big changes for the better, but at least I'm doing it now and I can't help but notice that my days are no longer boring.

'Can you handle things, if I go answer more of Seb's questions?'

Gaz pulls a face. 'Sure,' he replies. 'I'd tell him to shove off, though.'

After Seb left yesterday, I filled Gaz in on everything that is going on and, if he didn't like Seb based on first impressions, he really doesn't like him now that he knows he's going to knock the shop down.

'I just need to get enough money together to buy the place before he does,' I say under my voice. 'That'll tell him to shove off.'

'You're small but scrappy,' Gaz observes. 'I like it.'

Small, yes, but scrappy? I don't think so. Recent goings-on might have lit a fire under me, but this isn't how I usually am.

'Maybe I like it too,' I think out loud.

'Go on a date with me,' he says.

'Gaz, come on, stop it,' I insist.

'Just one drink,' he persists. 'Just one, and if you don't have fun, we'll never do it again.'

'Gaz…'

'OK, fine, if I sell the antique, will you go for a drink with me?'

'If you sell a £150 single decoration, will I go for a drink with you?'

Gaz nods. In recent weeks, I've struggled to make that in a whole day.

'I'll consider it.' I laugh. 'But it's been for sale for decades, so…'

Gaz laughs. When he does, the skin around his eyes crinkles up, making his eyes look almost closed. He might be a cheeky flirt, but there's a warmth to him that I find endearing.

I laugh to myself as I head into the kitchen, quietening down when I realise Seb is doing a video call. I notice, on his screen, two other men and a window with what I'd imagine are stocks – numbers and charts that look like every movie portrayal of the stock exchange I've ever seen.

Weirdly, I feel like one of the men on the screen is looking at me. He says something in a language I don't recognise, which causes Seb to turn around and look at me.

'Sorry, I won't be long,' he says, turning back to the screen, conversing with the men in whatever language it is they speak.

I leave the room, giving Seb some privacy. Not that I could tell what they were saying.

'Sorry if I disturbed you,' I say, heading back in once I'm certain he's finished.

'You didn't,' he replies.

'Another cup of tea?' I ask.

'That would be great,' Seb says.

As I fill the kettle I pull a face at my reflection in the window, wondering why I'm being so nice and accommodating with him.

'What language was that you were speaking?' I ask curiously.

'Dutch,' he tells me. 'I was talking to associates in Amsterdam.'

I suppose that's impressive, but what does it matter? Gaz might not speak perfect English, and Seb might speak several languages, but it doesn't dictate who is a good person and who isn't, does it?

I place his tea down in front of him.

'Thanks,' he says. 'Just what I need, after all the chocolate and biscuits I've eaten while I've been sat here.'

He sounds like he means it, so I smile.

'Have you started work on your eBay store yet?' he asks.

'I have, actually,' I tell him. 'Maybe it's just the time of year, but I've had a few sales already. Thank you for such a good idea.'

'You're welcome,' he replies.

Seb's phone vibrates on the table. 'Sorry, I'd better take this,' he says.

'No worries,' I reply.

Speaking of eBay, it's probably a good idea to put the antique bauble on there – maybe someone on the world wide web might be willing to splash £150 on a golden decoration.

'All going OK?' I ask Gaz as I walk past him.

'Really good, actually,' he tells me.

'Really good? Wow,' I reply, but my smile soon drops as I see that the cabinet door is open, and the antique bauble is missing.

With a shop full of people, I don't want to make a scene. Instead, I calmly make my way back to Gaz.

'Gaz, the bauble has gone,' I say quietly.

'I know,' he replies, all smiles.

'You know?' I reply. 'Have…have you taken it?'

'What? No! I've sold it.'

I furrow my brow. 'Gaz, it's been maybe 30 minutes since we spoke about it. You're telling me you've sold it?'

He nods proudly.

I step behind the counter and pop open the till and, sure enough, there does appear to be an extra £150 in cash, as well as a receipt to say we've sold it.

'Wh… How?' I ask.

'Just got the gift of the gab.' He laughs. 'Some woman came in and, you know when you can just tell someone has money? So I point it out to her, tell her we've got a guy flying in from Japan to see it. This lady, American she was, was suddenly interested. I told her it was an antique and real gold – and that it used to belong to the current Duke of Sussex.'

While the description and the value of the bauble are true, its origin story is not.

'The Duke of Sussex is Prince Harry,' I tell him.

'Is it?' he replies. 'I knew I'd heard it somewhere.'

'She believed we had an antique bauble that we got off Prince Harry?'

'Yeah. She really liked it though, very satisfied customer.'

I can't help but laugh as well.

'Gaz, that's amazing,' I say. 'That thing has been here my entire adult life. I never thought I'd shift it and you managed to while I was making a cup of tea.'

He gives a modest shrug.

'Come here,' I say, grabbing him for a hug.

I might've only hired Gaz because I felt bad that he'd lost his job, but it turns out it was a great decision.

Seb emerges through the door behind the counter, putting him in awkwardly close proximity to our hug.

'I just sold a bauble,' Gaz tells him, by way of an explanation.

'Do you hug every time you make a sale?' he asks. 'Wow, business must be bad.'

I frown, noticing a sudden change in Seb.

'It was a special bauble,' I tell him. 'An expensive antique.'

'Great,' he replies. 'Do you have enough money to buy the shop now?'

'What do you mean?' I ask.

'Come on, Ivy, don't play innocent,' Seb says. 'I just got off the phone with Mr Andrews. He told me you're working to outbid me.'

'I'm not trying to outbid you,' I tell him. 'I doubt I could, I'm not stupid. But Mr Andrews knows how much the shop means to me, and he said he'd sell it to me, if I could buy it.'

'You've been lying to me all this time,' Seb says. 'Pretending to help me.'

'I really don't think you can play the morality card,' I point out.

Seb exhales deeply. 'We need to talk about this,' he says. 'We need to clear the air. Why don't we go for a drink tonight, somewhere neutral, and talk about this like adults?'

'I can't tonight,' I say. 'Gaz and I have plans.'

I watch as Gaz's ears prick up, like a dog who has just heard the word 'walkies'.

'Really?' Seb asks in disbelief.

'Really,' I reply. 'I promised.'

It was never my intention to go for a drink with Gaz tonight, but I absolutely don't want to go for a drink with Seb, especially now he's on to me. I'm sure I can handle having one drink with Gaz – we can treat it as a sort of strategy meeting – if it means avoiding an awkward chat with Seb.

'And where are the two of you going?' he asks.

'Few drinks in The Hopeful Ghost,' Gaz suggests. 'See where we end up.' He gives that unsubtle eyebrow wiggle of his that he uses to make his flirtatious tone crystal clear.

'I see,' Seb says. 'Well, have a great night.'

'Cheers, pal,' Gaz calls after him in his strong Yorkshire accent, which seems stronger than ever, in comparison with Seb's

Oxfordshire accent. Gaz wraps an arm around me. 'Glad you came to your senses,' he says.

'Oi,' I say, wiggling free. 'It's just to celebrate you selling the bauble, nothing else.'

'We'll see.' Gaz laughs. 'No one can resist the Gazza charm.'

We'll see, indeed. Although I'm sure that, if I can resist Seb, with his Henry-Cavill-meets-Jamie-Dornan face, physique, accent, and bank balance, I don't think I'm going to struggle to resist a horny Santa with his own name tattooed on his arm.

Chapter 11

Of all the bars and pubs in Marram Bay, The Hopeful Ghost is the place to be. It's a large pub, with a massive circular bar in the heart of the main room, which you often won't even be able to make out for people on a busy night. It has a rustic charm and a roaring log fire, which makes it a wonderful place to be on a cold winter night, like tonight, sipping a glass mug of their secret-recipe mulled wine, listening to the male/female duo playing their acoustic guitars, singing Christmas songs in the corner.

A chunky pug comes running over to me, immediately throwing himself onto his back to have his tummy tickled in that adorable way dogs do. I happily oblige.

'I'm not much of an animal person,' Gaz tells me.

I don't know what it is about animal people that just makes me instantly more trusting of them. Similarly, if a person tells me that they don't like animals, I wonder what is wrong with them.

The owner calls the pug and he happily waddles back over to his own table.

'So,' I say.

'So,' Gaz replies. 'You look nice, by the way, I don't think I told you.'

'Oh, thanks,' I reply, glancing down at the red, off-the-shoulder peplum dress that I don't get much opportunity to wear. Well, I don't often go out for drinks, so I thought I'd dress up, curl my long blonde hair, and apply more make-up than I'd usually ever have cause for. When I applied my red lipstick in the mirror, I couldn't help but smile. I never get to dress up and I can't believe how different I look.

Gaz has made an effort too, wearing jeans and a white, long-sleeved T-shirt. His hair looks neater than usual and even his beard looks tidier, although no shorter. It looks like he's used some kind of taming product.

I glance down at my glass of white wine, examining the contents, considering whether or not I can leave if I down it. Gaz and I don't really have much in common so, now that we're done talking about work, we don't have much to say to each other.

'Are you sure you'll be OK managing the shop alone tomorrow?' I ask, breaking the silence.

'No worries,' he says, swigging his beer. 'You go knock 'em dead at the bank.'

I have a meeting tomorrow to find out where I stand with getting a mortgage, to buy the place myself. I'm nervous – very nervous – and had hoped that coming out tonight might help to calm my nerves, but no such luck.

'Ivy, Gaz, fancy bumping into you two here.'

I glance up from my drink, to see Seb standing there, along with a familiar face.

'Hi,' I say.

'Have you met Charlie?' he asks me, gesturing towards the brunette woman standing beside him, the quintessential 'girl next door', her arm hooked around his. 'We met a few days ago and she's been insisting she take me for a drink.'

'I have met Charlie,' I reply. 'I brought my niece and nephew's rabbit to you recently.'

Charlie is a vet at the local animal surgery, and it's not just animals she loves, it's people too – most specifically men, with healthy bank balances. The locals know all too well that Charlie is always the first to welcome wealthy men into town, although she's yet to snag one for keeps.

Charlie is short – maybe even as short as I am – and seeing how small she looks next to Seb gives me a glimpse of how little I must look next to him.

Charlie gathers her hair and lets it fall at one side of her head.

'I remember the rabbit,' she says. 'How's it doing?'

'It died.'

'Oh no,' she replies with perhaps more emotion than you'd expect. 'When?'

'The day after we saw you, actually. Although I'm sure it's not a reflection on your work,' I quickly add.

'Remind me of the name,' she says.

'Ivy,' I reply.

'No, silly,' she says with a snort. 'The rabbit.'

'Oh. Buddy.'

'Buddy,' she repeats back. 'Rest in peace, Buddy.'

'And this is Gaz,' Seb says.

Gaz does that weird pointing thing he does in acknowledgement of people.

'Nice to meet you,' Charlie says. 'Right, I'll go get our drinks.'

'I'll get them,' Seb says.

'No, no,' she insists. 'I said I'd buy you a drink, silly.'

Charlie's fondness for calling people 'silly' is really starting to annoy me. I also feel like rule number one in the gold-digger handbook is to make sure that you pay for something to get the ball rolling, to make you seem like less of a gold-digger. Or maybe I should just stop listening to rumours and admit that I'm weirdly jealous that she's here with Seb. But then again what do I care?

Charlie trots off to the bar in her green Hunter wellies, which sit at the bottom of her woolly-tight-clad legs. She's wearing a bright yellow raincoat which, given her height (or lack thereof) makes her look a little like the kid from It.

'Well, what a coincidence,' I say, with just a hint of sarcasm.

'I know.' Seb laughs, removing his long, black coat to reveal an outfit not dissimilar to Gaz's. Seb is wearing a pair of black skinny jeans, which look a little under pressure trying to contain his thighs, and a long-sleeved white T-shirt that clings to the ripple of each muscle – I didn't know that was lingering, under his suits.

Right on cue, the pug comes plodding back over, to inspect the new person at the table. I don't know why, but I don't expect Seb – who always looks so pristine and business-like – to be a dog lover, but I'm wrong.

'Hey, mate,' Seb says, dropping to his knees to get better acquainted with his new friend. 'Oh my God, aren't you gorgeous. Aren't you just the cutest thing.'

When the pug is satisfied with the amount of attention he has received, he waddles off again. Seb takes a seat next to me.

'What?' He laughs.

'Nothing,' I reply. 'You just don't seem like the kind of guy who would be friendly to animals.'

'What kind of guy do I seem like?' he asks.

'Erm, like the kind of guy who would steal a bunch of Dalmatians so a horrible woman could make a coat out of them,' I reply, honestly.

Seb just laughs again. 'No, I love dogs. My dog passed away last year, actually,' he starts, pausing to clear his throat, sounding genuinely cut up about it still. 'He had a good life; he was old.'

'What was his name?' I ask.

'Eric,' he replies, with a smile. 'Everyone always said it was a funny name for a dog. He wasn't the easiest dog to live with; he was a little devil. I think his worst crime was when he ate an irreplaceable souvenir that I brought back from Antarctica. It was a wooden carved penguin from the gift shop at Vernadsky station that sells homemade items. Eric ate my penguin and, do you know what, I wasn't even mad, I just loved him so much. I'm not close with my family – I never really see them to be honest – but Eric was always there for me. He went wherever I went; he was always pleased to see me. He might have ruined a few of my things, but he made my life.'

Oh, God, it's taking everything I've got not to cry right now. There is such a lump in my throat.

'That dog had you for a mug.' Gaz laughs.

'Maybe,' Seb replies with a sad smile.

'What did I miss?' Charlie asks, placing two pints of cider down in front of her. She removes her coat to reveal a white bodycon dress that isn't leaving all that much to the imagination.

I notice Gaz staring and give him a subtle jab with my elbow.

'Nothing,' Gaz says, snapping out of his trance. 'Just these two being depressing.'

'Oh, no, none of that tonight,' Charlie says. 'We're celebrating. Seb told me all about his plans and they're just wonderful, aren't they?'

'Hmm,' I reply, insincerely.

'With the environmental plans, especially,' she persists. Ergh, I'm really not in the mood for sitting here, listening to her butt-kiss Seb all evening.

'I'm thinking of getting a pet,' Gaz tells her.

'Oh?' she replies. 'What kind?'

I suspect Gaz is just looking for an excuse to talk to Charlie. They start to chat between themselves.

'We need to talk,' Seb says to me quietly, so that only I can hear.

'No, we don't,' I correct him.

'Ivy, it's crazy to think you can buy the shop and the land without any money.'

'You're just worried you'll lose your plot.'

'No, I'm worried you will,' he says. 'Don't ruin yourself for a business.'

'It's not just a business,' I remind him. 'It's my mum's.'

'Ivy...'

'Isn't that right, Ivy?' Gaz interrupts.

'Hmm?'

'I'm great with kids and animals, right?'

'Right,' I reply. Exclusively kids and animals, though.

'What are you two talking about?' Charlie asks, suddenly paying attention. 'You're looking a little intense.'

'We were just talking about business,' Seb says. 'Ivy makes all these amazing festive chocolates, sweets and biscuits.'

'I just make them for my niece and nephew,' I say.

'Yes, and I think she should sell them. They're incredible,' Seb stresses. 'I think people would pay a lot of money for them.'

'Yeah, they're great,' Gaz chimes in, not one to be outdone by Seb.

'You should take some home for your son,' I tell him.

'Who?' Gaz replies.

'Your son,' I repeat.

'I don't have a son.'

'Yes you do,' I tell him. 'You told me, when I hired you, that you were a single dad.'

'Oh.' Gaz laughs wildly. 'No, sorry, that was just to get me the job.'

I feel my jaw drop.

'Anyway,' Seb interrupts, changing the subject. 'I was just telling Ivy that, in business, you have to be flexible.'

'I'm flexible, FYI,' Charlie tells him, with an unsubtle flirtatious tone that Gaz is no stranger to.

'Well,' I say, knocking back the last sip of wine in my glass before standing up. 'We should probably get going, Gaz, right? Early night tonight.'

'Ooh, it's like that, is it?' Charlie teases.

It's not, at all. What I meant is that we need separate early nights, because Gaz is opening up the shop tomorrow and I'm heading out early for my meeting at the bank.

'Something like that,' I reply casually. I don't know why but suddenly I want Seb to think there's something between me and Gaz. Well, if he's turning up with Charlie, rubbing her flexibility in my face, why shouldn't I do the same? 'Bye.'

'See you tomorrow, Ivy,' Seb calls after me.

Outside the pub, away from the warm lighting and the even warmer log fire, it's so dark and cold. I tighten the belt on my coat.

'So, my place or yours?' Gaz asks. 'If we go to yours, I'll be ready for work in the morning.'

'What? Gaz, no!'

'You said we were getting an early night.'

'Yes, separately,' I point out. 'You're opening up the shop early, I'm at the bank – we need to be up early, so we need to get to bed early.'

'Oh,' he replies. 'So…you're not interested?'

'Gaz…I'm your boss – I like to think we're friends too, but when I say no, I mean no, OK?'

'Hmm,' he replies. 'OK. So…'

'So you go to your place and I'll go to mine.'

'OK.' He laughs. 'Night, love.'

'See you in the morning,' I call after him as he walks away, leaving me alone outside the pub.

I glance back at the window where we were sitting, where Charlie and Seb are happily chatting away. What was he thinking, turning up where he knew I'd be, with a girl in tow? Was that for my benefit? I don't know what he's playing at, but he needs to stop. My life is stressful enough right now. I don't need his games.

Chapter 12

'What now, Auntie Ivy?'

'I just need a second, Chloe,' I reply.

I'm sat in the driver's seat of my car, massaging my temples as I try to get my stressed-out ducks in a row.

'The bank was fun,' Chloe informs me.

'Yes,' I lie. It might have been fun for Chloe and Harry, who got to sit and play with toys. It was less fun for me, who was told that, due to her situation, getting a mortgage was going to be tricky. The fact that I am going it alone, along with my financial instability, means I'll need a much larger deposit than I thought, with much higher monthly repayments to really twist the knife. The advisor I spoke to did say that my business had drastically improved recently, but that I would need to sustain it.

Things don't look great, but I don't feel like my horse is out of the race just yet. Business is improving, and I've still got a few more tricks up my sleeve. Maybe, just maybe, with some sort of Christmas miracle, I can make the deposit, or perhaps what I do manage to make will be enough for the bank to take pity on me (not that anyone has ever known a bank to do that...) or if the worst does happen, at least I will have made some money to live on, until I figure out what I'm supposed to do with my life.

I don't think it helped my case that I turned up to my meeting with two fidgety children in tow. I'd only just got in my car, ready to set off, when Holly called and asked me if I could take the kids. She said that she needed to 'do some things' and that the kids needed someone to take them to buy her a Christmas present – none of which I buy, but no amount of asking got a different answer from her. She may not have sounded truthful, but she did sound desperate, so I agreed.

I picked the kids up, along with some money from Holly, that she told me to use on a present for her, from the kids, and then she got in her car and left. It was weird because, although she'd made an effort, she wasn't exactly dressed up, so I couldn't even guess where she was going. I feel like if she were going to battle her way through Christmas shoppers, she would've just gone in her trackies for comfort and for grabbing items with ease, but she's definitely spent a little time in front of the mirror this morning.

After my disastrous meeting, I took the kids shopping and now we're just sitting in the car outside my shop, because I called Holly 30 minutes ago and she said she wasn't home yet.

A knock on my car window causes me to jump out of my skin.

'Hey,' I say, winding my window down. 'You scared me half to death!'

'Sorry.' Seb laughs. 'How's it going?'

'Going fine,' I reply.

'You and Gaz get back safe last night?'

I ignore him.

'Who are these two little angels, sat listening ever so attentively?' he asks.

I glance in the mirror and see Chloe eyeballing him, listening to every word we're saying.

'This is Chloe and Harry, my sister's kids.'

'Hey guys,' he replies. 'You having fun with your auntie?'

'We're bored *now*,' Chloe tells him. 'But we had fun at the bank.'

'You've been to the bank?' he asks me.

'We've been to lots of places,' I say.

'Are you Auntie Ivy's boyfriend?' Chloe asks him.

I turn around in my seat at the speed of light. 'Chloe, no,' I tell her. 'That's a rude question to ask.'

'My mum says Auntie Ivy needs a man,' Chloe announces.

I turn back to face Seb, my cheeks flushing with embarrassment.

'Just for building bunk beds,' I clarify. 'Holly and I were having a bit of trouble, and their dad works away. We're just waiting for him to come home for Christmas, aren't we, kids?'

'When is he back?' Seb asks.

'Christmas Eve,' I reply.

'Do you know who is really good at building bunk beds?' Seb asks the kids, getting them all hyped up.

'Who? Who?'

'Me,' he replies. 'I could put them together in no time.'

I laugh it off.

'Can you do it today?' Chloe asks.

'How about right now?' he replies.

'What? No, you don't have to do that,' I tell him. 'You can't.'

'Why not, Auntie Ivy?' Chloe asks.

'Yeah, why not, Auntie Ivy?' Seb echoes, flashing those cheeky dimples of his.

'You're busy,' I say.

'No, I'm not,' he replies. 'Come on, let me do this.'

I think for a moment. If I know Seb's MO – which I think I do by now – he probably thinks that, by doing something nice for me, he'll win me over. He really does think his charm and his fake generosity will get him whatever he wants. Well, he's wrong and I'm going to play him at his own game.

'OK, sure,' I reply.

'Yeah?' He smiles.

'Yeah,' I reply. 'Thank you.'

Seb probably thinks he's playing me so good right now, but I'm playing him. This little stunt isn't going to sway me at all, but it is going to get my niece and nephew's bunk beds built, and that's all I care about.

'You kids ever been in a convertible?' Seb asks them.

'A car without a roof,' I tell them.

They both shake their heads.

'I know it's a bit cold,' Seb starts. 'But if you button your coats up, and I turn the heated seats up to full blast, we could drive over to your house with the top down.'

'Cool,' Chloe replies.

'Fancy going in my car?' Seb says. 'You did give me a lift on your train that one time.'

'OK, sure,' I reply, unable to fight off a small smile.

'OK, let's go,' he says, helping us out of my old banger and into his swanky sports car.

Chloe and Harry are mesmerised by Seb's car. I don't think they've ever seen anything like it in real life before. Seb fastens them into the back before getting in and putting the top down. The kids gaze up at the roof as it disappears, like a real-life Transformer. As their little jaws drop, I can't help but smile. I suppose it's nice of Seb to do this for them, but I'm not going to be swayed by it.

'You seem like a two-seater kind of guy,' I tell him as we make the short journey to Holly's, who has since let me know that she is home. When she learned that I was bringing Seb to help build the bunk beds, she got very excited.

'I seem like a lot of things to you.' He laughs. 'None of them are accurate.'

I'm pretty sure I've got most of them right.

'So, I finally get to meet your sister,' he says, as though that's where our weird working relationship was heading all along.

'Mummy and Auntie Ivy are twins,' Chloe tells him, shouting loudly from the back of the car.

'Oh really?' Seb replies. 'Can you tell them apart?'

'They don't look the same at all,' Chloe replies, with more emphasis than I'd like. 'They came from the same tummy, but not the same egg.'

'Oh wow.' Seb smiles at me. 'I don't think I knew what an egg was at that age. I'm not sure I know what one is now.'

I laugh. 'I don't think she actually knows what it means,' I say quietly. 'I think that's just Holly's way of explaining to her why we're twins, but we look different.'

'Not even a family resemblance then?' he asks.

'Erm, a little, I guess. Holly got all the height and the looks – and the awesome kids,' I say for the benefit of those in the back of the car.

'And what did you get?' he asks me.

'The shop,' I say, with a slight laugh. 'It's a left here.'

We turn onto the street where Holly lives and I direct Seb onto the driveway.

'This is a nice house,' Seb observes, as we get out of the car, outside Holly's detached house.

'It is,' I reply.

'What does your sister do?'

'She's a housewife,' I tell him. 'She looks after the house and the kids while her husband is away. He's got a pretty good job.'

'What does he do?'

'He works in the oil industry. He's an engineer. He's away a lot, working on oil rigs.'

'So he must go a long time without seeing his family?' Seb enquires. I nod. 'Wow, I'm not sure I'd want to be away from my wife and kids for so long – if I ever have them.'

'Hmm,' I reply, dismissively, ushering the kids towards the front door.

'Hello,' I call out.

'Hello,' my sister says as she emerges from the kitchen. She seems a little frazzled, and there's red sauce all over her apron, but when she spots Seb, her tone changes.

'Hello, hello,' she says, looking him up and down. 'You're Seb?'

'Guilty,' he replies.

Holly giggles like a little girl. And, here we go. Another woman falling for the supposedly irresistible Seb Stone charm offensive.

'It's nice of you to take time out of your busy schedule to come and help us.'

I notice my sister suddenly sounds distinctly less Yorkshire than usual.

'I'm happy to help,' he replies. 'I never get to build fun stuff and your kids are adorable.'

'My kids? Oh, yes,' Holly replies, as though she temporarily forgot she'd had them. 'You'll stay for dinner, won't you?'

'I'm sure Seb has to rush off,' I insist.

'Actually, I don't,' he replies. 'I'd love to stay for dinner.'

'Spaghetti Bolognese OK?' she replies.

'It's one of my favourites,' he tells her.

I roll my eyes. 'I'll show you where the room is, so you can get started,' I tell him. Sooner he gets started, sooner he can leave.

'OK, thanks. I'm going to need your help though.'

'Me?' I reply.

'No, Harry,' he jokes. 'Yes, you. Nothing difficult, I promise, I just need an extra pair of hands.'

Ergh, I was really hoping we could just shut him upstairs and leave him to it. When I thought I had his MO figured out, I didn't quite have it right. Yes, he's trying to use his faux nice guy persona to score points and get what he wants, but he's also only doing this to get me on my own, so he can talk to me when I have no choice but to listen.

'After you,' I instruct, gesturing towards the staircase.

Holly grabs hold of my arm. 'You two behave up there,' she whispers into my ear.

I shoot her a filthy glance before following Seb up the stairs. 'It's that room over there,' I tell him.

We walk into the kids' room, where the pile of bunk bed parts are exactly as we abandoned them.

Seb glances at the instructions before taking off his jacket and his tie, and unbuttoning his top shirt.

'First up, we need to attach the bed ends to the side rails,' he says. 'Simple enough.'

'Simple enough if you know how,' I tell him.

Seb arranges the parts where we need them and it's my job to hold the pieces together while he fixes them in place.

'I'm concerned about you,' he eventually says.

I shrug my shoulders.

'Ivy, I'm concerned about you,' he says again.

'If you were that concerned, you wouldn't be doing what you're doing,' I tell him.

'Building bunk beds?'

'Ruining my life,' I tell him.

'Ivy, it's business. Whether I buy the place or not, Mr Andrews is selling it, and unless things change, whether he sells it or not, your business is failing.'

'Things are really picking up,' I tell him.

'I know, you're doing an amazing job, but it's not enough to be able to afford to stay there – I'm sure the bank told you as much.'

I don't say anything.

'Is that why you went?' he asks. 'To see about a mortgage?'

Still, I don't stay anything.

'I know that it was your mum's place, and you don't want to say goodbye, but your mum's memory isn't in a shop, it's in you, and your sister. There's a term we use in business: the sunk cost fallacy. It's where you make decisions based on future values – the more you invest in something, the harder it becomes to stop investing in it. Say you're in a casino and you're gambling, putting money into a slot machine – gamblers believe that, once they've put a certain about of money in, it's better to keep going than it is to quit. When it's the right time to walk away, that's the time to walk away. Don't keep ploughing money and time into the business, just because it's what you've been doing for years. Do not ruin yourself, trying to save something that can't be saved.'

'Finished?' I reply.

'Ivy…'

'Sebastian,' I reply. 'Did you come here to build bunk beds or give me life advice?'

'Both?'

'Let's just stick with bunk beds,' I tell him.

Seb nods and carries on with his work.

'We can still chat though, right? Things will go faster if we chat.'

'Well, if it will make things go faster,' I reply.

'Your sister seems nice,' he says, as he screws two pieces of wood together.

'She is,' I tell him. 'She's a bit stressed at the moment; she's not usually so intense.'

'I like her,' he says. 'And, for the record, you can tell you're sisters.'

'Yeah?'

'Yeah, I'm not sure what it is…just a look you both have in your eyes.'

I feel a little flutter in my chest. That's something my mum always used to say, that we had the same glimmer in our eyes.

In no time at all, the bottom bunk is assembled.

'You didn't really need a man for this, did you?' he asks with a laugh. 'Was it just a ploy to get me here?'

'Yes, I am the kind of person to have hidden agendas,' I reply, with the sarcasm turned up to 10.

'You're the one trying to gazump me,' he points out. 'I've been honest since day one.'

'Erm, day three at best.' I laugh. 'Let me remind you that the first time we met, you came into the shop, didn't tell me who you were or why you were there – when you were, in fact, scoping out the joint. And then you kissed me, which is just so disgusting.'

'The kiss was disgusting or the timing was disgusting?' he asks me.

As much as I want to tell him that I was referring to both, I can't bring myself to be so mean to him.

'The timing,' I say.

'I kissed you because I wanted to,' he tells me.

'Yeah, and I tricked you into building bunk beds with me because I'm just oh-so enjoying the time we're spending together,' I say, again, with a healthy dose of sarcasm.

'I am on your side,' he tells me. 'We don't need to be enemies.'

'Yeah, OK,' I reply.

'I'm serious,' he says. 'If I can help you, let me help you.'

'Wanna buy the shop for me?' I joke. Seb laughs. 'Otherwise, there's nothing you can do for me. But thank you for the kind offer.'

'You're quite sarcastic,' he observes.

'I am,' I reply. 'Life has made me this way.'

Eventually, we have two beds in front of us.

'We just need to attach them to one another, and the ladder, and then we're done.'

'Great,' I reply. I just want this evening to be over with, and the thought of having to sit down and have dinner with him is filling me with dread. Eating dinner with Seb is the last thing I want to do.

'Can I just go and check on my sister, while you're doing that bit?' I ask, as he assembles the ladder.

'Of course,' he replies.

I take a welcome break from talking with Seb to pop to the kitchen and interrogate my sister.

'Hey,' she says brightly. 'Where is Seb?'

'Still upstairs working,' I tell her.

Holly quickly drops her bright and breezy act. 'Dinner is nearly ready,' she tells me. 'It'll be nice, to get to know him better.'

'Why on earth would it be nice?' I ask in disbelief.

'Well, you said he's going to be living there?' she replies. 'And, with Mum and Dad's ashes both being scattered in the garden...'

That's a fact I've been ignoring up until now, fighting furiously to keep it out of my mind because it's just too painful to consider.

'It would be nice if we could visit every now and then, that's all,' she says. 'And, well, you two seem close.'

'We're not close, I'm just stuck babysitting him,' I reply.

'If you say so,' she says as she places spaghetti into a pan of boiling water. 'I just thought I was picking up on some vibes, that's all.'

I feel myself blush.

'Ivy Jones, has something happened between the two of you?' my sister asks, her eyes wide.

'No,' I lie. 'Well, not really.'

'Spill,' she insists.

'On the day we met,' I start, lowering my voice to make sure no one can hear me. 'Seb...flirted with me.'

I decide not to tell Holly that Seb kissed me, because she'll get carried away, thinking it was way more than it was. I'm embarrassed that I let him kiss me before I knew who he was, and what he'd mean for the future of the shop. I never would have let him kiss me if I'd known what his plans were, and I can't stop kicking myself.

'He did?' she squeaks.

'Yep.'

'That's amazing,' my sister coos.

'No, it isn't,' I correct her. 'This was before he told me who he was, before he told me that he was buying the shop. He was just trying to butter me up.'

'I would let him butter me up any day,' she jokes. 'Seriously though, why are you so convinced he isn't genuine? Maybe, if you stop giving him a hard time, let him get on with what he's planning, something could happen.'

'Why would I even want that?' I ask, tearing off a piece of bread to dip it in the pasta sauce. 'He's the enemy, Holly. He's destroying Mum's shop.'

'Mum would want you to be happy with someone, not a shop,' she tells me.

I bite my tongue and turn the focus on her instead. 'Mum would want you to tell me what's going on,' I say.

'Are you changing the subject?'

'Yes, to a more important one.'

'I'm fine,' she insists.

'Except you're not,' I point out. 'You're keeping secrets, lying about where you've got to be and what you've got to do – I can just tell.'

'No, you can't.' She laughs. 'Stop deflecting and go and tell Seb his dinner is ready. You guys can finish the bunk beds after you eat.'

I exhale deeply before heading upstairs. 'Oh, wow, it looks almost finished,' I blurt as I walk into the room.

'I told you it was easy. You just needed a man,' he jokes.

'Well, Holly says your dinner is ready,' I tell him.

'Amazing,' he says, rubbing his hands together. 'I'm starving.'

Seb follows me downstairs.

'I've set the dining table,' Holly says when she spots us. 'Go, take a seat. The kids are already in there.'

When we eat here, we never eat in Holly's dining room apart from special occasions –we eat at the kitchen table. She's pulling out all the stops for Seb, which annoys me. Why doesn't she dislike him as much as I do? Why doesn't she care that he's going to knock down our mum's shop?

'Are the bunk beds done?' Chloe asks us excitedly as we sit down.

'Nearly,' Seb replies. 'You'll be in them tonight, for sure.'

'Cool,' she replies.

Holly brings in a large bowl full of spaghetti and begins serving it, playing mum to each of us, plating up our food, passing us bread and pouring us drinks.

'So, Harry no longer wants a bike for Christmas,' she tells us.

'Oh really?' I reply. 'Well, it's a good job Santa is working at my shop now – you'll have to go and tell him what you want instead.'

'I don't think Santa Claus himself could deliver on this request. He wants a convertible.'

Seb cracks up with laugher. 'Oh no, he's starting young.'

'I've tried to explain to him that he's still too young for a car – let alone a convertible like yours – but he's not having any of it.'

'I'll make a deal with you, Harry,' Seb starts, glancing at his mum for approval. 'I'll take you out in my car whenever you like, how about that?'

'That would be nice, wouldn't it?' Holly says. 'Say thank you, Harry.'

'Thank you, Harry,' he quietly jokes. Harry might not say much, but everything he does say is totally worth it.

'I like this kid.' Seb laughs. 'Both of them. You have a lovely family.'

'Thank you,' Holly replies. 'No kids of your own?'

'None yet,' he replies.

Imagine being a man, having the luxury of being able to have kids whenever you like. I am vaguely aware that my biological clock is ticking, but what can I do about it? Sure, I'd love kids one day, I just don't seem to meet the right men – or any men, for the most part.

More annoying than that, though, is the fact that Seb is here, offering to take my nephew out 'whenever he wants', like he's a part of the family – he isn't. Commandeering our family home does not make him a part of our family and, frankly, I find it weird that he has muscled himself in here tonight the way he has. It's weird, just plain weird.

'So, you're moving here alone?' Holly asks him.

'I am – this food is delicious, by the way.'

'Thanks,' she replies. 'It's one of the few things I do OK. Ivy is the real chef in this family.'

'Oh, I've tried her chocolates and her biscuits,' he tells her. 'Just incredible. I keep telling her she should sell them.'

'Oh, Hol, I still need to find you that Mary costume,' I say to change the subject.

My sister just nods in appreciation, before turning back to Seb.

'Are you spending Christmas here?' she asks nosily.

'I am,' he replies. 'I sold my place in Dublin a little while ago. I've been travelling around, hotel hopping, while I've been looking for somewhere to make my home. Here just feels right.'

'You'll be spending Christmas in a hotel?' she clarifies.

'Yeah, well, one of the B&Bs over on the island.'

'You're spending it *alone* and in a *B&B*?' she shrieks. 'I think you—'

'Holly, I think I can smell burning coming from your kitchen,' I interrupt.

Holly sniffs the air. 'I don't smell anything.'

'I think you should check,' I insist. 'I definitely smell something.'

'OK,' Holly replies, puzzled. 'I'll be right back.'

I give her a few seconds before saying: 'Actually, I'll go help her, make sure she checks properly.'

'No worries,' Seb says. 'I'm sure the kids will keep me company, tell me stories about their Auntie Ivy.'

As much as I want to stay and police this conversation, I hurry into the kitchen to find Holly, peering inside the oven.

'There's no burning anywhere. What are you talking about?' she asks.

'I just needed to get you on your own, to tell you to stop it, right now.'

'Stop what?'

'You were going to ask Seb to have Christmas dinner with us, weren't you?' I ask.

'Ivy, he's going to be alone – where's your Christmas spirit?'

I gasp. 'I have Christmas spirit in abundance, lady. You hate Christmas; what do you care if someone is spending it alone? Seb is Scrooge, pre-ghosts, OK? He doesn't care about us, he just cares about money and getting his own way.'

'I just feel sorry for him, that's all,' she says.

'Holly, promise me you won't ask Seb to eat Christmas dinner with us,' I insist.

'OK, fine, I promise,' she gives in. 'I just feel like if Mum were here, she would've asked him.'

I frown. My mum would be spinning in her grave – if she'd been buried – at the thought of some man muscling in and ruining everything she'd worked hard for. Holly seems to be suggesting that it might be worth giving up the shop if I get a man out of it, which is ridiculous. Not just because no woman needs a man so badly that she should give up her life, but also because Seb doesn't want me, he wants my shop. I feel like I'm the only person in this whole town who can see through him.

'What do you think Seb would like for dessert?' she asks. 'I've got all the stuff you'd need to make your famous Nutella soufflés.'

'Holly, please, don't offer him dessert. I just want this night to be over with, and to go home.'

She sighs. 'Well, you'll be setting off soon enough.'

I am reminded of the fact that Seb drove us here, which means I'll need him to drive me back home too.

After finishing dinner (without dessert) and completing the bunk beds (which, annoyingly, we did need a man for) we say our goodbyes and get in Seb's car.

It may only be a short trip but being trapped in such a confined space with him fills me with dread. He's tried putting the moves on me, flattery, pretending he cares, worming his way in with my family... Who knows what he'll try next?

Chapter 13

'Could you do me a quick favour?' he asks as he pulls out of the drive.

'What's that?'

'Could you check the causeway times, please?'

Oh no, don't tell me he's stuck over here, please! If the tide is in, the road will be closed, and there will be no way Seb can get back to his B&B.

'Sure,' I reply, crossing my fingers that it will be open.

'I didn't realise I'd be staying here so late and I forgot to check,' he says.

'Well, I'm sure Charlie will put you up,' I reply, doing everything I can to say each word without a tone of any kind.

'I don't think so.' Seb laughs.

'Oh?'

'It was just a drink,' he tells me. 'I thought it would be good to try and make some friends but we didn't have all that much in common.'

I don't say anything. I just hurriedly tap my phone to bring up the causeway times. 'Oh,' I say.

'"Oh" doesn't sound good.'

'It's not the worst news,' I tell him. 'It's closed, but it will be open again in an hour and a half.'

'Oh, OK,' he replies. 'Not too long to sit in the car and wait then.'

Ergh, the last thing I want is to spend more time with him, but I can't, in good conscience, let Seb sit in his car in the freezing cold for an hour and a half.

'Do you want to come in?' I ask.

'I don't want to keep you up,' he says.

'No, it's fine, I need to find a nativity costume for Holly anyway.'

'Well, I'll help then,' he suggests. 'Make myself useful.'

We head inside and upstairs in silence.

'I'll just get changed,' I tell him.

'OK,' he replies, hovering by my bedroom door. 'I could go up into the loft?'

I frown for a split second. I suppose he wants to scope it out, see what it's like before he buys the place.

'There's a stick thing propped against the wall over there,' I say as I point. 'It opens the hatch and pulls the ladder down.'

'OK,' he says. 'See you up there.'

There's so much stuff up there – a lot of it from my childhood – so I hurriedly get changed, worried he might see something I don't want him to.

'When was the last time you were up here?' Seb asks, blowing dust off a small trophy before examining it.

'I don't know,' I admit. 'Not that long, I don't think. It doesn't take dust and cobwebs long to take over.'

'So, what are we looking for?' he asks.

'It will be a box marked "nativity costumes" or something similar,' I tell him. I haven't just inherited my mum's sentimental need to hoard, I've inherited everything she ever hoarded too. Luckily my mum kept her things neatly boxed and labelled.

We take a side of the small loft each, carefully moving boxes, looking for the one I need. That's when it jumps out at me, a box with 'James's Memories' written on it. It's things like this that are the reason I don't come up here as much as I should. It's all well and good keeping things to help you remember what you've lost, but sometimes it's just too painful to think about. Sometimes, it's just easier to lock things away in the loft.

'Who is James?' Seb asks.

I pause for a second.

'James was my dad,' I say softly.

I rest my fingertips lightly on top of the box, wondering whether or not to open it, because I'd be opening up so much more than a box.

'Oh, right,' Seb replies. 'You want to take a look? I'm in no rush.'

'Maybe,' I reply.

There's uncertainty in my voice but the box is opened in a matter of seconds. Sometimes, even when we know something will hurt us, we still can't help ourselves, can we?

At the top of the box sits a photo album, which I carefully remove and lay on one of the sealed boxes next to me. As I open the first page I notice Seb curiously slink up alongside me.

'Are they your parents?' he asks. I'm sure he could've made an educated guess, but I feel like he's making an effort to talk to me.

'Yeah,' I reply. 'Audrey and James Jones.'

'It's weird, isn't it?' he muses. 'How pictures of our parents look like they were taken lifetimes ago.'

I nod. There are so many pictures of my parents from the Seventies, before they had Holly and me, before they were married. They look so young and carefree, but the fashion looks so dated, and the pictures all have a warm colouring to them, and a texture that you just don't get anymore. It makes me wonder if, when I'm older, I'll be looking back at pictures like this of myself, but then I realise that I'm already so much older than my parents were in this picture.

I flick through a few more pictures until finally Holly and I make an appearance.

'It was so nice, spending time with your family,' he says. 'I don't spend much time with families.'

I smile.

'Wow, even as kids, you and Holly didn't look alike,' he points out.

'I know.' I laugh. 'There's always been a running joke in the family that one of us got mixed up in the hospital. Holly always used to say it was her who got swapped, that my parents took her home, when her real parents were glamorous celebrities, not Christmas nerds.'

I flick through more of our family photos until we hit the awkward teenage years. I'm a little anxious, for some reason, about Seb seeing me when I was even less cool than I am now, but then it occurs to me that at some point while we were thumbing our way through the pages and laughing at the clothes and hairstyles, my dad just stopped being in the pictures.

'Wow, look at your sister.' He laughs, nodding at a picture of Holly at the height of her Steps obsession.

'I know. She was very fond of her cowboy hat.' I laugh too. 'And, you see those jeans she's wearing, she took a pair of scissors and cut the top couple of inches off, where the belt goes, and then used her friend's lighter to burn the edges so they didn't fray. My mum absolutely hit the roof.'

'I'll bet,' Seb says.

'Only the other day, Holly was talking about when Chloe grows up, and how it's a much scarier time to be a young woman. I reminded her about the house parties she would go to, where she would drink cheap alcohol with strangers, letting them drive her home. It's a miracle she wasn't murdered.'

'And what about you?' Seb asks.

'Me? Look at me. Holly has always stood out, whether it be because of her fashion choices or her wild behaviours, but I've always been boring.'

'You're not boring,' he objects.

'I am,' I say firmly. 'I have the shop, I read, I bake... There's not much else going on in my life.'

I am stopped in my tracks by something I find in the box – something I knew would be there, I suppose, but it just wasn't at the forefront of my mind. I remove two, not quite identical bean-filled cuddly dogs from the box. They're made from some kind of velvety material that feels just as soft as I remember it feeling the first time I held it to my face, when I squeezed it tightly and covered it in my tears.

Beneath the surface, I feel my emotions getting the better of me. I sniff hard and clear my thoughts.

'They're cute,' Seb says.

'My dad bought them for me and Holly when we were eleven – sort of a last-minute Christmas present to add to our Santa sacks. He'd seen them in some boutique shop on his travels and my mum says it was the fact that they were the same thing but looked different that made him think they'd be perfect presents for us. He was on his way home with them just a week before Christmas one night when he hit some ice, swerved off the road and...'

I don't want to finish the sentence.

'Ivy, I'm so sorry,' Seb says, wrapping an arm around me.

I try to shrug casually, although I'm not sure how convincing I am.

I think that, along with Christmas reminding us of Mum, losing Dad so close to Christmas is one of the reasons Holly hates it so much. That's why Mum tried too hard to make it special for us though, because she knew it would always be a hard time with painful memories attached.

'After he died, I clung on to this dog. It felt like my last connection to him. I wouldn't leave the house without it. I had it by my side when I ate, when I slept... It got to a point where my mum thought it might be best to...wean me off it, I guess. The less I depended on it, the more it made me sad to look at it. It was a painful reminder... I was just a kid,' I tell him, like that explains it.

'It's nice that you have it,' he tells me. 'And that you take care of Holly's.'

'Yeah, when my mum gave it to us and explained, Holly shunned it. All it did was upset her. Maybe one day she'll want it and when she does, it's here. I might keep mine out, actually...'

'I'm sorry you've had so much sadness in your life,' he says.

'Thanks.'

'But you still have Holly and the kids, and they worship you. That's a wonderful thing to have.'

'Yeah, they're amazing,' I agree, holding my dog close to my chest.

'You're really lucky to have them,' he tells me. 'Some people put so much emphasis on things – houses, holidays, cars, designer clothes – but, at the end of the day, it's just money that gets you those things. Money can't get you a family.'

At first I want to agree with him, tell him that everything he just said is right and that I've always believed that. But then I look for the hidden agenda and, sure enough, I find one.

'So, what you're telling me is that, because I have a family, I should let go of material things? Like, I don't know, say, my home and my business?'

'Ivy, that's not what I was saying at all,' he says hurriedly, holding his hands out in front of his body defensively.

'Sure it wasn't, Seb. Except you're about as subtle as a grenade.'

'Ivy...'

'Actually, could you go?' I say as I feel the tears stacking up behind my eyes.

'Ivy... OK, if that's what you want,' he replies.

'It is,' I say quickly. 'Thanks for your help.'

'It was nothing,' he insists. 'Goodnight then.'

Without much prompting, Seb goes. Leaving me alone in the loft, surrounded by the things that remind me of the life I had before it started to crumble around me. Maybe he was just being a gentleman, respecting my wishes, leaving me alone because I asked me to, or maybe he's worried that if a murder happens here, it'll be bad for business...

Chapter 14

As I puff air from my cheeks, I slump down in my chair behind the counter, after handing out my final plate of gingerbread truffles. When our first few customers of the day arrived, I thought it would be a lovely idea to hand out a few truffles from the batch I made last night. What I didn't anticipate was just how many customers were going to walk through the door today, and now my gingerbread truffle supplies are as exhausted as I am.

Seeing the shop teeming with people fills my heart with happiness – and neither my heart, nor the shop, has felt this full for such a long time, so I'm trying my hardest to savour it and focus on today rather than worrying about tomorrow.

All the happy faces, marvelling at the items in the shop, visiting our (surprisingly perfectly behaved) Santa Claus – and as people stroll around the place I can't help but hear them all buzzing from their trip here on the train. There's just this magic in the air, which I haven't felt since my mum was alive, when the shop used to be busy. If she could see the shop as it is today, she would be over the moon.

Happy customers and festive cheer aside, there is one other very important thing to note, and that's that, with all the money we're making from the increase in custom (both on and offline)

I can comfortably pay Gaz for working here, pay my bills, and still manage to put some money away to go towards the astronomically large deposit I'll need to get a mortgage to buy this place before Seb does. I might only be taking small step but, with only a couple of weeks until Christmas, at least I'm moving.

Gaz heads into the back room, after another successful shift playing Santa Claus, to hurriedly remove his outfit, which he says he's melting inside of because I have the heating on too high. Yesterday I caught him loosening his pants while he was still out here, so I had to give him a talk about how, best-case scenario, kids might realise he's not really Santa Claus if he's taking his costume off, and, worst-case scenario, it doesn't look great, Santa taking his pants off in front of children. After 15 minutes he re-emerges in his regular clothes, with two cinnamon lattes in his hands.

'I can't make them the same as you can,' he says, placing one down in front of me. 'But I thought I'd try.'

'Thank you,' I say. It looks a little rough around the edges, but it's exactly what I need right now – a little like Gaz himself, really. I do like that – when things appear one way, but are totally different on the inside. Gaz has really surprised me with the way he's stepped up, but I'm so delighted that he has because now I'm not sure how I ever coped without him.

'I still can't believe Seb invited himself over last night,' Gaz says, cradling his mug in his hands, gossiping like a housewife, which makes me smile.

'I know,' I reply. 'At least the kids finally got their bunk beds built, and Holly's husband didn't have to get in late on Christmas Eve and feel like he had to do it right then.'

'I could've built them for you on my own,' he insists. 'You didn't need him.'

'Oh really? Did you build your son's bunk beds?' I ask sarcastically.

Gaz laughs. 'I'm really sorry about that, Ivy, I just really needed this job and it was the only thing I could think of, to make sure you hired me. Little white lies don't hurt anyone, do they?'

'No, they just thoroughly embarrass,' I tell him. 'But it's fine, all is well that ends well.'

'This isn't the end,' he assures me, looking me square in the eyes. 'We're still fighting. We'll show that Seb he can't just muscle into *our* town and do what he likes.'

I smile. Seb has more experience and, more importantly, more resources than we do, so I very much doubt we will show him. Gaz's passion for the cause means so much to me though, because this isn't technically his fight, so he's in my corner because he wants to be.

After the final wave of customers leave to catch the last train back to town, I follow them to the door, wishing them all happy holidays before closing the door, locking it behind them and turning the sign around to show that we're closed. Finally. It's been an amazing day, but it's been a long day. I'll definitely sleep well tonight.

I've no sooner turned my back on the door when I hear a knock on the glass. Peeping out through the window I spot Charlie, standing there in her furry earmuffs, blowing into her cold hands. She raises her eyebrows to signal for me to let her in. Reluctantly, I open the door.

'Charlie, hello,' I say. 'What's up?'

'Hello, Ivy; hello, Gaz,' she says, waving over to him. 'I just wanted a quick word.'

'OK,' I say cautiously. 'What's up?'

Charlie edges closer to the counter so that Gaz can hear what she has to say too. We both stare at her until she eventually spits out exactly why she's here.

'The other night, when we were at the pub,' she starts, pausing to consider her words. 'I'd asked Seb out for a drink a couple of times already and he'd make polite excuses each time. But then, out of nowhere, he suddenly changed his mind and invited me to the Ghost. I figured he'd just seen sense and decided he did want to go out with me – and I felt like we had an amazing time together, even though we wound up spending a little time with you two out of manners or whatever.'

I literally hold my tongue between my teeth, to stop myself saying anything in response to this.

'Anyway, I thought we all had a great time,' she continues. 'But when it came to the end of the night, and it came to going home…he just wasn't interested, at all. He didn't want to go to my place, he didn't want me going back to his B&B – not even a kiss in the car park.'

I shrug my shoulders.

'Come on,' she reasons. 'He shot *me* down. Who does he think he is?'

A person capable of making his own decisions? 'So…'

'So, *he* invited *me* out, but then at the end of the date he goes cold on me. And it wasn't just that he didn't wanna spend the night – I actually tried to kiss him goodnight and he *turned his head.*'

It's kind of hard to understand exactly why Charlie is so upset. I mean, no one likes getting knocked back, but she seems to think that just because she's Charlie, men should be throwing themselves at her feet. If every man not wanting to sleep with you is an upsetting concept, I should constantly be in tears.

'Right,' I reply.

'You know him,' she says. 'I thought you might know what he's playing at – unless he's gay? Gay would explain it.'

I stifle a laugh. 'Nope, he's not gay, sorry.'

'Well, why would he mess me around like that?' she asks, her shoulders dropping as she pouts. 'Can I use your bathroom?'

'Of course,' I tell her. 'Just up the stairs, on the left.'

As soon as Charlie is out of earshot, I lean in to talk to Gaz.

'Is she really this upset over getting knocked back by one guy?' I whisper.

'Probably.' He laughs. 'She'll need to find another victim now.'

I snigger. I don't think Seb is the only one with a hidden

agenda around here; I think everyone in town knows that Charlie's ultimate game plan is to marry well and retire. Strange really, because it's not like she doesn't have a good job – not only is being a vet the perfect job for an animal lover like her, but it's not like she isn't being well paid, is it? I wonder, if the real Henry Cavill – or Jamie Dornan – wandered into the shop and asked me to marry him, if I'd happily say yes, sack off the shop, and go and live a life of luxury. I like to think the shop is more important to me than any of that – but I don't suppose it's ever going to be a dilemma that I need to face. I wish! Movie stars don't just wander into Christmas shops in the middle of nowhere, before popping the question to the frazzled-looking owner the second they clap eyes on them, do they?

'It is weird though,' he says. 'That he knocked her back.'

'Is it?'

'Yeah, well, sounds like she was offering it to him on a plate, and he said no…'

'You wouldn't have said no?'

'Of course not,' he says with a laugh.

I don't pass comment on this.

'What is he playing at?' I wonder out loud. 'Turning up at the pub with her, crashing our plans. He knew that's where we were going to be.'

'Do you think he was trying to make you jealous?' Gaz asks me.

'Me? No, of course not,' I reply. I think about it for a few seconds. 'Why would he want to make me jealous?'

'Maybe he likes you,' Gaz suggests.

'Or maybe it's another game,' I reply, the cogs beginning to turn in my head. 'Just another way to try and get inside my head.'

I hear Charlie walking back down the stairs and I quickly stop talking.

'Anyway, so I came here to tell you that I'm on your side now,' she says. 'I want his business to fail.'

'Well, that's sweet of you,' I reply. 'Thanks.'

'I was thinking,' she starts, twirling a strand of her hair in her fingertips. 'Wouldn't it be awful if everyone else turned on him too?'

'On Saint Seb?' I laugh. 'That's never going to happen; he has everyone eating out of the palm of his hand.'

'I just think that, if they had a little encouragement, that would be all it would take,' she says. 'Like, say, if someone were to spread some rumours about him, about what he was *really* like – maybe exaggerated rumours, that play with the truth just enough to legitimise them – we could kneecap him with that.'

I feel my eyes widen with horror. This is exactly the kind of woman that men are talking about when they talk about psycho women, isn't it? I thought they only existed in fiction but here's one, standing right in front of me, trying to drag me into her crazy 'woman scorned' scheme.

'If you wanted to do something to support the cause, we're going to have a stall at the Winter Wonderland, and we need as much help as possible,' I suggest to her in an attempt to change the subject from psychological warfare. 'If you fancy it?'

'OK, sure,' she replies. 'If it helps run him out of town.'

'Great,' I reply. 'I'll be in touch with the details.'

'She is one angry bird,' Gaz says once Charlie has left, closing the door behind her. After every crazy thing she's just said, he doesn't risk talking about her behind her back until he's certain she can't hear him. 'She's got good ideas though. We could easily spread rumours about him.'

I laugh. 'Like what?' I ask, thinking his funny suggestions might cheer me up a little.

'Like, maybe he's got a wife and kids somewhere – or loads of wives and kids.'

'Like a bigamist?'

'Is that what you call it? Yeah. Maybe he turns up in towns, gets married, runs up loads of debt and then runs away, leaving the poor cow to raise the kids and pay all the bills.'

'Brilliant,' I say, but then my face falls. 'Gaz, don't you dare.'

'Don't what?' he asks coyly.

'We're just joking around, right? You're not going to tell people that about Seb?'

'No?' he replies, his voice shooting up in pitch.

'Gaz, I do not want you to do this,' I say as clearly as I possibly can. 'This could land us in a lot of trouble.'

'OK,' he replies with a wink. 'I *won't* do it.'

'This isn't a nudge nudge, wink wink thing,' I stress, just to make sure he fully understands exactly what I'm saying.

'I completely understand,' he assures me with a nod.

Does he though?

'OK,' I reply. 'So we beat him fairly. Whatever happens, I want my hands to be clean. It's what my mum would want too.'

'Got you,' he replies. 'Clean hands.'

For a second, I wonder to myself whether or not there is a chance that Gaz might do something stupid in the name of saving the shop. I really don't think I could have made it any clearer, that I absolutely do not want him to do anything underhand – especially not making up lies about Seb and spreading them around town. Not only is it absolutely not what my mum would do in my shoes, but I just know that I won't feel proud of myself at all, if I resort to lies in an attempt to drive Seb out of town.

While I might not agree with Charlie's tactics, I am more than happy to have her onside, willing to help out, even if her motive isn't pure. Having an extra pair of hands at the Winter Wonderland Festival will be such a massive help; we always get so busy there. I just need to make sure that while I'm running things, I am able to keep Gaz in check, as well as Charlie, and watch that they don't do anything reckless. But not only do they both seem like loose cannons at the best of times, they're fuelled by emotion right now. There's no telling what they might do. I just really hope they listen to me when I say that I don't want to do anything shady in order to win. I guess I'll have to wait and see what happens now…

116

Chapter 15

It is finally beginning to look and feel a lot like Christmas – at long last. It always hits you all at once, doesn't it? At the start of the year it feels like there are so many possibilities for the year ahead, and it feels like Christmas is so far away...but then, all of a sudden it is Easter, then it's summer. The build-up to Christmas feels like it starts earlier and earlier each year (my shop excluded, obviously, it's Christmas every day here), with the town Christmas lights being switched on in November. It feels like there is all the time in the world to get prepared for the most wonderful time of the year and then, all at once, you realise Christmas is imminent, and you are not even remotely ready for it.

As soon as the clock strikes 12, and we are officially in December, that's when I put up my personal Christmas tree in my flat. Sure, there are plenty of trees in the shop, but those ones are up all year round, so they don't count. Growing up, my mùm always bought a real tree, so I make sure I keep up that Jones family tradition. There is nothing quite like the incredible smell that you get with a real Christmas tree.

Along with the family decorations that we've had for years, I cover my tree with strings of popcorn, candy canes, and choco-late decorations, which combined make the whole flat smell irresistibly festive and delicious. Obviously we don't eat the popcorn, because by the time Christmas is over it is not exactly fit for human consumption, but Chloe and Harry always come over to help me with the candy canes and the chocolate decorations. There are already a few gaps, where edible decorations have been prematurely pinched, but that is pretty much a family tradition too. As much as Holly hates the rigmarole of putting up the Christmas tree, she does like the fact that we've always made sure it was largely edible.

My impeccably decorated Christmas tree aside, I am in no way prepared for Christmas this year. These days I go to Holly's house to eat Christmas dinner with her, Lee, and the kids. Lee and I share the cooking on the big day, but in preparation for it, the food shopping is solely down to me. And not only do I need to shop for the ingredients to make the Christmas dinner still, but I need to finish my Christmas present shopping too.

I also need to start my present wrapping – something I've usually done by now because I'm always so eager to do it. I absolutely love present wrapping, and I like to think I'm good at it. You can wrap presents badly, you can wrap presents well, or you can wrap presents like I do – super extra. Present wrapping is an art form. I'm not very competitive, but if competitive present wrapping were a thing, that would be my sport.

It frustrates me to admit it, even to myself, but I've been so distracted by Seb and trying to save the shop that time seems to be passing me by so much quicker than it usually does, leaving me with less time to do more in. As if I don't have enough on my plate getting myself and my family ready for Christmas, I have the charity commitments that Prue roped me into to fit into my schedule now. That stuff will take up at least a couple of days, which I absolutely do not have. Normally I am all over charity work – what with my life being otherwise empty – but there's so much going on this year, and I've got my Winter Wonderland stall to open up soon. At least I'll have Gaz, and

118

hopefully Charlie, helping me out with that. Unless Charlie has calmed down and lost interest, that is.

I think it is safe to say that, when Seb first turned up, my business was not booming. I also think it's pretty fair to say that, if things had carried on the way they were, there probably wouldn't have been a shop left to save in the not so distant future. When the shop became harder for tourists to find, I became complacent. Business quietened down but I did nothing to wake it up again. I was bored most days, I wasn't making much money, but I just kept telling myself that it was my mum's shop and letting go of it wasn't an option. That feels more important now than ever, now that I can see it slipping through my fingers straight into Seb's hands.

At first, I was fighting to save the shop purely in memory of my mum, but things have changed now. Battling to save the shop lit a fire under me – I'm fighting for so much more. Now I feel like there really is something worth saving here. My wonderful, festive, cute, (and most importantly) busy family shop. I've been working so hard, trying to turn things around, to make the shop everything that it used to be when my mum was in charge – and more. I know that my mum would be so proud of what I've done with the place and, for that reason, I am even more determined to hang on to it for as long as I possibly can.

I look over at Gaz, sitting on his stool in the corner. He's in full Santa Claus mode right now, dressed in his red suit, with his surprisingly convincing fake beard carefully concealing his true identity. He's reading a story to a group of children who are all sat cross-legged in front of him, completely captivated by his animated storytelling.

Having Santa Story Time was actually one of Gaz's ideas and it's turned out to be a great one. Instead of simply having a grotto like most places do, where kids queue up for ages to tell Santa what they want for Christmas in their 30-second window, before it's on to the next kid, Gaz thought if he read stories, kids would come back again and again – especially if he reads a different story every day. So kids are turning up, day after day, to clock face time with St Nick and to hear his story.

So, now we have this edge. People are coming here to see Marram Bay's best (and technically only) Santa Claus – and some people are coming every day.

As I serve customers, I can feel my big, dumb smile pulling on the corners of my mouth. It's not always easy to find things to smile about but here, now, today, it's coming so naturally. I might not know how things are going to play out here but that's no reason not to feel truly content with each of my little victories. Whether the shop closes down or not, I am so, so proud of myself for everything I've done to save it. Whether I'm winning or not, I'm fighting, and that's the kind of daughter my mum raised.

My smile finally lets up, faltering as I notice Seb walk through the door to burst my bubble. He's never far away.

As he approaches the counter, I wonder what pointless, stupid distraction he has in store for me today. After countless tests on the land, measuring the plot, and using my kitchen as an office, I'm not sure what else he needs to do now – not until after he pulls the trigger, anyway.

It's only as I'm forcing my game face that I notice the look on Seb's. He looks absolutely fuming and it takes me aback. It suddenly occurs to me, as I look at the furious expression on his face, that I've never seen a hint of anger from Seb until today, and it gives me a sick feeling in the pit of my stomach. His steely blue eyes are narrowed in my direction, and there's an icy coldness behind them that I haven't seen before, which chills me to my core. His jaw looks tense, his brow is furrowed, and his usual charming, easy-going demeanour is MIA. Something must be really wrong.

'Hey, hey,' I chirp brightly, probably in an awkward attempt to overcompensate, which I instantly regret, because the only sight rarer than Seb appearing angry, is me appearing pleased to see Seb. I don't know why I thought acting uncharacteristically friendly might defuse this situation, so I quickly tone it down. 'Is everything OK?'

'Hello,' he replies coolly. 'No, it isn't. I need a word.'

Now I really am worried. 'Sure. Are we OK to talk here? Gaz – excuse me, Santa,' I correct myself, lowering my voice, 'is mid-story with the kids, so I can't really leave my post.'

'Fine,' he says with a sigh. 'I just received a call from Prue Honeywell and she was very upset. She said that some unsettling details of my life – from before I moved here – had come to light, and that she was reconsidering supporting me.'

'Oh?' I reply casually – well, as casually as I can force myself to sound.

'Oh, indeed,' he replies. 'The town rumour mill has gone into overdrive, with unfounded – and frankly very offensive – allegations about my past.'

I don't say a word. I just listen attentively and try my absolute hardest not to do anything with my face that might indicate even a hint of guilt. I don't want Seb thinking I played a part in this, or that I had any knowledge of these rumours because the truth is I think I might know exactly what the rumours are, and where they came from.

'Rumour has it I'm a bigamist,' he tells me, his eyes wide with horror. 'But not simply your run-of-the-mill bigamist, no, no, I'm a bigamist who travels from town to town, starting up businesses, running up debts, before marrying an unsuspecting victim and disappearing with all their money. Then I start up my life again somewhere else, running the same scam again and again. And now, here I am, in Marram Bay, ready to start the process again.'

Yep, I know exactly where these rumours have come from, and now I'm terrified he's going to figure out who started them and find me guilty by association.

'That's absolutely awful,' I tell him honestly – well, as honestly as I can afford to be right now.

'It is,' he replies. 'Supposedly I've done this no less than six times now. Except I've never been married at all, let alone married anyone for money. It did get me wondering though, why would someone start such horrible rumours about me? Who on earth could possibly want to run me out of town...?'

'Me?' I squeak, sensing an accusation. 'No, no, no. I would never do that – not to you, not to anyone.'

'Well, who else would, hmm?' he replies in disbelief.

I glance over at Gaz – *bloody* Gaz – only to realise that he's scarpered, leaving the kids in the capable hands of a 6-year-old, who has taken over reading the story to the rest of the kids. I listen to his chatter for a moment and I'm pretty sure that the words coming from his mouth are not being read from the pages of *The Polar Express*, unless it's just a huge coincidence that this kid's Uncle Andy and his cat feature heavily in the story.

'Seb, I promise you, I would never do something like this.'

'Ivy, who else would?'

'I...I don't know,' I lie.

Gaz is my rock right now. He's the only person truly in my corner, fighting to save the shop just as hard as I am. Not only that, but he's my friend. There's no way I'm throwing him under the bus.

'Ivy, I want you to listen to me very carefully,' Seb starts, sounding no less angry than he did when he walked through the door. 'I want to make something perfectly clear, just in case I haven't already. I *am* sorry for what is happening to you, and I *am* sorry for the part I am playing in it, but you just need to let it go, let it happen.

'It's great that you're fighting to save the place, but you've taken things too far now. I was happy to just leave you to it, but now you're badmouthing me around town... You just need to let it go, and let it happen.'

Now I feel angry. 'You could build your stupid holiday homes anywhere, why do you have to do it here?' I ask. 'Not just here in Marram Bay, but right here, in this exact spot, where my entire life is.'

'Because this is the best place to do it,' he replies firmly. 'If I don't buy it and you stay here, I'd bet every penny I have that you'll be done by next Christmas anyway.'

Ouch. 'If I were going to start a rumour about you, I'd find one more believable,' I start. I'm hurt and I'm angry, which means that the next thing that comes out of my mouth probably isn't going to be pretty or helpful. 'As if people would buy into a story where someone like you successfully dupes *six* women into marrying him.'

'Meaning?'

'Meaning there's a reason you don't have family around you,' I tell him. 'You might think I'm bad at business – and, you know what, maybe I am – but you're bad at people. And you don't even realise you're bad at people, you think everyone loves you, but your charm offensive is only ever going to get you so far. Sustainable relationships aren't built on charm and business transactions, they're built on sincerity, and you have none of that. And, no, you can't buy any of that unfortunately, no matter how much bloody money you have.'

Seb raises his eyebrows. For a few seconds, he just glares at me, staring so hard it almost feels like he's looking straight through me, like he's lost in thought. Eventually, he says something.

'I came here today to see if you knew anything about where these rumours could have come from, because I really couldn't think of anyone else with motive, but deep down, I really didn't think you were personally capable of something so vindictive. And then Poison Ivy rears her ugly head...' Seb quickly pauses and changes the direction his words were going in. 'From day one, I have been trying to do what is right by everyone, but if you want to play games, fine, just know that I am a much better player than you.'

'Are you finished?' I ask.

'No, you are,' he replies.

'Great, now get out of my shop,' I say angrily, while I still can.

As Seb storms off I remember where I am. I glance around the shop to make sure that our little tête-à-tête didn't attract too much attention from the customers. Thankfully, everyone seems to be completely captivated by the young storyteller, who is still commanding his audience, despite not actually having the book in his hand anymore.

As I'm glancing around the room, I double-take at the Christmas tree. I can't help but notice the bright red leg poking out from behind it. I march straight over, where I find my cowardly Santa Claus trying to hide.

'Oi,' I say, but Gaz just continues to stare at the wall in that guilty way dogs do after they tear up a cushion, hoping that if they can't see you, then you can't see them. It's unfortunate for Gaz that he is wearing bright red because he sticks out like a sore thumb.

'I need a word with you,' I say in hushed tones.

'Ho, ho, ho,' he replies merrily, loud enough for the room to hear him. Suddenly all eyes are on him again. 'Mrs Santa is on the phone, from the North Pole. I just need to go and have a quick chat, make sure you're all on the nice list. Keep reading, young man, you're doing a great job. Extra presents for you.'

Sometimes I think Gaz is a few baubles short of a Christmas tree, but other times, like now, when he's making a scene because he knows I can't yell at him or assault him with a giant inflatable candy cane with the children watching (he is Santa Claus, after all) I'm reminded that he does have his moments of intelligence.

I usher my babbling Santa Claus – who is absolutely on my naughty list now – into the kitchen. I hover in the doorway, just in case any customers need me while I'm telling him off.

'Gaz, what the hell did you do?'

'Huh?' he replies in an infuriating, faux innocent way, that isn't going to fool anyone.

'Don't "huh" me,' I tell him. 'You know what's going on – why did you hide, if you've nothing to worry about?'

'I was checking the star on the Christmas tree, like you asked me to? You said it looked a bit…' Gaz's expression changes all at once, when he finally stops lying. 'OK, I only said a few things to a few people. I'm surprised it got back to him so quickly.'

'Gaz, the local MP called him to voice her concerns. This could cause big problems for him.'

'Well, that's great, right?'

'No, it isn't, and I specifically asked you not to do this.'

'Yeah, I know, but only because you didn't want to get in trouble. I took the hint.'

'There was no hint, you idiot,' I reply. 'I said no, I meant no. You really need to learn to take a "no" – in all areas of life.'

'But it sounds like your problem is solved?'

'But it isn't,' I reply. 'Because he can easily refute these six wives he supposedly has, because it's all lies. It's just going to make us look pathetic, bitter, and like we're losing. And now, Seb is firing on all cylinders, he's so angry.'

'Six wives?' he replies. 'I didn't say anything about him having six, I just said he was a biga-whatsit.'

It is both fascinating and terrifying, how information is shared in small towns like Marram Bay. Rumours really do travel like wildfire here, equal in speed and sometimes equal in destruction too.

'Well, he's gunning for me now.'

'So, we try harder,' Gaz insists.

I massage my temples. 'Promise me you won't go rogue again, Gaz. It's only making things worse.'

'OK, fine,' he replies, and this time I think he means it. 'But tell me you didn't enjoy seeing him brought down a peg or too.'

If I'm being completely honest, I didn't enjoy it at all. Not even a little bit. It was awful, I just felt so guilty, and so sorry

125

for him. I remember what it was like when my dad died, especially with it being such a tragic accident. Even though I was a kid, I couldn't help but notice that people were talking about us, nudging each other in the street, saying, oh look, there's that poor family who lost someone in that bad accident just before Christmas.

And later on, when my mum died – my mum was like a local celebrity, known for being the bright and bubbly lady who ran this shop; everyone used to call her Mrs Christmas – the Marram Bay Facebook group filled up with locals saying 'RIP Mrs Christmas' and sharing stories from times when they had visited the shop... I should have been happy, comforted even, to see that she had touched so many lives while she was with us, but all it did was upset me. She was just some fun lady in a shop to everyone else, but she was my mum. She was the most important person in my life, and I still miss her, every single day.

The point is, I know what it's like to be the talk of the town, and in a small town like ours, the voices only seem louder. So I know exactly what Seb will be going through right now.

And even though he upset me, I feel guilty for hitting back. Perhaps he only said what he did because he was upset...or maybe there was some truth in his words. Maybe that's why I hit back twice as hard.

I know that he wants this place, and I know that he thinks my crappy little shop is going under – and maybe it is – but I won't stop trying to save it. I'll never stop. The only thing is, I feel like doing that is about to get a whole lot harder.

Chapter 16

'It's Ivy, isn't it?' I hear a voice call over to me. 'Chloe and Harry's aunt?'

I turn around to see Mrs Snowball, the head teacher at Acorn School, towering over me. Mrs Snowball, who must be in her fifties now, is a tall, broad woman, who I want to say would terrify me if I were a kid here, but even as a 5'3" adult, she towers over me, and I can't help but find her intimidating.

Her short, sharp, dark bob – teamed with the grey shirt she is wearing – instantly puts me in mind of Cate Blanchett's Irina Spalko character from *Indiana Jones and the Kingdom of the Crystal Skull*. I imagine Mrs Snowball's character to be not all that dissimilar either.

'Yes, hello,' I reply. 'Is everything OK?'

Today I told Holly I would pick up Chloe and Harry from school. I was in the process of quickly ushering them towards the car when Mrs Snowball caught up with me. I wouldn't usually be in such a hurry, but I'm still a little worried about Gaz and his guerrilla tactics.

'I was hoping to speak to your sister really,' she says.

'Oh, sorry, just me today,' I reply, waiting to see if that's good enough. 'Can you talk to the monkey, instead of the organ grinder?'

'Oh, no, I'm sorry, I don't think that's a PC thing to say anymore,' she starts.

'Why?'

'Because, animals are not here for our amusement. Because, PETA, and…anyway, just a quick word,' she says, quickly changing her tune.

Mrs Snowball seems like the kind of prim and proper person who could get upset over just about anything.

'Yes?'

Mrs Snowball hesitates for a moment.

'Kids, why don't you get into the car?' I suggest, unlocking the door.

Once they're safely inside I close the door, ready to hear what Mrs Snowball has to say, away from curious little ears.

'So…'

'Just a quick word about Chloe, that's all,' she says. 'She's been talking a lot recently about, about the things she wants for Christmas.'

'OK.'

'She's talking an awful lot about presents, telling the other children what she's getting this year from Santa Claus and from her parents.'

'And…'

'There's an expectant tone to her voice, like she knows what presents are coming her way, and she said something about a Kardashian, and while I'm not all that well versed on current events in the entertainment sector, I know that's not good – they are not good role models for young women.'

'To that, I'd probably point out that the Kardashian-Jenners are all multimillionaires in their own right, so they must be doing something well, but this isn't a hill I'm prepared to die on. As for Chloe…I mean, she's 7 years old, and it's December – what kid doesn't have Christmas on their minds?'

'Children in third-world countries,' she says.

I do my best to stifle a laugh, at her attempt to channel Bob Geldof. 'Right, so...'

'I just think perhaps her mum needs to have a word with her, about what Christmas is really about.'

'Mrs Snowball, she's 7 years old,' I repeat. 'She's excited about presents and I guarantee none of them will be remotely Kardashian.'

'Another thing is that, with her saying she's getting something from Santa Claus, and other things from Mum and Dad – it's causing some debate, amongst the children.'

'It's causing debate amongst the 7-year-olds?' I laugh. 'Why?'

'Some children only get gifts from Santa Claus, and with Chloe saying this, it's making the other children think that their parents don't buy them gifts which is, of course, completely untrue.'

I can't help but roll my eyes.

'If you could ask your sister to have a word – maybe we'll leave it up to Mum, yes?' she suggests. 'And if I don't see you before, a very Merry Christmas to you.'

'You too,' I reply through gritted teeth.

I get into the car and fasten my seatbelt, but I hesitate for a few seconds before I set off.

'Are we in trouble?' Chloe asks.

'No, of course you're not,' I reply. 'Mrs Snowball was just telling me how well you're both doing at school. Let's get you home.'

When my sister called and asked me if I would pick up the children, she assured me that it would only be a quick favour. She said if I picked them up, she would be at home in time for me to just drop them off at the bottom of the drive, so I could hurry back to work. I wonder whether I need to hurry back, to keep an eye on Gaz, but there's no way he'd do anything daft again, is there? Not after I told him off for it. I'm sure I'll be fine to pop in for a few minutes and give Holly a heads-up on what Mrs Snowball is going to talk to her about.

I park in the driveway and help the kids out of the car.

'Do you want to watch a Christmas movie, Auntie Ivy?' Chloe asks as we walk up the drive.

'Yeah,' Harry says excitedly.

'Aww, sorry kids, I've got to get back to work,' I tell them. 'I'm just popping in for five minutes, just to say hi to your mum. The good news is, you'll be breaking up for your Christmas holidays soon, and then we'll have all the time in the world for watching Christmas movies, and we can bake some Christmas biscuits, sing some carols. And I'm so excited for our trip to the Winter Wonderland Festival.'

'Us too,' Chloe tells me. 'You're so much fun at Christmas. Mummy hates it.'

'Mummy is just busy,' I reassure her.

Chloe is definitely very perceptive for her age. She's intelligent, but she isn't...whatever it is Mrs Snowball is suggesting she is. She's only 7, for crying out loud. I didn't think 7-year-olds could be materialistic – or, maybe materialistic is all a 7-year-old can be. I don't know. There's a reason people say 'like a kid at Christmas' and that is because kids love Christmas, and they love presents, and when they're that small, they're not burdened with the guilt that there are other children in other countries who are far less fortunate than them, but that's not something they need to worry about – because they are kids, because there is plenty of time for them to find out the world stinks when they are older.

'Hello,' I call out, as we walk through the door. 'Hol?'

I hear a loud clatter upstairs.

'Hello?' I call again.

Within a few seconds my sister appears on the landing, buttoning her jeans. She seems all flustered.

'Ivy, kids, sorry, I...I didn't realise the time,' she says.

'Everything OK?' I ask.

'No, I mean yes, I'm just...I'm wrapping presents. Could you take the kids out for a walk or something? Just for fifteen minutes.'

'Erm, OK, sure,' I reply. 'You sure you're OK?'

'I'm fine, I'm fine,' she assures me.

I don't know what to say, other than that I will. 'Come on, kids, let's give your mum a minute, while she finishes wrapping presents.'

'I don't want to go for a walk,' Chloe whines. 'It's too cold.'

'How about we go to my place? I'll make us hot chocolates, we can eat some of the festive treats that I've made and, if you're lucky, Santa might be stopping by!'

'No way!' Chloe replies. 'Do you know Santa?'

'I do,' I reply.

Harry's cute little eyes widen with surprise.

'Come on, let's go,' I say, ushering them to the car.

As we make the short trip to the shop, I wonder about how I can ask the kids questions about their mum, without them getting suspicious. Instead of blurting out the first thought that comes into my head, I wait until we're in the flat, cuddled up on the sofa, with big mugs of hot chocolate piled high with whipped cream and marshmallows. I've also put out a few of my Christmas chocolates for the kids. I know that this might spoil their tea, but I feel like they deserve it.

'So, how's your mum been recently?' I ask.

'Ergh, she's so weird,' Chloe informs me. She's like a little old lady, gossiping with her cup in her hands. It's absolutely adorable.

'Weird?' I reply. 'How is she being weird?'

'She's always whispering,' she tells me. 'And she's always too busy to play with us.'

Harry nods.

That's kind of odd.

'I need to talk to Santa,' she informs me.

'Oh really?' I reply.

'Yeah,' she says confidently. 'Because my mum keeps talking to him on the phone, and...and I think she's gonna tell him I can't have a lip kit, so I want to check.'

And that's really odd.

'Baby girl, you do not want a lip kit, trust me.' I laugh.

'Why not?'

I think carefully about what to say next, because if I tell her she's too young, she'll only want one even more, and if I tell her they're not cool, she'll only think I'm uncool for saying that and I'll lose my cool auntie influence.

'Because there's going to be plenty of time for stuff like that when you're older. I would love a collection of dolls like yours, but I'm too old now. Sure, I can buy lip kits, but they're so boring. With your dolls, you can play with them, dress them up, do their hair... Adults don't get to play with dolls. I only have my own hair to play with now.'

'You can always play with my hair, Auntie Ivy,' she assures me. 'Or you could have some babies, and you could do their hair, and I could have some cousins to play with.'

Wow, one problem at a time, kid.

I sip my drink thoughtfully, as I try to put the pieces of the puzzle together in my head. Holly is being secretive, she's lying, we clearly caught her by surprise today and, now that I think about it, it was weird that she was buttoning up her jeans, unless... Suddenly it all makes sense. I think Holly might be having an affair.

Chapter 17

'I just don't get it,' Gaz says, sitting on his stool in the corner, ready for story time, except there are no children here today. Usually, around this time, there would be a crowd of children sitting on the floor, waiting for St Nick to tell them a festive story.

'It is odd,' I say, glancing around, only noticing a handful of grown-up patrons in the shop. 'We're definitely much quieter today.'

'The festival?' Gaz suggests.

'No, that hasn't started yet,' I reply. 'Hmm...'

It's strange, to be quiet suddenly after days of being so busy. The train keeps turning up practically empty, which is even weirder, because *everyone* loves the train.

I tap my fingernails on the counter, one after the other.

'It's just so weird,' I say again.

I grab my phone and load up the Marram Bay Facebook group, to see if anything is happening that might slow down business. The Facebook group is the single best source of information in this town. Need a plumber? Facebook. Trying to sell your old sofa? Facebook. Wondering why you can't drive down Sycamore Lane today? Facebook will tell you all about the group of rogue sheep blocking the way.

'Oh…my…God…' I say.

Gaz jumps up from his stool and hurries over. 'What?'

'You're not going to believe this,' I say, turning my phone so we can both look, before I read aloud. 'Wilson's Garden Centre have a brand-new Santa Claus, thanks to a generous donation from a local businessman. Wilson's, who recently parted ways with their usual Santa, will be working with the anonymous businessman, to raise money for charity. Thanks to the generous contribution, they've got A-list actor, Donald Hale, who recently played Santa Claus in hit movie *A Christmas Wish* playing the role.'

Ergh. Gaz might be brilliant at dressing up as Santa but, as far as kids are concerned, Donald Hale *is* Santa. His belly is real, his beard is real, and it's all legitimised by the fact they've seen him on TV.

Gaz takes my phone from me to get a closer look.

'They're only doing bloody reindeer rides,' he says. 'Reindeer are better than train rides.'

'Oi,' Mick, our steam train driver, calls out from behind us. I forgot he'd popped in to use the loo before his next trip.

'Sorry,' I call after him as he heads back outside. It's true though: real reindeer and *the* Santa Claus are way cooler than what we've got going on here.

'Do you think Seb did this?' I ask Gaz once we're alone again. 'He did say it was game on…'

'I'll deck him,' Gaz says angrily.

'No, you won't,' I insist. 'We're not hitting him, and we're not retaliating.'

'Why not?'

'Because it won't help us,' I reply. 'He's probably hoping we'll waste our time and resources hitting back, because if we do, we'll be distracted; we won't be focusing on saving the shop. So we won't retaliate, we'll focus on working hard – I told you, no underhand tactics.'

'I'm fuming,' Gaz says. 'This Santa gig is everything to me – he's attacking *me*!'

'He's just...I don't know. But we'll rise above it, right? No underhand tactics?'

'No underhand tactics,' he replies, sounding disappointed. I get the feeling Gaz would love nothing more than to punch Seb in his smug little face.

I can see how upset Gaz is so I'd never admit this to him, but Seb has severely wounded us today. If everyone is going to the garden centre to ride the sleigh and see their Hollywood Santa, they're not going to be coming here, and that's going to have a big impact on business. Still, I have my eBay money coming in, and our stall at the Winter Wonderland Festival should do well. I don't think we're out of the race just yet...we are definitely limping now though.

Chapter 18

'Do you want to do a good thing today?' I ask Gaz.

'Well, there's nothing to do here, is there?' he replies, glancing around the shop.

Today has been another quiet day so far, which is probably thanks to Seb's little stunt.

'My sister just called me. She says the kids have their nativity play this afternoon and it slipped her mind – she can't make it. She's asked if I'll go. I thought we could maybe shut up shop; you could come with me... I'm sure the kids would love it, if you came as Santa Claus. Chloe and Harry keep telling everyone that their auntie knows Santa, and that they got to meet you.'

'Yeah, why not,' he says. 'Shame your sister can't make it. She got work?'

'No, she doesn't work,' I tell him.

'Oh, right. Where is she?'

'She just said she's held up,' I tell him. 'She might be out Christmas shopping or something – she probably drove to the city.'

'Oh, that's a shame. Well, yeah, come on then, let's go.'

I quickly dash upstairs to smarten myself up a little, because I always feel so plain around the yummy full-time mummies at that school, before Gaz – sorry, Santa – and I hop in the car and head straight over.

Acorn School is possibly the smallest school I've ever laid eyes on. It's a beautiful, old Victorian stone building, with a slate roof and sash windows – it even has its own tower. Back in the day, it used to belong to the richest family in Marram Bay, but now it's a school, home to just 39 pupils – two of which I am so excited to see today.

Gaz and I walk through the large wooden doors into the hallway, where I glance around until I clap eyes on the lovely Mrs Snowball. At first, she doesn't look all that pleased to see me, but then she notices I've brought Santa Claus with me, and hurries over.

'Chloe and Harry's auntie, hello,' she coos, all sweetness and light. 'And, St Nicholas, hello.'

Mrs Snowball curtseys in the presence of Santa, which a) I didn't know was a part of Christmas etiquette, and, b) I can't understand why she's doing it, because all the children are somewhere else, getting ready for the play.

Gaz takes Mrs Snowball's hand and kisses it.

'Hello, gorgeous,' he says.

I feel my eyes widen with surprise. I was not expecting him to do that.

'Oh my, hello,' Mrs Snowball says. 'What a lovely surprise.'

'Well, I was coming to see the kids and I thought it would be nice if I brought Santa too,' I tell her. 'Holly is stuck in traffic – she apologised. But I'm here to support the kids.'

'How lovely,' she says.

'How many kids you got?' Gaz asks her.

'None,' she replies, with a flirtatious tone. We both stare at her for a second. 'Oh, you mean in the school?' Mrs Snowball laughs wildly.

Gaz laughs too. 'Yeah. How many in the school?'

'We have 39,' she tells him. '38 present today.'

'Well, I'll happily stick around after the play, talk to the kids?'

'Oh, marvellous, marvellous,' she replies. 'The mums, dads and parental figures of other titles will be pleased. Come with me, let me get you both a space on the front row.'

Once we're in our seats, Mrs Snowball disappears to check on the children.

'Bloody hell, she's acting like you're George Clooney,' I say, baffled. 'You could be anyone under there.'

'I guess Mrs Snowball has a thing for Santa Claus,' he jokes.

'Each to their own,' I reply. 'I prefer tall, dark and handsome to old, fat and wearing bright red.'

'I never knew you were so superficial,' Gaz replies, in a faux serious tone. 'Oh, look.'

Gaz points towards the stage, where the kids are finally making their way into their starting positions. Chloe is – of course – the star of the show, playing Mary, wearing the same costume I wore when I was her age. Holly did tell me that, when they were assigning parts, she didn't just ask for the lead role, she asked to play Jesus. Apparently Mrs Snowball told her that a doll would be playing the baby, to which Chloe told her that girls can play Jesus as well as boys. She did settle on playing Mary in the end though, when she found out she had far more lines. Harry, the little cutie, is playing a sheep, and he looks absolutely adorable in his outfit. Costume making isn't exactly Holly's forte, so I bought him a black onesie and covered it with cotton wool balls – it's actually turned out way better than I thought it was going to.

The play starts, and we're only 15 minutes in when Gaz gives me a nudge.

'What?' I whisper.

'Is this it?' he replies.

'What do you mean?'

'Is this as good as it gets?'

'Gaz, they're little kids, this isn't the Royal Shakespeare Company. What were you expecting?' I reply.

'I dunno, just something more entertaining.'

'There's not long to go, just suck it up,' I tell him, noticing him fidgeting with his belt, like a bored child at a wedding.

'Oh, look, it's Harry's bit,' I say, giving him a nudge.

All of the animals line up at the front of the makeshift stage, but as the piano starts to play and the other animals start their dance routine, Harry doesn't move. He's glued to the spot, staring straight ahead, paralysed with stage fright. To be honest, he's such a shy kid, I'm surprised anyone put him up to this in the first place.

'Harry,' Mrs Snowball calls out. I look over and from where I'm sitting, I can see her crouched down behind the piano. 'Harry, dance.'

The lady behind the piano starts the song again, but Harry still won't move. Once again, the music stops.

'Ah, no, that poor kid,' Gaz says.

Before I have chance to think it through, I am standing up from chair and climbing onto the stage. There are maybe 50 people in the audience, and now that I'm up here, I can feel what Harry is feeling. There may as well be 50,000 people out there; it wouldn't make a difference.

I crouch down next to him.

'Hey, you OK?' I ask. 'Don't you want to do your dance?'

Harry shakes his head.

'Why not?' I reply softly. 'You see all those people out there? They only came here because they heard that this is the best dance routine in the world, and they wanted to watch. Look, even Santa came.'

I watch Harry's eyes widen as he realises Santa is on the front row.

'I'm scared,' he tells me.

I wrap an arm around him and squeeze him tightly.

'Hey, you don't need to be scared; it's no big deal. I could dance with you,' I suggest.

139

'OK,' Harry replies.

'What's that?'

'OK.'

'You want me to dance with you?'

He nods.

Crap, I wasn't expecting him to go for that.

'Yeah, OK, why not?' I say.

I hurry over to Mrs Snowball.

'He says he'll dance if I dance with him,' I tell her.

'OK, just…try and be good,' Mrs Snowball whispers. 'I've got a man from the paper here; he's writing a review.'

Oh, wonderful, no pressure then. No wonder Harry is so scared, if she's giving everyone this pep talk. I'm not entirely sure how I'm going to dance to a song that I've never heard before, with an already choreographed routine that I don't know, when I've never been any good at dancing.

The music starts up again, and before Harry will make a move, he looks to me, to see if I'm dancing too. There's no time to overthink things, and given that I don't know any dance moves, the only thing I can think to do is to perform the only dance routine I know, one that I have seen my sister do a million times, which is the only reason I've committed it to memory. A dance routine so simple, with only a handful of moves…'5, 6, 7, 8' by Steps.

As soon as I start dancing, Harry joins in the dance routine he's supposed to be doing, and for what feels like the longest few minutes of my life, I dance the same few steps again and again and again. If Harry is still feeling stage fright, he shouldn't, because I don't think anyone's eyes are on anything else, other than the grown woman, who turned up with Santa, line dancing to a song called Little Donkey.

The final bar of the song can't come soon enough. As I hop down from the stage, a huge round of applause is bestowed upon me, with Gaz cheering the loudest. As I sit back down in my seat, sinking down as low as possible, I feel my cheeks burning up with embarrassment. Gaz can't control his laughter.

'Oh my God, that's one of the funniest things I've ever seen,' he tells me.

'Oh, God, don't, please,' I beg quietly, as the play continues. 'That's the most humiliating thing I've ever done. I just didn't want Harry to feel embarrassed, or for people to think he'd ruined the play.'

'Well, people will say you ruined the play now,' he cackles. 'But, seriously, I think that might be the nicest thing I've ever seen anyone do for anyone.'

Gaz's tone changes, from amused to sincere. 'Honestly. You're an amazing lady,' he tells me.

I smile. 'Thank you, Santa.'

I take Gaz's hand, and give it a big squeeze, before sitting up a little straighter, ready to watch the last part of the play.

As soon as it is over, Gaz and I hang around, while all the other parents filter out, because we said we'd stay so that the kids could meet Santa Claus – something I deeply regret now, because it has allowed almost every last member of the audience to come over and congratulate me on my dance routine on their way out. At least people are commending me for stepping up for Harry like that. No one seems to be just straight-up laughing at me, which is of some comfort. I can't wait to tell Holly all about it. I always used to tell her how pointless I thought it was, her learning dance routines to songs that I did not think would stand the test of time. Well, today one of those silly dance routines saved one of her kids – she'll take real joy in her being right and me being wrong, even if it was an argument we had 20 years ago.

With the parents finally gone and the children changed out of their costumes, they all charge towards Gaz, ready to meet Santa Claus.

'OK, OK, children, we need to do this in small groups so that everyone gets a turn. If you all sit on the floor in your colour groups, I will bring you one at a time.' Mrs Snowball turns to us. 'Santa, if you'd like to stand on the stage, I'll bring the kids to you in groups.'

'OK, sure,' he replies.

'No more dancing,' she jokily calls after us.

'Oh, man, I am never going to live that down,' I say quietly.

Gaz and I sit on the stage, on plastic chairs, as Mrs Snowball brings up small groups of children to meet him. Eventually, it's Chloe's group's turn.

'Auntie Ivy, is Santa your boyfriend?' she asks.

'What?' I laugh.

'I saw you two holding hands,' he says.

'But what about Mrs Santa?' another kid asks.

'Maybe they got divorced,' a small boy with big brown curls suggests. 'Couples get divorced sometimes. Maybe Santa is with Chloe's auntie now.'

I glance over at Mrs Snowball, who looks like she's about to have a heart attack.

'No, Santa isn't my boyfriend,' I quickly chime in.

'But doesn't he live with you?' Chloe asks.

'No…'

'But he's at your house a lot.'

'Because my house is above my work, and he works with me,' I assure the kids – and Mrs Snowball, because she looks the most concerned by all of this.

'And his clothes were in your bedroom. I saw them the last time we were over,' Chloe persists.

God, I wish this kid paid less attention.

Mrs Snowball's jaw drops.

'Another perfectly innocent explanation: I wash Santa's suits for him,' I say.

This is completely true. A couple of days ago, Gaz spilled a full cup of coffee all over his suit – luckily it was cold, because he's still not quite mastered the coffee machine, but it left a big,

142

brown stain all over his pants, that you just don't want to be there, not if you're inviting kids to sit on your lap all day.

'Maybe they're having an affair,' a tall brunette kid suggests.

'Emma Parker, that's enough,' Mrs Snowball snaps at her. 'We don't say such things in this school. Chloe's auntie and Santa Claus are obviously just friends and work colleagues. That's all there is to say.'

There's an awkward vibe, for the rest of our time at the school. Mrs Snowball keeps giving us evil eyes – me specifically. I think she thinks I'm having a fling with Santa now, and she's not happy about it. I don't know if she's jealous, or if I've just ruined her festive spirit by supposedly getting it on with Santa Claus as well as ruining her nativity by dancing the Steps routine.

As soon as we're done talking to the kids, Mrs Snowball shows us straight to the door.

As she opens it she purses her lips, and gestures for us to leave.

'Never meet you heroes,' I tell her with a serious shake of my head, as I walk past her, hurrying in the direction of my car.

Chapter 19

I know what you're going to say, that I have enough on my plate at the moment, but no matter how many problems of my own I have, I am worried about my sister.

Holly is my twin – we've been together since before we were even born. If something is wrong with her, I need to help her, whether she wants me to or not.

That's why, today, Gaz is running things at the shop while I spy on my sister. I parked outside her house, hiding just out of sight, waiting to see if she went anywhere – or if anyone came to see her. Eventually, after a couple of boring hours, Holly headed out in her car and I followed her, and now here we are, on the way into town.

Holly pulls into a car park in town, and I make sure to park on the street much further away. I get out of my car and watch her, and she buys a parking ticket and places it in her car. But, rather than walk in the direction of the shops, she heads into the doctor's surgery.

I begin hurrying across the road, when I hear the screeching of brakes.

I turn around to see Seb jumping out of his car, angrily walking over to me.

'There you are,' he says.

'Not now, Seb,' I say.

'You've gone too far this time, Ivy,' he replies.

'What have I supposedly done now?' I ask, keeping one eye on the surgery, in case Holly walks back out. Perhaps she's just popping in for something, like painkillers, or…I don't know. 'Come on, what?'

Seb points towards his car, so I walk over to it and look. His previously pristine black Porsche has red and green glitter paint all over the bonnet.

'Well?'

'Well?' I echo. 'Wait, you think I did this?'

'I know you did it,' he replies.

'What are you talking about?' I laugh. 'No, I didn't.'

'I've seen this paint somewhere before,' he says. 'On your hands, and on the sale signs you put up in the shop.'

I examine the bonnet again and, unlucky for me, it does look like the same paint.

'Seb, I wouldn't do that,' I insist. 'Come on, you know I wouldn't.'

'I don't know that at all,' he replies. 'When I first met you, I thought you were this nice, cool person, and now…you're spreading rumours about me, you're trashing my car.'

I glance over at the doctor's surgery, wondering why my sister hasn't come out yet.

'Ivy? Are you even listening?' Seb asks.

'Look, I'm not saying it was me – it wasn't – but if it really is the same kind of paint, it's kids' paint. It should just wash off.'

'Really?'

'Really,' I reply.

'I'm still angry,' he says, heading back to his car. 'I never thought you'd resort to this.'

I just ignore him, instead waiting until he has gone and then calling Gaz.

'Ivy,' he sings as he answers the phone.

'Gaz,' I reply. 'What did I say about no underhand tactics?'

'Not to do them,' he confirms. 'And I didn't.

'You didn't cover Seb's car with the red and green sparkly paint from the shop?'

'Well, I did,' he replies. 'But that wasn't an underhand tactic, that was just because I was pissed off.'

'I see. Well, you're in luck on two counts. First of all, because it's kids' paint, it should just wash off, and second of all, he thinks it was me.'

'Do you want me to own up?' he asks.

'No, just leave it to blow over,' I reply. 'No real damage was done.'

'Are you sure, because—'

'Gaz, I need to go,' I say quickly, spying my sister heading back to her car.

I hang up and hurry across the road, where I find my sister, sitting in her car with her head in her hands, crying her eyes out.

I tap on her car window, making her jump.

'Ivy, what are you doing here?' she asks, wiping her eyes, as though that might disguise her tears.

I hurry around the other side of the car and climb in the passenger's seat. 'Holly, what's wrong?'

'Nothing, nothing,' she replies.

'At some point, you're going to have to stop saying that and talk to someone,' I tell her. 'I'm your sister, please let me help you.'

She nods as tears flood her eyes again.

'Are you ill?'

'I had a few, erm, women's issues,' she tells me. 'I thought maybe I was pregnant, so I took a test and it was negative. I had some bleeding.'

'Right,' I reply, feeling sick to my stomach at the thought of anything happening to my sister, but doing my best to keep cool.

'When you came in yesterday, I was taking a pregnancy test,' she says. 'Sorry if I seemed odd.'

'Don't apologise,' I tell her, taking her hand. 'What did the doctor say?'

'Well, I was terrified about cancer. I think I'd pretty much resigned myself to the fact that I had it and that was that – it was all I could think about. The doctor checked me out and couldn't find anything wrong. She gave me a pregnancy test today and...it's positive.'

'It's great news that you're not ill,' I tell her, unsure whether or not to enthuse about her pregnancy, because she's giving nothing away with her emotions. She looks terrified.

'It is,' she replies. 'I know so many people are less fortunate, and that I should be on top of the world, being pregnant, but... it's just so hard already, looking after two small kids on my own, with Lee being away all the time.'

'I know it is, but you have me,' I reassure her with a smile. 'And, let's face it, my life is pretty empty anyway, but it's about to get a whole lot emptier.'

Holly laughs. 'Your life is not empty,' she says with a smile. 'You're amazing and we'd be lost without you.'

'Thanks, sis. Just know that, whatever you decide to do, I am here for you, OK?'

'OK,' she replies. 'I guess it would be nice to have another baby. I've really missed having a cute little baby.'

I smile. 'It would be amazing to have another baby around – you're an incredible mum, and I would love to be an auntie again.'

Now that Holly isn't freaking out, it's so nice, to see her getting excited about it. I feel a combination of exited for my sister and weirdly envious. Baby news before Christmas...it's the stuff of dreams for some women.

'This is great, isn't it?' she says, possibly for reassurance, but she does seem like she's come around to the idea now.

'Have you told Lee?'

'I haven't,' she replies. 'I'll call him now.'

'I'll give you some privacy,' I say. 'I need to get back to work.'

I hug my sister and say goodbye, and as I walk towards my car I glance back and see her on the phone, smiling widely, obviously gushing about her news to Lee, who must be just as excited as she is. It's amazing to see her so happy, with her perfect little family. I know that I'm a part of it but I can't help wanting what Holly has, and I just don't feel like I'm ever going to get it.

Chapter 20

'So amazing of you to donate your time, as always, Ivy,' Prue says as she leads me through the town hall and into the room full of tables, all heaped high with wrapping paper and various other wrapping supplies, like bows, ribbon, and tape.

'Always happy to help,' I lie – the truth is, I'm *usually* happy to help, but this year it would be easier not to.

'Turn the music up, Roger,' she says as she passes a man sitting at a desk. Roger obliges, cranking up Shakin' Stevens' 'Merry Christmas Everyone'. Ergh, normally I'd be in my element here, but I'm just not feeling the festive spirit today at all.

Prue leads me to a table, where my wrapping partner is already waiting for me, and just when I think things can't get any worse for me, it turns out that I'll be working with Seb.

'I figured, what with you two already having a working relationship, you'd be perfect together, to fly through wrapping your pile of presents.'

At the end of each table sits a mountain of presents that people have brought in to get wrapped, in exchange for a 'pay what you like' donation. I take part in this event every year and we always raise a ton of money for good causes, but all I want to do today is run out screaming.

'I'll be back to check in on you soon,' she sings, leaving us alone.

I reluctantly sit down next to Seb.

'I didn't think this would be your scene,' I say, noticing the poorly wrapped present on the table in front of him. 'Or your forte.'

'It isn't,' he replies. 'But after Prue had words with me, I had to do something to get back on her good side. This is it.'

'Oh.'

'My car cleaned up, in case you were wondering,' he tells me, as he gets to work on a second present.

'Good,' I reply.

'It's a good job that, even though you didn't do it, you knew all about the kind of paint it was.'

'Just a good guess,' I reply.

'Right.'

The atmosphere here is as frosty as the weather outside, but only at the table. Everyone else is dressed up in festive jumpers, Santa hats, elf ears, and various other sparkly bits. I turned up in a black jumper dress, because I felt like it matched my mood this morning, and Seb is, of course, wearing his suit, with his jacket off, sleeves rolled up and his tie loosened. So, with everyone else dressed up, and Seb and I looking like we're about to attend a funeral, this is very much the gloomy end of the room.

My phone vibrates on the table in front of me. It's a message from Gaz, which reads: '*Train missing. Seb?*'

I angle my phone, to make sure Seb can't see our conversation.

'*What do you mean, the train is missing?*' I reply.

'*Someone has stolen it!*' he punches back.

I feel my brow furrow in puzzlement.

'*Did the driver leave it unlocked?*' I ask.

Gaz is typing...

'Everything OK?' Seb asks.

I nod.

'Do you think you can help then?' he suggests, nodding towards the present in front of him.

A message from Gaz finally comes through.

'What are you talking about? The little train from the shop.'

Oh! I thought he meant the one we hired to ferry people back and forth from town. He means the antique steam train from the shop, the one my mum has had since before I was born. Is this some kind of petty revenge act from Seb then? He thinks I've ruined his car so he's stolen my train? If he thinks he's going to get a rise out of me here, he can think again. If Gaz hasn't noticed, I'm not sure when I would have. Which means, if Seb has stolen it, if he wants a reaction, he's going to have to prompt one out of me. Let's see if he brings it up.

I take the present Seb has already attempted wrapping, and loosen the edges with my finger before refolding them and sticking them down in place, much neater than it was done before.

'Wow,' he replies. 'Did you just re-do that?'

'It's just...present wrapping is an art form,' I tell him. 'And people donate good money to get their gifts beautifully wrapped.'

'OK, so show me,' he insists.

'Erm, OK,' I reply self-consciously.

I cut a piece of wrapping paper to size before placing a box of chocolates down in the centre. I borrow Seb's finger, as I fold each piece with delicacy, before sticking it in place.

'This is called a four corner tie,' I tell him, wrapping red ribbon around the gold paper, forming a diamond shape on each side. 'Then, you can tie a bow with the ribbon, trim it to shape, and you don't even need a stick-on bow.'

'You're really good at this stuff,' he tells me.

I smile.

'I imagine Christmas has always been a really big part of your life?'

'It has,' I reply.

'I can probably handle the wrapping, if you want to be on decorating duty?' he suggests.

'Sure,' I say.

We only get through one present before Seb speaks again.

'Was it you? Who did those things?'

'It wasn't,' I answer. 'It could possibly have been someone who thought they were acting in my best interest, who is very sorry about what they did...'

'I see,' he replies with a smile. 'That's nice, that you have someone willing to do that for you.'

'Yeah, I guess.'

'You have a lot of good people around you – like your sister.'

'She's pregnant again,' I blurt, unsure why I'm telling him.

'Yeah? That's great news,' he replies. He wraps an arm around me and gives me a squeeze. 'Congratulations, Auntie.'

'Thanks.' I smile, feeling my cheeks flush as he hugs me. Real physical contact is not something we've had since our peck on the day we met.

'You OK?' he asks.

'Yeah, I'm fine. It's great news. And Chloe and Harry are amazing – I can't wait to meet their brother or sister.'

It suddenly occurs to me that Seb and I just had a normal conversation, like normal people, and it was kind of nice.

'Do you have any siblings?' I ask curiously.

'Only child,' he replies.

'Ahh, that explains so much,' I reply.

'Does it?' He laughs.

'Aren't only children spoilt and bad at sharing?'

'Hey,' he says defensively. 'I don't exactly come from a well-off family, so I absolutely wasn't spoilt growing up – except with affection, maybe.'

'Really?'

'Yeah, totally. Everything I've got, I built up myself, which I think is why I can be a little new money sometimes.'

'I wouldn't say you were new money...'

'Not even with my sparkly Porsche?' He grins, passing me another present to wrap ribbon around.

'I am so sorry about that, really.'

'It's OK,' he replies. 'I'm guessing it was Gaz and I'm pretty sure he's got your best interests at heart. That and that he maybe wants to sleep with you.'

'Yeah, but he wants to sleep with everyone.' I laugh. 'What makes you so sure it was him?'

'Because it turns out a witness saw the guy who did it – he was dressed as Santa Claus. So, that wasn't a date you guys were on the other night?'

'No, no,' I say. 'Sorry if we ruined your date with Charlie.'

'That wasn't a date either,' he tells me. 'She kept insisting she take me for a drink and tell me all about the town. She said she'd fill me in on everyone, so I didn't see the harm. Plus, it was nice, bumping into you outside work.'

'I bet you hardly recognised me, not surrounded by Christmas lights.'

'Yeah, you definitely looked different. Good though.'

'As did you,' I reply. 'I think that's the only time I've seen you in something other than a suit.'

He laughs. 'I'm pretty much constantly in meetings here – with council officials, contractors, et cetera – or on Skype business calls, so I dress smart. Plus, I just kind of like wearing them. I feel like a nice sharp suit gives me a nice sharp mind.'

'Hmm, maybe I need to try that,' I reply.

'But you work so well in your pyjamas.'

I can't help but admire the pile of perfectly wrapped presents we've amassed already. We actually make a pretty good team.

'I don't know if Charlie maybe assumed – or hoped at least – that the other night was a date,' he says. 'I never said it was or anything but…'

'Yeah, I think she might've thought that but don't worry too much. She bounces back easily.'

'That's all right then,' he says.

'Must be par for the course,' I reply.

Seb just laughs.

It feels good, to be getting on so well, but I can't push out of my mind that he's going to knock my shop and my home down, and even if it was just in retaliation, he knows how hard I've been trying with the business so his stunt with the garden centre Santa Claus was especially cruel.

'Wow, what a great job the two of you are doing,' Prue says, admiring our handiwork. 'You make a great team.'

'Ivy is a great teacher,' Seb tells her. 'I was hopeless at wrapping, until today.'

'Do you two want to be on a team for the tasting competition later?'

'Yes,' we both reply at the same time, glancing at one another in surprise.

'Tasting competition?' Seb enquires.

'Every year locals can enter whatever festive food is selected into a competition,' I say.

'It's all for charity,' Prue explains. 'Entrants pay a fee to enter, and the winner gets Marram Bay's prestigious "Festive Favourite" award.'

'Wow,' Seb say. 'Lots of responsibility then.'

'It is,' I agree. 'It's also one of my favourite festive traditions, because I get to enjoy a little bit of everyone's variation on festive favourites. It's loads of fun.'

'I can't wait,' Seb replies.

'I'll see you two tonight then,' she says. 'And the auction tomorrow, will you be there too?'

'Yes,' we both say.

'Marvellous,' she replies. 'Did I mention what a great team you make?'

As Prue walks off, I feel my cheeks blushing.

'Oh no,' Seb jokes. 'Two days, spent with me. Do you think you can handle it?'

'I'm sure I'll find a way,' I say.

Chapter 21

The tasting competition has long been one of my favourite festive traditions...until this year, because this year, the food in question is Christmas cake. I *hate* Christmas cake.

Seb and I are sitting at our table, waiting for plate after plate of Christmas cake to be placed in front of us. If it were a Yule log, or stuffing – I'd even take Brussels sprouts – just anything but Christmas cake.

Two identical plates are placed down in front of us, with neat little squares of Christmas cake topped with white icing.

I can't help but eyeball it with disgust.

'You OK?' Seb asks with a laugh, obviously clocking the look on my face.

'I hate Christmas cake,' I tell him.

'Uh-oh.' Seb chuckles. 'But you love all things Christmas – how can you hate Christmas cake?'

We're interrupted by a little old lady, standing in front of us.

'Hello,' she says. 'I'm Clara, from Clara's Café, and this is my entry.'

'Marvellous,' Seb replies.

'I made it back in August, using my mum's recipe. I've been feeding it brandy every two weeks. Enjoy,' she says with a smile, wandering over to the next table, to tell them all about her old cake.

'See what I mean, that's so gross,' I tell him quietly. 'People make it months in advance, it never goes off – even the cake needs getting drunk.'

Seb laughs. 'I take your point,' he says. 'Maybe try a little?'

I raise the cake to my mouth but the smell – month-old, booze-soaked fruitcake (with way too much fruit and not enough cake) turns my stomach.

'I can't,' I tell him.

'It's OK,' he assures me.

'It isn't, look at that sweet old lady,' I say, pointing over at Clara who is bursting with pride, telling everyone about her cake. 'I feel so guilty.'

Seb pops his cake into his mouth. 'I'm not the biggest fan of Christmas cake, but it's all right,' he says. 'Tell you what...'

Seb stealthily switches our plates around, then proceeds to eat my piece too.

'You can't do that.' I laugh. 'You'll be sick.'

'I'll be fine,' he says. 'They're only small pieces.'

'They're only small, but they're many,' I tell him.

He glances around the town hall, noticing all the entrants standing by tables covered in samples of their cake.

'Oh boy.' He laughs.

'Hello,' a tall, thirty-something man says as he approaches our table. He places another two pieces of Christmas cake down in front of us, except his are round and simply dusted in icing sugar, instead of a piece of icing, which if anything must make it go down easier – like a spoonful of sugar.

'Hey,' Seb replies. 'So, when did you start making your cake?'

'I actually start mine on Boxing Day,' he says.

I am almost sick in my mouth. This cake is nearly a year old and I know that I of all people should be fine with this, but it just makes me feel squeamish.

Seb raises the cake to his nose. 'And the alcohol?' Seb asks.

'Red vermouth,' the man replies. 'Enjoy.'

One again, Seb eats his piece before swapping our plates, taking mine down too.

After the fourth round, Seb starts looking a little worse for wear.

'You can't do any more,' I insist with a laugh. 'You'll be sick.'

'I'm good,' he says, not sounding good at all. 'How many more?'

'Four, I believe.'

'Oh, God, no, I can't eat eight more. We could just say we're full?'

'Everyone has worked so hard though,' I say. 'I'd feel so guilty – I feel so guilty already.'

'Any ideas?' he asks.

I glance around where we're sitting, to see if there's anywhere we can subtly dispose of the next *eight* pieces of cake, but there's nowhere. Apart from...

I grab my handbag from the floor and glance inside – luckily there's a plastic, 10p shopping bag in there, which should be more than enough to contain the next four rounds.

I open the bag up wide inside my handbag, leaving the bag open on the floor between us.

'Just drop them in there,' I tell him quietly.

'OK.' Seb laughs. 'Good idea.'

Two at a time, cake samples are brought to us, and with an impressive subtlety, we swipe them into my handbag. It's like a military operation, Seb watching my back, me watching his.

It pains me that I haven't maintained the integrity of the competition, but of the entries Seb tried, he tells me which is best and we both cast our vote for that one. It's another entry that wins – one that Seb didn't taste.

'Maybe I'll fish it out of your bag and eat it later,' he jokes.

The event comes to an end. After we're all dismissed, we head out to our cars.

'I feel sick,' Seb tells me, as we hover by my car. 'But that was a lot of fun.'

'It was,' I reply, all smiles. 'But it would've been more fun if I'd got to eat some chocolate or something.'

'Excuse me, everyone,' Prue calls out, grabbing the attention of everyone in the car park. 'I forgot to say that we thought it might be nice if tomorrow we all dress in black tie and ball gowns. I'm sure you've all got something hanging in your wardrobes.'

'Well, my tux is in storage still,' he says.

'I don't think I have a ball gown at all.' I laugh awkwardly.

'Excuse me, please,' I hear a man's voice say behind me. 'Are you about to drive that car?'

'Yes,' I reply, turning around to see a policeman standing in front of me.

'Miss, I'm going to have to ask you to take a sobriety test,' he says.

'Why?' I ask, absolutely baffled.

'There's a bracelet on the ground. I assumed you'd dropped it, bent over to pick it up and noticed how strongly of alcohol you smell,' he explains.

'Everything OK, Ivy?' Prue calls over.

'Everything is fine,' I call back, trying to sound like everything is fine, but I can't help noticing I have most of the car park's attention.

'I haven't had a drink,' I say under my breath.

'Well, you won't mind taking a sobriety test, will you?' he replies.

I'm not worried about taking the test, because I know that I'm sober, but this is a small town, and this is how rumours start. If people see me taking a sobriety test, no one will be talking about whether I pass or not, they'll only mention the fact that I had to take one.

'Oh, Ivy, it's probably all the cake in your bag,' Seb says.

'Oh, my gosh, yes,' I reply. 'Officer, I have a bag full of Christmas cake, it's probably that you can smell.'

The policeman gives me a suspicious stare.

'No, really,' I insist.

'What's going on?' Prue asks.

'I'm going to need you to show me inside the bag,' the policeman says, ignoring her interference.

Now I'm in a pickle. I can show the officer inside my bag – my handbag full of Christmas cake – and put an end to this drunk driving nonsense, but now that Prue is watching, it's going to make me look bad...although perhaps looking like I'm driving under the influence will look worse.

'Fine,' I say, holding my bag open in front of me.

During the walk from the town hall to the car park, the pieces have all kind of bashed together and either crumbled off or merged with a different one. It looks horrific, but it's obviously the source of the boozy smell.

The officer takes a chunk out of the bag and sniffs it.

'Pooh,' he exclaims. 'Yep, that's what I could smell. Sorry for the accusation, miss.'

'Don't worry,' I say, hurriedly closing my bag, but it's too late.

'Ivy,' Prue starts. 'What was that?'

'Er...'

'It was just our leftover cake,' Seb says, stepping in. 'We tasted them all but, rather than eat every last bit, we just wanted to take them home and enjoy them. They were all so great.'

'Oh, I see,' Prue says. 'You should've said so. I have all the untouched leftovers in my car. Come with me, I'll give you both some to take home.'

'Oh, yay, thank you,' I say as convincingly as possible.

We follow Prue over to her car, giggling together like naughty little kids, to collect more Christmas cake which neither of us will be able to eat. I'm hoping that Gaz likes it, because I know that Holly doesn't.

Seb gives me that cheeky smile of his as Prue hands us sandwich boxes filled with a variety of festive fruitcakes. I smile back because I'm having such a great time with him, and it's nice to forget about my problems for a little while. Of course, thinking about how I've forgotten about my problems only reminds me of my problems, and that Seb is the root of them. I might be having fun with him, but I need to keep reminding myself who he is. He's the man who is ruining my life, and while he might eat a few pieces of cake for me, he's still more than happy to take my home and my business. I just need to keep telling myself that.

Chapter 22

'Santa's been,' Gaz announces.

Now that I'm able to rely on Gaz to open up of a morning, I don't need to rush down first thing, which is great – not because I get to lie in, but because I have an eBay business to run now too.

'Oh?' I reply. 'We're not expecting anything.'

'Postman Pete dropped it off this morning,' he says. 'He told me to tell you that he misses your chats now that I'm here opening up. I told him I didn't take any offence.'

Gaz places the large cardboard box, addressed to me personally and not the business, on the counter and hands me a pair of scissors to open it.

'It's probably a symbol of Postman Pete's love for you,' Gaz suggests. 'A sculpture of you made out of the hair that gathers in his bath drain.'

'I thought you said you didn't take offence.' I laugh. God, I really hope that's not what it is.

After carefully cutting the tape, I lift out three identical garment bags from the box. Inside each garment bag is a ball gown – all three gowns are identical, and absolutely stunning.

Each gown is made of silky rose-gold material, with cold

shoulders, a V-neck at the front and a cowl back. The skirt part of the dress is pleated and, upon closer examination, has a split at the front on one side, which goes up to the thigh.

'Oh my God! This…is…maybe the nicest dress I've ever seen,' I blurt. 'But I didn't order them.'

'There's a card,' Gaz says, peering into the box. He takes it out and reads it out loud. "*Ivy, I was buying a tux for tonight and saw this. Thought you might like it but didn't know your size – hope one of the three fits. Seb.*" Ergh, the smarmy git is trying to buy you.'

'These are from *Seb*?' I ask in amazement.

'Yup, like, he gets you a dress, and you'll just let him do whatever he wants, right?' Gaz says sarcastically.

'Yeah, that's not gonna work,' I say firmly, but something different is going on in my head, which I don't dare say out loud to Gaz, because he'll think I'm an idiot.

'We're going to destroy him, aren't we?' he says confidently. 'He's got some town hall meeting in a few days. I thought we could go, make clear to everyone that we're not happy about what he's doing.'

'Sure,' I reply. While I still feel confident that we're going to fight this, the thought of kicking up a fuss at his meeting just feels wrong, especially when I've been getting on so well with him recently.

Yesterday we had a great day together, we put all our issues to one side and just got on like normal people, and it was amazing. Seb, out of business mode, is actually a great guy, and the more I see that side of him, the more I wonder if he can even still go through with his plan after befriending me.

'So this thing is tonight?' Gaz checks.

'Yeah,' I reply. 'Early evening.'

'You look all dopey, staring at that dress,' Gaz points out with a sigh. 'Just to refresh your memory, the bloke who bought it is gonna knock this place down. And, as soon as he realised you were trying to stop him, he made things even harder for you by ruining what we'd done, getting a famous Santa Claus to replace me at Wilson's.'

'I know, Gaz, don't worry. You don't need to remind me. It is a beautiful dress, though. No harm in wearing it, is there?'

'Suppose not,' he replies. 'You'll look fit in it – or beautiful, or whatever isn't sexual harassment in the workplace.'

I smile, proud of Gaz for making an effort to be more politically correct. I don't think he's a bad person, or a sexual deviant; I think he's just been brought up around *lad* lads, thinking it's OK to talk to women like that. I'm sure he thinks he's being harmless, but I'm glad to have steered him away from that mentality.

'Would you mind if I finished early today?' I ask. 'I could go to Holly's, see if she'll do my hair and make-up for me.'

'Of course, boss,' he replies. 'It's not like we're gonna be busy, and it's not like anyone is gonna be here to see Santa – thanks to your buddy, Seb.'

'True,' I reply. 'I appreciate it.'

After a quiet half-day in the shop (which Gaz was constantly reminding me is all Seb's fault) I figure out which of the three dresses fit me best, carefully zip it back up in its bag, and head for Holly's, because she's way better at hair and make-up than I'll ever be.

'Oh my God!' Holly blurts, seeing me in my dress. 'That's… like something from a movie. And surprising you with it is like something out of a movie.'

'Yeah, except he didn't just magically know my size, he sent me three different ones.' I laugh.

'What a man,' she says with a sigh. 'Sexy, loaded, built like a *Men's Health* cover model, romantic – remind me what's wrong with him?'

'He's knocking down our childhood home?' I offer. 'And he's not being romantic, he just feels sorry for me because I'm a poor

Cinderella with no dress and no money to get one.'

'That makes him Prince Charming,' she points out.

'Does that make you my ugly sister?' I tease.

'Oi, I'm nothing less than your fairy godmother,' she replies.

'And I'm Perla, the mouse,' Chloe joins in, which I think is a reference to the Disney movie.

'Wow, you really are always listening, aren't you?' I laugh, having not even realised she'd entered the room.

'Chloe, why don't you go get your princess dress, and I'll take a picture of you and Auntie Ivy together.'

Holly waits for Chloe to charge off before speaking.

'That should buy us five minutes,' she says hurriedly. 'I told Lee about our little surprise. He jokes that next time he leaves for work, maybe we should keep our clothes on…but, really, he's just as over the moon as I am now.'

'That's amazing,' I tell her, squeezing her hand. 'When are you going to tell the kids?'

'We thought we might wait for the 12-week mark, just to be safe,' she says.

'Good idea.'

'OK, what are we doing with this hair?' she asks, wrapping a towel around my shoulders.

I already have a face full of make-up – like something from a YouTube tutorial, that I'd never be able to get right on my own – and now I have my dress on, which Holly insisted I do before she did my hair, just in case I ruined my hair, putting my dress on.

'What do you think?'

'I'm thinking red carpet waves,' she suggests, clipping up my hair in sections.

'I trust your judgement,' I reply.

'So, what did you say to Seb?' she asks.

'I didn't know what to say; it was so unexpected. I texted him and thanked him so much for helping me out.'

'And what did he say?'

'He said I was welcome and asked me if I wanted a lift tonight. So he's picking me up here.'

'Ooh,' Holly teases. 'Things are getting serious.'

'Shut up.' I laugh.

What he actually said was, in light of my recent near miss with a driving ban, maybe it would be best if he drove me there tonight. Which reminds me...

'Oh, I've got a box full of Christmas cake in my bag for you.'

'Me?' Holly replies. 'I don't like the stuff.'

'Do the kids?'

'They kids would sooner eat Play-Doh.'

'Lee?'

'You know, I don't know,' Holly replies.

'Well, the stuff lives for years without going off, it seems. If he doesn't, you're welcome to chuck it.'

'Thanks.' She laughs. 'You didn't make it then?'

'No, no, no,' I say quickly, not wanting my name put to such a repulsive dessert. 'I did the charity tasting thing yesterday – well, I didn't, Seb ate mine for me.'

'Ivy has a crush,' Holly sings. 'Look at you, you're all doe-eyed and your cheeks are all rosy.'

'That's just the make-up,' I say.

'Sure it is,' she replies. 'Except I didn't use blusher.'

Holly finishes my hair and blasts me with hairspray.

'There we go,' she says, holding up a mirror for me to examine myself.

'Wow...' I blurt. 'Holly, thank you. I look so...not like me.'

'You should glam up more often,' she tells me. 'You look amazing.'

'It'll be an improvement on the reindeer dressing gown Seb saw me in the first time we met.'

'Erm, what?' my sister asks.

'It's not as bad as it sounds...or maybe it is. I'd overslept, and the shop was never busy that time of day, so rather than rush to get dressed, I made myself a warm drink and got stuck into my new book…'

'Oh, you and books.' My sister laughs. 'So he walked in on you like that?'

'He did,' I say. 'And…never mind.'

'No, go on.'

'It's nothing,' I insist.

'My twintuition is telling me it's something.'

'No, you're just prying.' I laugh. 'OK, fine…he kissed me, under the mistletoe, before he left.'

My sister's eyes light up and her jaw drops. 'Sexy Seb kissed you?'

'Yes,' I say. 'Shhh.'

'He's kissing you, he's buying you dresses – he likes you.'

'No, he's trying to get me onside,' I tell her. 'I told you he's donated loads of money to the garden centre – they've got a movie Santa Claus there, raising money for kids.'

'That's just business.' She dismisses me with a bat of her hand.

'Yeah, I keep hearing that, but it's *my* business that his "just business" is having an effect on.'

We're interrupted by a knock on the door.

'That's probably Seb,' I say. 'Do *not* say anything.'

'Of course I won't,' she replies, hurrying to the door to let him in.

'Seb.' She beams. 'My gosh, look at you, you look amazing.'

'Thanks,' he says, flashing his dimples.

Seb steps inside and when he turns to see me, I see his jaw drop.

'Oh, God, do I look daft?' I ask.

'You look incredible,' he tells me. 'Mesmerising.'

'You have great taste in dresses,' Holly tells him.

'I'm glad one of them fit,' he says. 'I had no idea about women's sizes, so I just bought three.'

'"Just bought three", Holly teases.

'Just three.' He laughs. 'I'm not a billionaire.'

'Anyway, shall we go?' I interrupt.

'Yes, of course,' he replies.

'Well, have a good time, behave yourselves, don't keep her out too late, and don't get her pregnant,' Holly jokes.

By the time we get to Seb's car, I'm blushing again.

'So, remind me what's happening tonight?' he asks.

'It's just dinner and a silent auction,' I tell him. People pay for tickets, to raise money for charity. You don't pay for tickets if you donate a thing or a skill to the auction.'

'I'm giving an hour of one-on-one business coaching,' he tells me. 'Prue came up with it.'

'Yeah, she came up with one for me too: an "expertly" decorated Christmas tree, for next year.'

'Yours sounds more fun,' he replies. 'Where am I headed?'

'Yorkshi,' I tell him. 'Over on Hope Island. Don't worry, I've checked the causeway times – we're good until 1.30 a.m. They have to plan these sorts of things in advance, if they're expecting people to attend events on the island.'

'I don't mind, my B&B is there,' he says. 'What's Yorkshi?'

'It's a Yorkshire-themed sushi place. I've always wanted to go, but I've never really had the excuse.'

'I've always eaten out,' he tells me. 'Never really been able to cook. But I've never had Yorkshire sushi, so this should be interesting.'

We arrive at Yorkshi, where a red carpet has been laid out. Everyone is having their photo taken on the way in, so Seb and I have ours snapped together, arm in arm.

Inside, the large room has been decked out with silver and blue Christmas decorations, with twinkling fairy lights in all directions. Tables and chairs are set out, but there's no assigned seating. Servers are doing the rounds with plates of both bizarre and incredible-looking things to eat – a mixture of sweet and savoury.

I take one of the sweet strawberry rice flavoured cones from the plate – in a rush to get straight to dessert, as always. It's just amazing. Such a cool and unique idea, and executed to perfection.

Prue comes rushing over to us.

'Ivy, Sebastian, hello,' she says. Prue is wearing a floor-length silver dress, embellished with blue glitter, making her look like part of the décor. 'The silent auction has started, so make sure to get your votes in.'

'Oh, we will,' I tell her, although I won't. I don't exactly have disposable income at the moment.

'Everyone has been so generous this year,' she says. 'Wilson's recently had a large donation from a mystery businessman, which they're very kindly using to help us with our chosen charities too.'

'Oh, I heard about that,' Seb says.

'Yes, it's so amazing. Between us—' Prue leans in to whisper, first glancing either side to make sure no one else is listening '—it was Alfie Barton. His cider business has been doing really well lately and he wanted to share some of his success.'

I swallow hard. So it *wasn't* Seb.

'That's very generous,' Seb says.

'Every little bit helps,' Prue tells us, leaving us to schmooze with more people.

'You OK?' Seb asks me. I smile at him as I watch him swipe a mini Yorkshire pudding stuffed with gravy. 'Want one?'

'Oh, in this dress, I'd better not.' I laugh.

Seb grabs one anyway. 'Here's the plan,' he starts. 'You're going to open your mouth and I'm going to carefully feed you this Yorkshire pudding. I not only promise not to get any on your dress but, if I do, I'll go get one of the backup dresses.'

'OK,' I say with a smile. 'I, erm, I sort of owe you an apology.'

'Oh?' he replies.

'When I found out someone had donated to the garden centre

so they could get a new Santa Claus, I thought it was you, and that you'd done it to thwart my efforts.'

'I wouldn't do that,' he assures me. 'I was just upset the other day when I thought you were spreading rumours about me, but it was an empty threat.'

'I'm glad we've cleared the air,' I tell him.

'Me too,' he replies. 'Now, if you'll excuse me, I have a silent bid to make.'

I smile as I watch him head over to the auction table. There are a few things up for auction that I would absolutely love – a spa weekend, dinner here, a haircut at the swanky new place that's just opened up on the island – but there's no way I'd win anything. This place is full of Marram Bay's richest residents (and little old me).

I pop to the ladies' room, where I'm delighted to find a koi pond. The sides are clear, providing an unobstructed view of the pretty coloured fish. It's mesmerising really. I sit and admire them for a moment, with the dumbest grin on my face. Suddenly, Seb seems like a different person. He's sweet and charming, but in a way that feels genuine. He isn't mentioning the shop or his project at all – and given the recent news that it wasn't him who funded the new Santa Claus, I can't help but feel like he might have had a change of heart. I don't know; I just feel like there's something between us. Something more important than business.

I check my make-up in the mirror – it's still flawless. I don't know how my sister does it. When I do my own, it never looks amazing, and it gets steadily worse as the day goes on. Then again, I don't spend as much money as Holly does on things like primers and finishing sprays. With everything where it is supposed to be, I head back out into the main room in the hope of eating some more Yorkshire sushi.

As the evening goes on, there's a real merry buzz in the air, the kind you only seem to get at festive parties. It's a wonderful kind of merry too, not the debauched kind you see in the movies, at wild office Christmas parties. I've never had a work Christmas party – I suppose because, not only is it Christmas every day, but for the most part it's only me working there. I might do it this year, although the idea of celebrating, just Gaz and me, when there really is nothing to celebrate, is probably going to be more than a little awkward. Perhaps I'll have something for my inner circle: Gaz, Holly, the kids…maybe even Seb.

Speak of the devil. Seb walks over to me and hands me a glass of champagne.

'Someone just bought me this, but I'm driving,' he says. 'It's all yours.'

'Thanks,' I say, taking the glass from him. It's very kind of him not to drink, just so he can drive me home later.

'If I could have everyone's attention, please,' Prue calls out. 'Now that the silent auction is over I want to tell everyone that this year we've raised a record-breaking amount of money, and it's largely down to one very generous bid. Congratulations to Mr Sebastian Stone, who has donated a whopping £5,000 for a Christmas tree decoration session with Ivy Jones, from Christmas Every Day. A round of applause for Mr Stone, please, ladies and gentlemen.'

I look at Seb, my eyes wide with shock – my mouth even wider.

'You paid £5,000 to have me decorate your Christmas tree?' I ask in amazement.

'It's for charity,' he says casually. 'Anyway, it's a big job. I'm sponsoring the big Christmas tree, at the top of Main Street, next year. Except I'm going to see about getting an even bigger one, and I want you to decorate it.'

I just blink.

'Not physically,' he insists. 'I don't expect you to climb a 30-foot tree, to place a star on top. But I want you to design it, decide what should go on it, et cetera.'

'That's…amazing,' I tell him. 'I thought I was going to wind up in a stranger's living room, putting tinsel on an artificial tree. This is amazing!'

I grab Seb and hug him. Even in my heels, I'm still much shorter than he is, so my face just presses into his body, but I squeeze him as hard as I can.

'It's nothing.' He laughs, wiggling his arms free from mine to wrap them around me.

'Sebastian,' Prue interrupts. 'We were hoping to get a photograph of you.'

'I'll be right back,' he tells me.

I watch as Seb disappears with Prue. That was so generous of him, in so many ways. Not only has he given a huge amount of money to good causes, but it is also going to be an absolute honour to dress the town tree. My head is so full of ideas already – I can't wait.

I know what I need to celebrate: more sweet sushi. Now that most people are bored of eating, servers are no longer circulating with plates; instead plates are just lying around so that guests can help themselves.

I move from plate to plate, trying to find the sweet ones, finally spotting them at the end of a table. As I approach the plate, I see Seb chatting with a few of the town's other businessmen.

'Hoping to finalise the purchase in the New Year,' he says. 'And I'll move the bulldozers in that week. I'd like a speedy turnaround.'

And just like that, it feels like a knife has been driven into my heart. Seb, who I thought was being so lovely with me – who maybe might be changing his mind about knocking down my shop – never had any intentions to change his plans. He's just been keeping me sweet, distracting me while he carries on making business moves. I've been such an idiot.

I fetch my coat from the cloakroom and ask the host to call me a taxi. All I want to do is get out of here.

I'm nearly home when Seb texts me, asking where I am. I send him a blunt message saying that I've gone home. A lift home from him would be just another one of his empty gestures. I feel so stupid for thinking he was being nice to me, but I'm glad that I have realised now, before it's too late.

I just need to put this out of my head and be up bright and early tomorrow, ready for the Winter Wonderland Festival. Our stall is booked, so all we need to do is get there early and set up. Now, more than ever, I am determined to wipe the smug smirk off Sebastian Stone's face.

Chapter 23

'I don't want you to get mad,' Gaz says cautiously, using his hands to keep distance between us, as we make our way through the unopened Winter Wonderland, to where our stall is based.

It's cold today – I know, it's December, but it's probably the coldest day we've had this winter so far, and I'm not in the mood for spending the day outside. I'm definitely not in the mood for any of Gaz's shenanigans.

'OK,' I reply, pretty sure I'm going to get mad.

'When I booked the stall, I booked an extra bit too.'

'OK…'

'So, the bloke I spoke to, he tells me no one wants to run the kissing booth this year. He says people think it's too old-fashioned. They don't want anything to do with it.'

'That sounds right,' I reply. Well, a kissing booth – as cute as it sounds – is basically when strangers pay to kiss you, right?

'So, he said if we wanted to use it, we could for free. Isn't that great?'

Gaz smiles widely, like he's bagged us an awesome freebie.

'Gaz, he only did that because there's still a few perverts out there, willing to pay a stranger for a kiss at a fairground – and no one else wants to play pervert wrangler, so he talked you into doing it. No, *us* into doing it.'

'But it's not even for charity,' he says. 'We can keep the money.'

I sigh.

'Trust me,' he says. 'It's going to be great.'

'We're not using it.' I laugh but, as we approach our stall, I can see not only that our sign is up, but that it advertises both the Christmas Every Day Christmas shop, and the Christmas kissing booth. Our fates are tied now, thanks to Gaz's naivety and this bloody sign.

'I don't suppose we can take that down and just have no sign at all?' I suggest.

'No.' Gaz laughs.

'Cover it maybe?'

'With what? We can't cover our shop sign; people won't know it's us.'

'I'm not sure I want people to know it's us now,' I confess with a sigh. 'Well...OK, fine, but you're running it, right? I don't have to kiss any strangers.'

'Sure, sure,' he assures me. 'I'll do all the kissing. I was born to do this job.'

He probably was.

There's a large open space, down by the seafront, where the town hosts a variety of festivals and conventions, but the Winter Wonderland Festival, which we host every year, is the biggest and it's definitely the most popular, with people travelling from all over just to check it out.

The Winter Wonderland Festival is a real mixture of all sorts of things. We're here because there are always lots of stalls – the kinds of things you'd expect to see at a Christmas market – for almost every local business here in Marram Bay, as well as a variety of other shops that travel from all over, just to sell things at the festival.

A personal highlight for me is all the amazing places to eat and drink. As well as local businesses – like my new favourite place, Yorkshi, and the team from Apple Blossom Deli – we also get traders from outside town, serving up festive favourites from all over Europe. Then there's the street food vendors, the baristas and, right in the heart of the festival, they build a wooden lodge, where people can go get drinks from the bar.

The festival also boasts a variety of games and rides, from the stunning, old-fashioned carousel to the Christmas tree maze. There's something about mazes that truly fascinates me, but as this one changes each year, it's impossible to learn the layout. I suppose this is a good thing, but it does frustrate me a little when I inevitably can't find my way out – especially when there are kids doing it with their eyes closed. Luckily for me, Holly hates the idea, which means I get to take the kids in, which is the perfect excuse.

We set up our stall with the items we brought from the shop, and Gaz preps his kissing booth, which I can't help but roll my eyes at.

'Is Charlie still coming to help out?' I ask him.

'She is,' he replies. 'She'll be here in five.'

'How about I go and get us some gingerbread lattes?' I ask, nodding towards the cute little gingerbread house, that sells flavoured hot drinks and, of course, biscuits in various festive shapes. I can smell the gingerbread drifting across the cold fairground, and it smells glorious. It's just what we need to warm ourselves up.

By the time I'm back with the drinks, Charlie has arrived.

'Here we go, team,' I say, handing out drinks and gingerbread men. 'The festival gates open in ten minutes. Any questions?'

'Just one: how much do we need to make to ruin Seb's life?' Charlie asks.

'A lot.' I laugh.

'Let's do this,' she says confidently, securing her faux fur pillbox hat, ready for action.

Once the festival is open, people begin pouring in almost straight away. Men, women, children, pensioners – lots of people have even brought their dogs. Our stall gets a lot of attention, like I hoped it would, but I can't help noticing that the kissing booth is fast becoming the star attraction.

Gaz and Charlie have taken a side each, standing behind their own pieces of mistletoe, and they have attracted quite the crowd of curious people already.

'Roll up, roll up,' Gaz says. 'Welcome to Marram Bay's kissing booth – the perfect way to warm up on a cold December day like today. Here's what you do. You join the queue of your choice, you hand over £2, you get a peck – no tongues, no saliva, no touching, no dirty talking.'

The crowd laugh.

Gaz proceeds to hand over £2 to Charlie, before demonstrating what an acceptable kiss is like. It's nothing, really, just a fleeting peck. Everyone cheers, when they kiss.

Soon enough, people begin forming lines in front of them both, happy to trade £2 for a quick peck. There's such a diverse crowd of people here today. I've seen what I'd guess is a 16-year-old lad queue, for a peck on the cheek from Charlie, and the only thing more amazing than the fact that there are men queuing up to kiss Gaz is the fact that he is happily obliging. It's all just a bit of fun, and everyone is having a wonderful time. Perhaps kissing booths aren't as dated or as seedy as I first thought.

'Ivy, come and have a go,' Charlie insists. 'It's so much fun!'

'Me? No, no, no,' I say. 'No one wants to kiss me.'

'They will,' she replies. 'You look much prettier than usual.'

I think that was a compliment, and I think it's largely down to the fact that my hair still has gorgeous waves in it from last night (apparently sleeping on it only makes it look more like natural curls) and, encouraged by my sister's efforts, I made a really good attempt at doing my make-up this morning. It's not as good as when Holly does it for me, but at least I tried today.

'What do you think?' Charlie asks the man at the front of the queue. 'You wanna kiss Ivy? She reckons no one would kiss her.'

'I'll kiss her,' the twenty-something man replies keenly.

I pull a surprised face. I didn't think that anyone wanted to kiss *me*.

I don't know if it's down to peer pressure, the fact that I am encouraged by a single man wanting to kiss me for money, or just good old festive spirit, but I edge towards the kissing booth, take the man's £2, and plant a peck on him.

'Whoo!' Charlie cheers. 'See, it's fun.'

'It is weirdly fun,' I admit.

'It's liberating too,' she insists. 'It feels kind of feministy.'

'Who's next?' I say, clapping my hands.

'Hello, Ivy,' the man says.

I double-take, because at first it just seems like a stranger who knows my name, but then I realise it's Pete the postman.

'Pete,' I say. 'I didn't recognise you out of your uniform – in your regular clothes, I mean. What are you doing here?'

Pete holds out his hand to reveal two pound coins.

'Oh, right,' I say. Kissing strangers is one thing, but kissing the man who brings my post is another. 'OK.'

I lean forward and peck Pete on the cheek. He instantly places a hand over the spot I kissed and smiles.

'I miss you of a morning,' he says. 'Now that you have the man opening up for you.'

I laugh at his use of 'the man'.

'That's Gaz,' I tell him. 'He's great.'

'He doesn't brighten up my day like you did,' he says.

'Oh, stop,' I say with a bat of my hand as Pete walks away.

'Who's next?' I say cheerily, turning my attention back to the queue of people in front of me. My face falls as I realise Seb is the next person in line.

'Slow business day?' he jokes, nodding at the sign above us.

I don't laugh.

'Just kidding,' he says, handing me a £5 note.

Today I am immune to Seb's faux charm and his generosity. His dimples are no longer attractive to me; they are a sign of his smug self-assurance, and I'm sick of the sight of them.

'Charlie,' I call. 'Isn't this the end of my shift and the start of yours?'

I watch as Seb's face falls.

'It is,' she says, taking my place. 'Hello, Seb.'

'Er, hi,' he says.

'Wow, £5? Does that mean you want two and a half kisses, or change?'

'Erm, just the one,' he says, glancing over at me, and then back to Charlie.

Charlie, ever the professional, gives Seb a peck, while I take up my position on the stall again.

After an awkward kiss with Charlie, Seb shuffles over to the stall, making his way to the front of the crowd so he can talk to me.

'What was all that about?' he asks with an uncomfortable laugh.

'Nothing,' I reply. 'Nothing at all.'

A customer hands me the baubles she has chosen from the selection we have on display, so I ignore Seb while I carefully wrap them, take the money from the customer and hand over her purchase and her change.

'You disappeared last night,' he says once I'm done, starting to sense that something might be up. 'I looked all over for you – I tried to call you a couple of times too, actually.'

'Yeah, I'd had enough,' I tell him, turning around to pretend I'm doing something with the cashbox.

'Ivy?' he says. 'Ivy…what's wrong?'

'Seb, can you just go away, please?' I say quietly, making sure that no customers hear me.

'OK, something is definitely wrong,' he says. 'Please tell me what's wrong.'

'I heard you,' I tell him. 'I heard you bragging, about how you'll have my shop knocked down in no time.'

'Ivy, listen to me—'

'I know what you're going to say, "it's just business",' I say. 'So, let's just skip that, and you can go, and I can enjoy my business while it's still my business, OK?'

It hurts me to be so cold with him, especially after we were getting on so well, but I very much doubt he even cares. This really is all just a business venture to him, and I'm just the annoying little nuisance that's getting in the way.

'Ivy, we need to talk,' he says firmly.

'Seb, I'm too busy,' I tell him.

'Too busy to talk about something that's important?' he asks.

'It's just business,' I reply.

Chapter 24

Today was an amazing day...until it absolutely wasn't.

Our stall at the Winter Wonderland Festival was a roaring success, and despite Seb's little interruption distracting me for a few minutes, I had an amazing time.

Not only did I set a record for the most money I've ever made at one of these festivals, but I think I've kissed more people today than I have in my life to date. OK, fine, they were only pecks, but I'll take what I can get these days. That said, I have to admit, my favourite kiss of all was the freebie I gave to the happy golden retriever who came bounding up to the booth, standing tall on two legs so that I could plant a kiss on his face. In return he gave me a lick – a possible violation of the kissing booth rules, but I won't tell anyone if you don't.

I left Gaz and Charlie running the show this afternoon, after receiving a message from Mr Andrews, asking me to call him as soon as possible, so I hurried home to call him, unsure of the time difference between here and Australia. I was desperately hoping I wouldn't wake him, because I need him in my good books.

I'm pretty sure I had my breath held for the duration of the phone ringing, but when he finally answered, everything I had been dreading came true. It turns out Mr Andrews has found a house in Australia that he wants to buy, and he needs to act fast...which means he needs to sell the shop fast, which means he's going to sell it to Seb, and even though I've saved up a little pile of money, it's nowhere near enough to secure a mortgage.

The first thing I did was what any sound-minded northerner would do – I went to put the kettle on, but while it was boiling I opened the fridge to get the milk out and noticed the bottle of Prosecco sitting in the door, which has been there for a few months now. I'm not usually much of a drinker, but today just felt like the right time. To toast my time here, to drown my sorrows – whatever. Around my third glass was when I had this *great* idea – that there might well still be a way to save the shop. I just need to appeal to the businessman in Seb, not the human, because Seb doesn't think like a human; Seb thinks like a money-hungry, life-ruining machine.

So I grabbed my coat, hopped in a taxi and headed over to Hope Island, to the Lighthouse B&B where Seb mentioned he's been temporarily living. I'm currently waiting in reception for him to come down and see me, standing by the log fire, hugging myself with my arms, because there is one hell of a storm going on outside. As my taxi drove along the causeway, the car was being lashed with water. It was kind of scary, really.

It's getting late, it's getting colder, and I'm getting to the end of my rope – where is Seb? I want to get this over with.

'Ivy,' he says, sounding a little surprised to see me. 'What are you doing here?'

'I have a proposition for you,' I say confidently.

'OK,' he replies with a smile. 'I was just about to have dinner. Do you want to join me?'

'No, thanks,' I reply. 'This won't take long.'

'OK, let's sit in the bar then,' he suggests.

I take a seat at the table, opposite Seb, before removing a piece of paper from my pocket. On this piece of paper is a number. I slide it across the table to Seb, like I've seen in the movies.

'What's this?'

'This is how much I've saved, for a deposit, to buy the shop,' I tell him.

'That is more than I expected you to have raised,' he tells me.

'Unfortunately, it's not enough,' I admit. 'Banks don't exactly want to lend money to single women with nothing going for them.

Seb opens his mouth to speak, but I stop him.

'Don't,' I say. 'Just listen. I want you to take it.'

'You want to give me this money?'

'Yes,' I reply. 'Well, what else do you want in life, apart from money?'

'Ivy…'

'Listen,' I say. 'It comes with a catch. You take this money and you leave town. You can do what you're planning somewhere else, and I can keep working hard, and start from scratch raising money for a deposit. If I pay you off, and Mr Andrews doesn't have anyone else lined up, it will buy me some time. Things are going well, I just need more time.'

Seb sighs. 'Ivy, no,' he says. 'I've planned everything here. I want to move here.'

'Please,' I say. 'This is my last option.'

'Ivy, I'm sorry,' he says, taking my hand. I snatch it back and storm out.

Outside, I huddle under the Lighthouse canopy, taking shelter from the rain as I call for a taxi on my mobile.

'Can I get a taxi from Hope Island Lighthouse, to the mainland, please,' I say.

'Now?' the woman on the phone replies.

'Yes please,' I reply.

'Sorry love,' she says apologetically. 'Causeway is closed.'

Crap, I completely forgot to check. 'Until when, please?' I ask.

'Coming up to 4 a.m., love, sorry,' she says.

'Thank you, never mind,' I say softly, but I'm screwed, trapped here on the island until morning.

I head back into the Lighthouse, to shield myself from the freezing cold wind and rain.

'Do you have any rooms?' I ask reluctantly.

'Sorry, we don't,' the receptionist tells me.

'Can you recommend anywhere that might?' I ask.

'I doubt you'll find anywhere, I'm sorry,' she says. 'I can call a few and check for you, but at this time of year everywhere is usually booked up.'

'I see,' I reply. 'If you wouldn't mind checking, thank you.'

I hover for a second, while the receptionist calls other B&Bs, to see if they can fit me in.

'Ivy?' I hear Seb's voice behind me. 'You rushed off.'

'I did,' I reply. 'Bizarrely, I didn't want to be around you.'

'No, sorry,' the receptionist says. 'Everywhere is full.'

'What's wrong?' Seb asks.

'The tide is in and I can't get home,' I admit. 'And everywhere on the island is booked up.'

'Stay in my room,' he insists. 'You can have my bed; I'll sleep on the floor.'

'No, thanks,' I say quickly. 'I'm sure I have other options.'

'Such as?'

'Maybe I could hire a boat to take me – it's only a mile – or…'

'You could swim?' he suggests sarcastically. 'Ivy, there's a wild storm out there. You can't cross, not until it's safe.'

'If you know him, I'd suggest taking up his offer,' the receptionist suggests. 'I don't think you have any other options.'

I exhale deeply.

'Have you eaten?' Seb asks.

I shake my head.

'Have dinner with me and, if you still don't want my bed, I will swim across the sea with you – OK?'

'Fine,' I reply, quickly remembering my manners. 'Thank you.'

'Would you like a table now?' the receptionist asks.

'Yes, please,' he replies.

'Head straight through, I'll call them and tell them you're on your way.'

'Thanks,' he replies. 'After you, Ivy.'

Seb gestures towards the dining room, ushering me with his arm.

I can't believe my plan to pay Seb off didn't work. I can't believe I'm stuck here with him now. I can't believe I've agreed to have dinner with him, and I really can't believe I'm going to have to sleep in his room.

One thing I know for sure is that if he starts getting on my nerves I probably will just wade into the sea and see where I end up. Anywhere has to be better than here.

Chapter 25

My life these days is just a series of awkward and disappointing circumstances, with me bouncing from one horrible situation to the next.

In what is potentially my fourth uncomfortable situation of *the day*, I've decided that the best thing I can do is just go with the flow. If I'm trapped here with Seb, what else can I do? I might as well weather the storm here and have dinner with him.

That said – and as I'm sure you can imagine – given the fact that Seb is the man who is ruining my life, the conversation is not really up to much.

Darren is our waiter this evening. He dutifully and gleefully introduced himself before taking our order. But poor Darren fast realised he'd happened upon something awkward. I don't know if he thinks this is some kind of mismatched blind date, or an awkward Tinder meet-up, but Darren knows something is wrong here. That's why, when he comes to our table, he does exactly what he needs to do, before scarpering as fast as he can. He's probably terrified he's going to get caught in some kind of cross-fire.

Darren brings us the bottle of white wine that Seb ordered and pours us both a glass.

Having sank a few glasses of Prosecco before I got here – and being quite the lightweight when it comes to drinking – there's a strong chance the effects of my previous drinks haven't quite worn off yet. That said, if having a couple more glasses will make this evening go faster, I'm all for it.

'Something you said earlier is really playing on my mind,' he finally confesses, filling the silence.

I glance down at my food – salmon in a white wine sauce with asparagus, baby carrots and new potatoes, which smells incredible. I wish I were here under different circumstances so that I could really enjoy it. It's hard to care about the *one* thing I said earlier that is playing on Seb's mind, because ever since he turned up in Marram Bay, he's said a lot of things that have been playing on my mind near constantly.

Seb ignores the steak and chips in front of him. The steak that he's only been given a regular knife for, because I'm pretty sure Darren thinks a steak knife might be a risky thing to leave between us.

'When you offered me that money earlier, you rhetorically asked: "What else do you want, apart from money?"'

'I did,' I confirm.

'It sounded to me like you thought that money was all I cared about.'

I gasp theatrically for effect. Seb just ignores my sarcasm and carries on talking.

'I was thinking about it, in the ten minutes while you were contemplating whether to swim home in a freezing rainstorm, or be trapped on an island with me, and something occurred to me… I've never actually told you why I want to move here.'

'I assumed it was to flash your money around town and ruin lives,' I say – or rather, the wine says.

Seb laughs a little. 'Can I explain?' he asks.

'Why not, eh?' I reply, sipping my drink. 'I'm all ears.'

'I'm not really in touch with my old school friends,' he starts.

'I have them added on Facebook though, so I do have an insight into what they're all doing with their lives, and they're all following quite similar paths.'

So far – annoyingly – I can relate to what Seb is saying. Holly still meets up with a couple of the girls we were friends with at school, but only because their kids all go to school together now. I – not a real adult – don't get invited to the mummy meet-ups, obviously, but it does remind me that everyone is taking that same road. Everyone but me.

'They've got husbands, wives, kids. They're working steady jobs, making enough money to have a nice house – which they relish taking pride in. They spend their free time on family holidays, at kids' parties, visiting their in-laws...'

'Is everything OK with your food?' Darren interrupts reluctantly.

'It's great, cheers, mate,' Seb replies, but while he sounds convincing, Darren isn't buying it.

'Neither of you has touched it yet...'

We both make an effort to tuck into our food, giving a relieved Darren the reassurance he needs so that he can leave us alone again.

'For as long as I can remember, my life has been all about work,' Seb confesses. 'I haven't put down real roots, I haven't had real relationships – I realised that I have pretty much nothing real to show for my life. Just work. And when I realised that, I also realised how unhappy I was, and that was that, I knew I'd need to make a change.'

I give Seb a half-smile. I suppose I can relate to that because I'm in a similar situation. For years, my life has been all about the shop. I haven't had proper, meaningful relationships – with men or friends outside my family – and, while I did have my own little house what feels like a million years ago, I sold it to buy Holly out of the shop, so that I didn't have to sell it to a stranger after our mum died.

'The truth is, I want to get married. I want to have kids. I want to care way more about my porch extension than anyone should ever really care about a porch extension. I'm not moving to Marram Bay because I thought you seemed like easy pickings for another business venture, I'm moving here because I want to move *here*. Yes, building holiday homes is a business decision, but I want it to be my last one. It's a business that I can set up and run myself, here, in one place, where I can become part of the community. I don't want to move here for work, I want to move here for good. I want my life to start here.'

With a little less reluctance than before, I relate even more to what Seb is saying. He could be talking about me. I've put finding love and starting a family to one side – not even intentionally, it's just what happens when you give everything you have to something else.

'Do you know what I mean?' he prompts.

'I do,' I reply. 'The only problem is that you can't just force yourself to fit in here – that's not how fitting in works. You want to be one of us – try acting like one of us, instead of an out-of-towner who just wants to come in and capitalise on our tourism. But otherwise, I understand. I've done exactly the same thing – watch everyone around me settle down and start a family, while all I've done is focus on the shop.'

'So we want similar things?' he replies.

'I suppose we do. The difference is, you're an eligible bachelor with all the time in the world to get married and have kids. I'm a soon to be unemployed and homeless spinster, with a biological timeline I need to stick to.'

Seb just smiles.

'In the interest of honesty,' I start – because what else do I have to lose – 'I would be upset about anyone buying my mum's shop and my family home, no matter who they were, or what my circumstances, but I think the reason it's hitting me so hard is because it's all I've ever worked for. It's all I've got, and that's probably why I'm so terrified of losing it. Because then what? Forget about where I'll live or what I'll do for money – why will I get up in the morning? What will my purpose in life be? Without the shop, there's nothing.'

'Ivy...'

'Nah, don't,' I say. 'There's no point. I get it. You feel bad, I feel bad – everyone feels bad.'

'I've bought a lot of buildings and businesses,' he tells me. 'I've never spent much time with the person I was buying them from so, as far as I know, they've never been reluctant to leave.'

'So?'

'So, I've never had any kind of...moral burden before.'

'Let's not talk about it,' I insist. 'You're buying the place – it's a done deal.'

'I'm giving a presentation at the town hall tomorrow, for the general public, so they can come along and learn about the plans.'

'And, what, you want me to show up, kick up a fuss, call you a monster, just like old times?'

Seb gives me an almost sympathetic smile.

'Shall we not talk about it?' he suggests.

'I think the night will be much more bearable that way,' I reply.

An awkward silence falls upon us, just in time for Darren to take our plates. Poor, innocent Darren, caught in the crossfire of a war he has nothing to do with.

'It's stopped raining,' Seb muses. Brilliant, we've resorted to making small talk about the weather. 'I'm looking forward to summer. Being able to explore the place. It's been pretty much nonstop work.'

'It's a beautiful place, lots to see,' I tell him. 'It's good being so close to the sea, to the beaches. I don't think I'll ever get tired of walks on the beach – not that I've had much time for it recently.'

'I could not tell you the last time I went for a walk on the beach,' he admits. Then he must notice the look on my face. 'I'm always working. That's why I made this change, more time to do the stuff I want to do, less time hunched over my laptop or on the phone.'

'You still seem like a money-talks, always-busy businessman to me,' I point out. 'Let me know when the change kicks in.'

'Let's go for a walk on the beach,' he suggests.

'When?'

'Now,' he replies. 'The rain has stopped, the wind has calmed. This place is on the coast – 30 seconds out the door, we can be walking on a beach.'

'OK…'

I'm a little taken aback by his suggestion but, after we pay the bill, we put on our coats and head outside.

With the rain halted and the wind calmer, it's much nicer outside, although still a little chilly. We walk down a small grassy hill until we're on the beach.

'It's an amazing view,' Seb says.

To the right you can see Marram Bay, looking more attractive than ever with the multi-coloured lights from the Winter Wonderland being reflected on the water. Straight on, you can't see anything. Just sea until you can't see sea anymore…nothing but black.

'Look at all that nothingness out there,' Seb muses, looking out to sea.

'I like that though,' I tell him. 'Looking one way to see everything that has felt familiar to me my entire life, and then looking the other and seeing nothing. It doesn't scare me or depress me; it gives me hope. It's a blank slate, which makes my imagination go wild with possibilities and hope. Anything could be over there.'

'I think Amsterdam is over there.' He laughs. 'But there *are* lots of possibilities in Amsterdam.'

Seb gives me that cheeky laugh of his, and that flash of his dimples that I can't help but adore, and with the moonlight reflecting in his eyes, I keep feeling my anger slipping away. If I could just let go of it...

'Christmas soon,' he says, changing the subject as we stroll along the sand. 'You must be buzzing.'

For the first time in my life, my excitement for Christmas has been quashed, and it breaks my heart a little. I don't say this out loud though.

'I am. Do you like Christmas?'

'Meh,' he replies. 'Never really had anyone to spend it with, not since I was a kid.'

'Not even girlfriends?'

'Never really had a girlfriend long enough to spend Christmas with her,' he tells me.

'There's a time period you have to wait before you can ask a person on his own for Christmas dinner?'

'Apparently,' he says with a chuckle.

'I think my sister was going to ask you to have it with us, the other night,' I tell him. 'And she'd only known you a couple of hours.'

'I did build furniture for her,' he says. 'Why did she only *nearly* ask me?'

'That's Hope Abbey down there, or what's left of it,' I tell him, changing the subject. 'Want to stroll around the ruins? It's weirdly beautiful. Supposedly it's haunted.'

'Haunted?' Seb asks cautiously as we walk towards it.

'Yeah, you're not scared of ghosts are you?' I tease.

'No,' he replies, not entirely convincingly. 'Let's go.'

'Seeing as how you're not scared, I'll tell you the story as we walk around it,' I suggest. 'Legend has it that a young couple once tied the knot here – as many couples still do. They had a big, beautiful wedding – an absolutely perfect day until the bride realised the groom had vanished. Still not scared?'

'Still not scared,' he tells me, twirling around to take in his surroundings.

'So, she doesn't panic, instead she just walks around to see if she can see him – he can't have gone far.'

'Let me guess, she never saw him again?'

'No, she did,' I tell him. 'She found him hidden behind a crumbled abbey wall, kissing her younger sister, telling her how she was the one he really loved.'

'Tale as old as time. Is that what's supposed to scare me? Infidelity?'

'The bride decided she would teach her no good, cheating groom a lesson. To show him that she was the one who was important to him, and to give him a scare, she climbed into one of the rumoured secret tunnels that run underneath the island.'

'Secret tunnels?'

'Yeah, I think the monks used to use them, to escape the abbey when they needed to. No, you can't buy them,' I tease. 'So she found her way into the tunnels to hide…but she could never find her way back out. None of her family or friends ever found out what happened to her and her husband married her sister in the end. Apparently the bride's spirit is trapped here, and many people have reported seeing her ghost rise up from the ground, intent on inflicting pain and suffering on any happy couple she sees.'

Seb doesn't say anything. His face is straight and his eyes are blank. Suddenly his head snaps up to make eye contact with me, his eyes wide as he screams: 'Boo!' at the top of his voice. The loud sound echoes around the remains of the abbey and I jump out of my skin.

'Oh my God, what is wrong with you?' I ask, my hands clutching my chest.

'You were enjoying trying to scare me, so I thought I'd give you a scare.' He laughs. 'And it worked. And, look, no ghost.'

'She only comes out for happy couples, not mortal enemies,' I correct him.

'Is that what we are?' he asks, straight-faced.

I shrug.

'Why did you sister only nearly ask me to have Christmas dinner with you?' he asks curiously. 'You never said before.'

'Because I asked her not to,' I tell him. 'The whole mortal enemies thing. Maybe it's a pregnancy symptom, to empathise with people.'

People who maybe don't deserve it, but I don't say that out loud.

'You must be buzzing about that too,' he says. 'Being an auntie again.'

I take a second too long to answer.

'Ivy?'

'I am – of course I am,' I stress. 'I just...I don't know, it made me a little sad. Not for Holly and her family, for me. Holly and I are twins, we had the same upbringing, all the same chances in life...and she has an amazing husband and two wonderful kids, with another on the way. She lives in a nice house and she goes for coffee mornings with her mummy friends. And I'm just me, all alone, with nothing to show for my life at all.'

'Single-handedly running a shop is a huge commitment,' he tells me. 'Especially one in the middle of nowhere, with zero footfall and minimal traffic. If you'd been in a different place, you'd be in a much better position now, and, no matter what, I guarantee your mum would be so proud of you.'

At the mention of my mum, I feel my eyes fill with tears.

'Hey, sorry, I didn't mean to make you cry,' Seb insists, grabbing me for a hug, pressing my face into his body with his arms locked tightly around me. 'You don't realise how amazing you are, how much you've achieved, how much you do for everyone.'

'How come I'm going to end up with nothing?' I ask in between sobs.

'Sometimes people – through no fault of their own – just end up with nothing left. But the tough ones fight through it, and they build themselves back up. But even so, you don't have nothing. You have an amazing family who love you so much, and one day you're going to have kids of your own. Trust me.'

I glance up at Seb, looking into his eyes, and in them I just see something…something that tells me he means everything he's saying.

And just like that, I let go of my anger.

And then we kiss.

Chapter 26

I did wonder, after the few occasions I've had a drink recently, why I don't drink more. It tastes nice, it helps me relax – why haven't I been doing this more often?

Spoiler alert: it's because of the hangovers. I'd forgotten about hangovers – they really are a truly unique and unpleasant nuisance, aren't they? My head hurts, my eyes hurt – even my teeth hurt.

I rub my tired eyes as gently as possible, opening them slowly to adjust to the bright morning light in the room.

'Morning,' Seb says cheerily.

I snap my eyes open and stare at Seb, lying in bed next to me. He's already wide awake, tapping away on his computer.

'Hi,' I say cautiously. Oh, that's right, I didn't dream that. Last night, after a few drinks and getting a little caught up in the romance of the moonlit abbey, I kissed Seb – or maybe he kissed me. Then we ended up back here, and here we are. The awkward moment to end all awkward moments this month, and I've really outdone myself this time.

'I'm going to take a quick shower. Room service is on the way. And then we need to talk, OK?'

I just nod.

As soon as Seb is out of the room, I dash out from under the covers and hurriedly wrestle my clothes back on. Once I'm on my feet, I see that Seb's room is also doubling up as his office. All over the walls are pictures of the shop as it is now, and different artists' impressions of what it will look like when it's gone. I remember Seb's words, about how soon he'll knock it down once the land is his, and the fact that he could do it so quickly, so easily, without so much as a second thought, especially after how close we've become…well, that breaks my heart all over again.

No matter what I'm feeling for Seb – and I'm scared to admit it, but my feelings are pretty strong, and I think perhaps they have been for some time now – I can't get past what he's doing because, if he felt about me the way I feel about him, there is no way he could do this to me. All Seb cares about is Seb, and once he's got what he wants, he'll find some woman to give him the picture-perfect life he wants, that he thinks he can get by just investing enough money in the right place.

That's not how you start a family. You start a family by being a decent person and finding someone who loves you for it. Seb can't love me, or he wouldn't be doing this to me, and I can't love him because he's doing this to me. As Gaz would say, it's a catch-33 situation.

Seb's laptop is open on the bed still. I could get my revenge? Maybe even have one last attempt at putting a stop to his plans? I could delete his presentation or, better still, edit it, put something inappropriate in one of the slides – something that will make everyone hate him.

Now that I'm thinking about it, I can think of a much better way to get revenge. All I need to do is grab my things and get out of here, before he gets out of the shower. The only thing more awkward than waking up in Seb's bed would be debriefing what happened last night, having one of those awkward 'what are we?' conversations. We are nothing, and it's time I acted that way.

Chapter 27

'Kids, you remember Gaz, don't you?' I prompt.

'No?' Chloe replies, while Harry shakes his head. There isn't a glimmer of recognition from either of them and, especially for a child as observant as Chloe, this puzzles me.

'Yeah, you met him...' My voice trails off as Gaz frantically shakes his head behind them, his eyes wide with something. Then I remember. 'My mistake, you must not have met him. Kids, this is Gaz.'

I introduce them to Gaz because it suddenly occurs to me that even though the kids have spoken to him twice, both times he was dressed as Santa Claus.

'Gaz is running the stall here for me. Why don't you guys pick a candy cane each?' I suggest, trying to bag myself a few minutes alone with Gaz, so we can talk.

'You're not going to crash Seb's town hall meeting then?' he asks once we're alone.

'Nah,' I reply with a smile. 'Are you?'

'Can't, I'm working.' He laughs. 'Plus, I think we're late.'

'Ah, and we had such big plans to take him down too,' I joke.

'Not worth our effort, is he?' Gaz replies, and he's absolutely right.

'I have wasted this whole month, fighting something that has been obviously inevitable from the start,' I admit. 'Today I decided that enough is enough. I'm not going to let it ruin my life anymore. And I did promise the kids I'd bring them to the festival so, here we are.'

'Here we are,' he agrees with a smile. 'And, I know things might suck now, but we'll make a comeback. We'll start the shop again and it'll be bigger and better than ever.'

'We will,' I agree. I don't know when, or how, but we absolutely will. 'Right, time to take the kids into the maze.'

'Have fun,' he says. 'Ooh, by the way, I have a date with Charlie tonight.'

'What? No way!'

'I know, I guess that £2 kiss did something for her.'

I smile. It's nice to see him happy.

'Right, kids, let's get lost,' I say excitedly, calling them over so we can finally go in the maze they've been so excited about for weeks.

After pulling on my clothes, putting my shame on the back-burner, and hurrying out of the B&B this morning, I spent the short journey home thinking about something Seb said to me recently. Ever since he said it, I haven't been able to get it out of my head – the sunk cost fallacy concept he told me about. I hate to admit it, now more than ever, but Seb is right. I *am* fighting a losing battle here, and there's no point in my throwing any more time, money or effort into saving something that can't be saved. Sure, I could turn up at his meeting today. I could object. I could kick up a fuss. I could tell everyone about how he seduced me last night – just for fun, or to manipulate me, or pretty much whatever exaggeration or flat-out lie popped into my head, to make him look bad.

But what's the point? All that time and energy, which I shouldn't be wasting on him – especially not at Christmas. Christmas is a time for spending with the people you love – the people who make you happy, not the people who make you sad. And when I really think about it, I don't think my mum would want me to bankrupt myself to save the shop. I think she'd want me to be happy, surrounded by my family, enjoying Christmas the way she would. Today I should be chasing my niece and nephew around a festive maze, not chasing after Seb, or trying to destroy him. Not going to his meeting is the right thing to do – I've missed it now anyway, so I'm not going to waste another second thinking about it.

I think Seb's sunk cost fallacy can be applied to so much more than gambling or business, more than things involving money – I think it can be applied to relationships too. Sure, I've had moments of thinking that there was something real between me and Seb – and maybe there was at one point – but just because we have had our moments where we get along, where we feel things for each other, where we have fun and forget about our differences…that doesn't mean I should stick with it, continuing to emotionally invest in him, hoping things will get better if I just keep trying, wasting all the love I have to give while I blindly hope that things will get better.

All of this needs to stop, right now. I need to stop wasting time, money, effort, tears and thoughts, on the shop, and on Seb. It's time to let go, to move on and find myself again, in a life that's about to change from everything I've ever known. And the first step to finding myself, is finding my way out of this maze.

The Winter Wonderland Maze changes with each festival, which is easily done given that it's made of real Christmas trees, all laid out side-by-side, in a new and confusing pattern each year.

It's made from over 300 Christmas trees, all decked out with pretty fairy lights. It's 3.30 p.m. now, so it's starting to get dark, which only makes the maze look even more beautiful. It would be a spectacular sight to behold, were it not for the fact I always feel so anxious in mazes, like I'll never find my way out. I know, that's supposed to be what makes it fun, but for some reason, I've never been any good at finding my own way.

Chloe and Harry charge off ahead of me like they always do, and as I walk through row after row of tall trees, I am reminded that this always happens, and that they always find the centre before me. Thankfully they usually come back to find me and help me find my way. That's what families are for, right?

It is also only now that I'm walking around it, that I recall just how frustrating it is – it's amazing how quickly the tress go from beautiful to irritating, when you suddenly find yourself lost.

A child (who is not one of the ones I brought with me today) charges past me. I attempt to follow him but he's just too fast, and before I know it I am face to face with a leafy dead end again.

I sigh deeply. Perhaps, if they did keep it the same every year, I might eventually learn my way around it, and save myself the inevitable embarrassment of getting lost, while my niece and nephew charge in, find the centre, and charge back out again – before realising I'm still in here somewhere, and coming in to find me.

I suppose it's good, that the maze has been made so safe that children can go in unattended, but it also means that there's no way I can cheat. I can't duck out the sides or climb over a tree. The only way in is the only way out, which is why I don't lose the kids – they lose me though.

I turn another corner and…I'm here. I'm in the centre of the maze. It's a relatively wide-open space, given how narrow the tree aisles are. The trees that face into the centre are covered with different-coloured lights, with lit-up reindeer and snowmen sitting on the grass. Right in the centre, hanging above me, is a disco ball, bouncing lights off in all directions, with a sparkly piece of mistletoe hanging from it. The best part of all though, is the snow falling, just here, just in this little square. They have a snow machine hidden away somewhere, which means that if you didn't know it wasn't really snowing, you could be forgiven for thinking you were in a real flurry.

The important thing is that I got here first, so I'm going to wait here until Chloe and Harry find me, to show them that their auntie isn't as useless as she seems sometimes.

'Ivy,' I hear Seb call from behind me.

Ergh, what is he doing here? Perhaps I won't stay here and wait after all, I think I just found the motivation to find my own way out.

'What are you doing here?' I ask angrily. 'Don't you have your town hall meeting?'

'I've had it already,' he says breathlessly. 'I thought you'd be there.'

I thought being trapped on a small island with Seb was bad, but it's nothing compared to being trapped in a literal maze with him.

'Nah,' I reply.

'Why not?' he asks, and I realise that the only way I'm going to get rid of him, is with an explanation.

'When I woke up this morning, I saw your plans scattered around the room. It made it feel so real, seeing which bits you were going to destroy, what you were going to replace them with… I almost got upset, but what's the point? So I just let it go.'

'You just let it go?' he repeats back to me. 'Just like that?'

'Yes, and I realised that you were right about one thing… I have my family. That's what is important to me – they'll always be there for me. So, sure, I could've turned up at your meeting and kicked off, but the kids wanted to come to the maze with me, so here I am. I just want to be happy and being with my family is what makes me happy.'

'Well, I'm happy that you're happy,' he tells me. 'You're absolutely right, with everything you just said.'

'Yay, I'm so happy to have your approval,' I say sarcastically. 'Now, if you don't mind.'

I go to leave, but Seb puts an arm out to stop me.

'Just hear me out, OK?'

'Do I have a choice?' I ask. I probably don't. Not because he'll force me to listen to him, but because I doubt I'll find the maze exit as quickly as I found the centre, and that will give him plenty of time to follow me, banging on at me with whatever it is he wants to say.

'Are you following me?' I ask, suddenly curious how he knew to find me here.

'Your sister told me you were here – Gaz told me you were in the maze.'

'I wish I'd known that before I bought them Christmas presents,' I reply with a sigh.

'I got out of the shower this morning, expecting you to be there, but you disappeared before we had chance to talk. I figured you would be at the meeting, so what I had to tell you could wait until then. In fact, I thought it would be better if you heard it at the meeting.'

'But then I didn't turn up and I ruined your plan – how selfish of me.'

Poor Seb, he's getting full-blown cynical, sarcastic Ivy today, the likes of which he hasn't witnessed until today. He isn't letting it throw him off though, which only fans my flame even more.

'I have lots of things in the world, plenty of money, but not many people. And you're absolutely right, I can't buy those, and that makes them even rarer than large plots of land in coastal towns, that already have planning permission,' he jokes. 'Humans get used to their situations, even if they're far from ideal. Without realising it, I became lonelier and lonelier, which is why I wanted to move to a small town in the first place.'

I raise my eyebrows impatiently. When is he going to tell me something I don't know?

'Last night was…amazing,' he blurts. 'I've never had a night like that before. Not just because of you, and my feelings for you, but because you gave me a piece of advice that I'd been in

202

desperate need of: I can't just turn up here and force myself to fit in; I need to change, to make myself the right kind of person who can fit in.'

'Right…'

'You got me thinking, when you asked me what was more important to me than money. I've been thinking about it all night, and I've realised that I want you more than any business. I've been trying to make a positive change in my life, but I've been going about it all wrong, thinking that the business is my reason to be here – it isn't. It's just the thing that's going to allow me to stay here, without having to worry about money.'

'So, what, you've had a change of heart and you're not going ahead with it?' I say, my cynically sarcastic tone reaching its peak.

'I am still going ahead with it,' he replies. 'But I revised my plans this morning, and I was hoping to show you them before you left. Then I thought, I don't know, that it might be romantic if you saw them for the first time at the meeting…but then you didn't show up to see them, so, here we are.'

'Seb, I'm so confused,' I admit, so exhausted with it all.

Seb opens his briefcase and takes out a rolled-up piece of paper. He opens it out onto the floor in front of us. I look down at it as fake snowflakes slowly fall on top of it. It's the same plan I've seen before – the beautiful, colourful artist's impression of the modern townhouses with dark cladding and grassy roofs, surrounded by blooming gardens and smiling faces…except it's changed. On the right-hand side of the plot are a series of small units, and on the front of one of them is a sign for my shop, Christmas Every Day.

'Erm…'

'The money you offered me last night,' he starts. 'You could invest it in the holiday community I'm building, and you can reopen a new and improved version of your shop there.'

'What?' I glance down at the plans again.

'We'll have your shop, a café, maybe a couple of other boutique shops. Then we'll have the holiday homes, and with the new bus route – you won't need to bring the customers to you, they'll already be there. What do you say?'

'You changed your plans?' I say.

'I did,' he replies.

'For me?'

'Of course for you.' He laughs. 'You think there's a lady with a café I'm trying to impress?'

'That's amazing,' I gush. 'Yes, I would love to invest.'

Ever since I learned that Seb was buying the shop, things have seemed so black and white. Either I was going to buy the place or Seb was. Sharing the space never occurred to me, not even once, which is crazy because there's definitely more than enough room on the plot for both of us. But the thing that is surprising me more than anything, is the fact that Seb is offering me this opportunity at all – that he's made this opportunity, just for me. I can't quite believe it. I didn't think he had it in him, to be kind like this. I am seeing him in a whole new light now (and it's not just because we're under a disco ball). I feel like I'm looking at him – the real him – for the first time.

I throw my arms around Seb, who picks me up and twirls me round, holding me in his arms when we finally stop spinning.

'I know that it won't be exactly the same shop as your mum's shop, but I'll do everything I can to make sure that it keeps all the charm and the warmth of the current place. But, either way, know that your mum would be so proud of you,' he says. 'I was chatting with Holly and—'

'You were chatting with my sister?' I interrupt.

'I called her to find out where you were,' he says. 'She, erm… she invited me for Christmas dinner. I hope that's OK.'

'It is now.' I laugh.

'Phew,' he replies. 'Don't know what I would've done other-wise.'

'That's a lot of work to ensure you have somewhere to spent Christmas,' I joke, nodding towards the plans.

'Oi, listen,' he says with a laugh. 'I'm trying to tell you something. We were talking about the shop, and about your mum, and I just know that she would be so proud of you, working so hard to save the place, and then with everything you're going to do with the new place. I promise, we'll make it even better. Maybe even set you up a kitchen, so you can make and sell your Christmas chocolates and sweets,' he suggests.

Wow, that would be amazing – to get to keep the shop, but to be able to go back to doing what I used to do, too. He's thought of everything.

'You did all this for me?' I say again, quickly wiping tears from my face. I've been so strong all day, but one mention of my mum and I'm blubbing like a baby.

'I did it for you, for the town, and for me,' he says seriously, before adding, 'and so you guys will let me have Christmas dinner with you.'

'Thank you,' is all I can say.

'Thank *you*,' he says. 'For helping me realise what I needed to do, to get what I've always wanted.'

'Well, I guess you're welcome.' I laugh, not that I had any idea I was doing anything.

'And, look at that, here we are again, underneath the mistletoe.'

I look up. 'So we are,' I reply. 'Is it my turn to kiss you first this time?'

'That only seems fair,' he replies. 'And safest. I wouldn't want to upset you – Gaz might find out and try to destroy my car with glitter again.'

'I like the sparkles,' I tell him. 'They're classy and festive.'

As Seb starts to laugh, I reach up and place my hands on his face. I'm too short to reach his face with my own, so Seb lifts me up into his arms so that I can kiss him. The snow falls down on us as our lips lock, and it's a passionate, loving kiss that means so much more than any of our others have (thanks to the anonymity of the first or the animosity surrounding the second). It's only as our lips part that we realise there's a small crowd of children watching us, and the two I brought with me are at the front.

'Auntie Ivy,' Chloe says, all smiles. 'You said he wasn't your boyfriend.'

'Erm, he wasn't before,' I say.

'But I am now?' he asks me.

'I feel like the parents of these children would be more comfortable – and have far less explaining to do – if I answered yes.' I laugh. 'So, yes?'

It occurs to me that it might be a weird way to enter into a relationship, with us both asking each other a question, but nothing about our relationship so far has been at all normal.

Yesterday, things felt so bleak. I felt like I was going to lose everything I had – which, admittedly, wasn't much. Now, not only do I get to keep it all, but I'm getting so much more too, and it looks like it's going to be everything I've ever wanted.

Chapter 28

Glancing out of the flat window, I look at the tree in the garden, where we scattered our mum's ashes.

'Ivy, can you sort the carrots, please?' Lee asks me.

'Yeah, sure,' I reply.

On this Christmas Day, just like on many of the ones that came before it, Lee and I are cooking the Christmas dinner. We actually make a pretty good team because when it comes to cooking, we share similar values.

We both agree on many important issues: that Brussels sprouts can taste amazing (if you cook them with bacon, chestnuts, and smother them in honey), that Christmas pudding is just as gruesome as Christmas cake (again, why doesn't it go off?!), and that – if you're doing things properly – under no circumstances should you cook your vegetables ahead of time and simply reheat them the next day (because half the fun is running around like a headless turkey, trying to make sure everything is ready at the same time).

While it may be tradition that Lee and I cook, we usually eat at Holly and Lee's house. This year is different though, what with it being the last Christmas before the shop as we know it is demolished. We thought it would be nice to have one last Christmas here, to honour our mum.

I strain the carrots before placing them in a dish. Then I do the same with the peas.

'You have Yorkshire puddings with your Christmas dinner?' Seb observes.

Oh, that's another change in tradition this year – no, not the addition of Yorkshire puddings, we always have those. This year, I'm not alone. I have Seb.

'You're in Yorkshire now, lad,' Lee tells him, in an overly exaggerated Yorkshire accent. 'Par for t'course.'

'I'm not complaining.' Seb laughs. 'I love Yorkshire puddings.'

'Dinner is ready, kids, come to the table,' Holly says, tearing them away from watching *Elf* on TV.

My dining table isn't very big, which is why we're using a pasting table that Holly and Lee brought with them. However, covered with my beautiful red and gold festive tablecloth, you'd never know the last time it was used it was for hanging wallpaper.

'Well, the number of people around this table is just going to keep growing and growing, isn't it?' Holly observes with a big smile.

'There's just one more, mummy,' Chloe says. I wonder how she'll react, when she finds out her mum is pregnant. Holly says she'll be fine, so long as she's expecting a girl. She doesn't think Chloe will want another brother.

'It's weird, having Christmas dinner here – it's been so long since we had Christmas dinner here,' Holly says. 'Do you remember the last time?'

'Yes.' I cackle. 'It was while Mum was still alive, but it was so disastrous. In fact, we'd had a few disastrous ones – that's why we started having them at your place.'

'What happened?' Seb asks curiously.

'Well, that last one…we had these crazy snowstorms in the run-up to Christmas. It wasn't so bad, until Christmas day, when we all gathered here and then the power went out. As soon as it got dark, we had to do everything by candlelight. Luckily we still cook with gas here, or we wouldn't have been able to eat Christmas dinner.'

'We'd bought loads of microwave stuff, telling my mum how much easier the cooking would be, if we could just bung half of it in the microwave.' Holly laughs. 'And then we had to do it the old-fashioned way.'

'It was kind of nice though, with all the candlelight, having to play board games to keep us entertained,' I say nostalgically.

'Until Lee got so mad playing Monopoly that he flipped the board,' Holly says.

'Yeah, all right,' Lee says embarrassed. 'They're not even mentioning the worst bit.'

'Oh yeah?' Seb asks.

'Yeah, not only was the power out, but we also got snowed in for two days. Luckily, this was before the kids were born, but there isn't much room here, and we had to eat Christmas dinner leftovers for more meals than I would've liked.'

'Oh yeah, I forgot about that.' Holly laughs.

'I suppose you've forgotten about the year you wore a cowboy hat to Christmas dinner,' I remind her.

'Oh, God, I was obsessed with Steps,' she says.

'You still are,' Lee says under his breath.

'It's nice.' Seb chuckles. 'That you guys have so many stories like this. I don't really have any stories…'

'Well, we've got loads,' Holly reassures him. 'And many more to come, I'm sure.'

'I know what Holly's worst Christmas was,' I offer.

'Oh, God, so do I,' Lee says. 'I'll be in the dog house if she tells this one.'

'Well, then I have to hear it,' Seb says, grabbing his drink.

'It was the first Christmas Lee was going to be spending with us – with me, Ivy and my mum,' Holly explains. 'My mum didn't know him all that well and, of course, she was worried that he might not be good enough for her daughter.'

'Holly warned me to be on my best behaviour, so I was,' Lee chimes in. 'I met up with a mate for a drink beforehand – and neither of us drank alcohol, to make sure I was in a good state when I turned up for dinner.'

'Except the idiots forgot to check the causeway times, so when it came time to leave, the tide was in,' Holly says. 'And what did he do? Did he call ahead and make a polite excuse? No. He drove into the bloody sea, got stuck there, and had to get the coastguard to rescue him.'

'You've seen the causeway, right?' Lee says, in his defence. 'It just looks like a big puddle.'

'Someone told me it was 6 feet deep at high tide.' Seb laughs.

'Whose side are you on?' Lee asks. 'We need to stick together, buddy. There's finally the same number of boys as there are girls at this table.'

'Maybe.' Holly laughs. 'Anyway, I was so, so angry with him for showing up late, and I was terrified of Mum finding out the reason why.'

'Did she?' Seb asks.

'I told her,' I confess. 'I was worried he wasn't good enough too.'

'Anyway, I was raging – at Lee, and at Ivy, but my mum just laughed. She calmed me down, Lee turned up eventually, and she approved.'

It's so wonderful, eating dinner together as a big family. Seb might just be one more person but, after Mum died, and it was just me going to Lee and Holly's for Christmas dinner, it felt like I was crashing their family dinner. Now, with Seb here, it feels like I'm bringing something to the table too.

We might be surrounded by boxes, ready for me temporarily moving out in the New Year, but this is the happiest Christmas I've had in a long time.

When we're finished with dinner Seb disappears for a few minutes, before returning with a box.

'One last present,' he tells me.

'Another one?'

'Last one, I promise,' he insists, handing me the box.

It's heavy so I place it down on the table in front of me, opening it carefully in front of my audience.

'My train,' I squeak, before my smile quickly falls. 'So you did steal it?!'

'I didn't steal it,' he replies. 'I...borrowed it.'

'Well, erm, thanks,' I reply.

'I got it fixed,' he tells me.

'What?'

'I told you before, I know a model train guy. I took it, hoping you wouldn't notice, so I could put it back – fixed. He only got it back to me yesterday, actually.'

'Seb, that's amazing! I thought it would never get fixed,' I chirp, running over to him to throw my arms around him.

'You're welcome.' He laughs, squeezing me tightly. 'When the new shop is ready, we'll see about extending the track maybe. My guy said he'd service the whole thing for you.'

'You're amazing,' I tell him, grabbing him for a passionate kiss.

'OK, you two, get a room,' my sister jokes awkwardly.

After dessert, Seb offers to do the dishes, even though I told him I don't have a dishwasher. And much to my surprise, Holly offered to dry them, saying that as Lee and I cooked dinner, it was only fair.

I walk up behind Seb and wrap my arms around him.

'You're wonderful,' I whisper into his ear.

'You're not so bad yourself,' he says, turning around to kiss me. 'Now, go put your feet up.'

I head for the sofa, where Lee and the kids are watching *The Grinch*.

Holly chases after me and gives me a big hug.

'What's that for?' I ask with a laugh. My sister isn't usually one for hugging.

'This is just nice,' she tells me. 'It feels like an old-fashioned Christmas, having it here.'

'I thought you hated those,' I remind her.

'I thought I was cooler than Christmas.' She laughs. 'And then Mum died and...it just reminded me too much of her.'

'It's not the same without her, is it? She was always the life and soul of Christmas and, now she's gone...'

'And now you're the life and soul of Christmas,' she tells me, squeezing my hand. 'You make Christmas just as amazing as Mum did when she was alive. She'd be so proud of you.'

Chapter 29

I pierce the whipped cream topping of my drink with a straw and take a big gulp.

'Wow, this is amazing,' I say, quickly going in for another sip.

'Do you really think so?' Sophie, the girl who runs the café asks. 'I made it in honour of your shop.'

I've never tried an iced gingerbread latte before. I suppose people don't usually want festive flavours in the heat of summer. It's so sweet of Sophie to think of me and my shop, when it comes to her menu.

'Honestly, it's delicious,' I insist. 'Just what I need on a hot summer's day like today.'

'It's me who should be thanking you,' she says. 'Relocating here is the best thing I ever did; there was a bit too much competition for me over on the island. And, selling your sweet treats is just the icing on the cake – no pun intended. People are going crazy for them.'

'Thank you for giving me an outlet to sell them,' I reply. 'It's nice to make them for more than just my friends and family.'

'They're incredible,' she says. 'It's so hard not to snack on them all day.'

I thank Sophie one last time before grabbing the two drinks

from the counter and heading next door, to the new and improved Christmas Every Day.

As I walk through the new door, the first thing that hits me is the air con, which is a welcome new addition. While there was always something fun about being around Christmas things during the summer months, I never did quite adapt to sweating my face off while surrounded by fake snow.

I make my way to the counter, which takes longer than it did in the old shop, because the new one is much bigger, and it's already full of customers, despite the holiday homes not being quite finished yet. Seb doesn't think it will be too long before they're finished and then the project will finally be complete. It's been a busy, full-on year so far, but it's the happiest I've been in a long time.

As I approach the counter, the steam train whizzes past me on a track above my head. It had been broken for so long, I'd forgotten just how amazing it was to see it in action. It's become the star of the shop again, and with new life breathed into it, I feel that little bit closer to my mum. It was her who bought it and set it up in the shop originally, after all.

I hand Gaz an iced gingerbread latte, which he swigs between serving customers.

'This is bloody good,' he tells me when he gets a few seconds' downtime.

I smile. I like to watch Gaz working; he's a real natural in the shop now, and a true expert in all things festive. He seems to love it too because, other than promising to dress up as Santa Claus for me again this coming Christmas so he can resume his Santa Story Time gig, he's given up travelling around, dressing up as different people. He says he's happy just being Gaz for a while, although I think that might be something to do with his flowering relationship with Charlie the vet.

'Oh, your balloons arrived,' he tells me, nodding towards a box.

'Great,' I reply, picking it up. 'I'll set them out.'

It's strange, because I know that we're in a new shop, but it still feels like we're in the old one. The building is much bigger, with a more modern feel, with big glass windows that give the place more natural light – of course, before, with our one little window at the front, I didn't have much room for showcasing all of our different types of window decorations and lights, so it's nice to have more space to do that.

While everything may appear different, I think it is that unmistakable Christmas atmosphere that we have here that has carried on, and that's why everything feels so familiar. It just goes to show, when I was so worried about relocating the shop before, that it wasn't the four walls that made it what it was, it was everything that I put inside it.

With more space, more opportunities have arisen for the shop. Now, we have a small section devoted to things from other seasonal occasions, so you can pick up things for Easter, Halloween, Valentine's Day, et cetera.

I head over to our little seasonal section, a little corner tucked away from all the Christmas stuff, open up the box and begin placing the special edition snow globes on the space I made for them earlier. They are made by the same man who makes the Marram Bay Christmas snow globes that I sell in the shop, but these aren't Christmassy at all. The intricate scene inside shows Marram Bay in all its sunny glory, at the height of our forthcoming Hot Air Balloon Festival. It truly is a spectacle, with hot air balloons dotted around in the sky. The snow globes depict it perfectly, and if you shake it up, it sparkles instead of snows. The snow globes have always been so popular, so I'm hoping these will be too, with all the tourists who will be coming to town especially for the occasion.

I feel a pair of hands on my hips.

'Hey, gorgeous,' Seb whispers into my ear.

'Hello,' I say brightly, turning around to face him.

I close my eyes and pucker up, just like I always do when I want to kiss him. It's not that I'm needy, or being especially sickly, but with him being a foot taller than me, it's my way of asking him to come down to my level so we can kiss.

'How's it going over there?' I ask.

'Good,' he replies. 'Although northern builders terrify me. I'm pretty sure Rich just broke his finger – he says "it'll be reet" though.'

'That sounds about right.' I laugh. 'We're much tougher than you southerners.'

'Says the woman who has to ask me to bend over so she can kiss me,' he teases.

'Well, I'm not exactly going to leap into your arms in front of all these people, am I?'

'Shame,' he jokes. 'I need to get back but, before I forget… You know how, by some miracle, you've managed to stand me for more than half a year now?'

'It has been tough,' I reply, faux seriously.

'Hmm,' he replies. 'Well, I thought we should celebrate, and what better way than to go to the place where we had our first date. The Lighthouse has reopened again, after their big refurbishment. I thought we could go there. We could even stay over, go a day without waking up on a building site.'

'God, you're amazing,' I say, practically in awe. I don't think a day has gone by since we got together, when Seb hasn't pleasantly surprised me in some way. He definitely isn't the ruthless businessman I thought he was to start with.

'Yeah,' he agrees with a cheeky laugh. He leans forward to kiss me again. 'Right, I'd better go make sure Rich hasn't lost a finger; see you this evening.'

'See you,' I call after him.

I sigh happily, before turning back to stacking the shelves.

After a couple of minutes, I feel someone grab me again. This time it's two people, my niece and nephew, who take a leg each and squeeze me.

'Hey, kids, how's it going?'

'They're driving me mad,' my heavily pregnant sister says.

'Wow, you get bigger every time I see you,' I exclaim.

'Thanks.' She laughs. 'You sure know how to make a girl feel good about herself.'

'Baby big, not big-big.' I laugh.

My sister flashes me a cheeky smile to let me know that she's joking.

'Kids, go see if Gaz has any candy canes,' Holly tells the kids, who gleefully charge over to see Gaz, ready to eat some seasonal sweets – off-season. That was always one of my favourite things about growing up here.

'Good news,' she starts. 'Lee is changing his job – well, his role, not his job. He's going to be working in Aberdeen, two weeks on, two weeks off. And that's after his generous paternity leave.'

'Hol, that's amazing,' I say, grabbing her, pulling her close for a hug. Well, as close as I can get to her, with her massive baby bump.

'It's definitely a huge weight off my mind,' she says. 'I don't know why I was so worried. I'm so excited now.'

'Me too,' I reply. 'I think Seb is as well... He keeps talking about gifts we can get you and asking questions.'

'Eek,' Holly says excitedly. 'It'll be you next.'

'Don't get carried away.' I laugh, placing the last snow globe on the shelf. 'Have you decided what you're going to call her yet?'

'I have,' my sister replies, looking down at her tummy, cradling it in her hands. 'We were thinking Audrey.'

A huge lump forms in my throat, at the mention of my mum's name. I feel my eyes well up.

'No, no crying,' my sister insists firmly. 'My hormones have got me crying every five minutes anyway, I don't need you setting me off.'

'That's a beautiful idea,' I tell her. 'A beautiful way to honour Mum.'

'I was always disappointing her, it's about time I did something that would make her proud,' Holly jokes.

'Mum knew you were just being "young and cool",' I say, making bunny ears with my fingers. 'You never disappointed her.'

'She'd be so happy, if she could see this.'

'What, a bigger, better version of her shop?' I reply, glancing around to admire our handiwork. I just can't stop looking at the place – it's amazing.

'No, she'd be happy seeing you, living your life, happy and in love,' my sister replies. 'That was always all she ever wanted for us.'

Acknowledgements

I cannot believe I am writing the acknowledgements on my tenth book! I can't believe my luck that I've been able to write ten, and not just write ten, but have people read them and enjoy them... I know how lucky I am, and I'm living proof that, if I can do it, anyone can. I don't want to say anything as cheesy as 'always follow your dreams' but do. Do what makes you happy, no matter how difficult it seems.

Thank you so, so much to Nia, the best editor an author could have. Nia is such a talented joy to work with and I feel so fortunate to have her on my team. Thank you to everyone at HQ Digital for their amazing work on all of my books. I couldn't imagine doing this with anyone else.

A massive thank you has to go to the people who take the time to read and review my books. Without readers I wouldn't be doing this – and without the fantastic reviewers who share such wonderful reviews of my books, reaching readers would be much harder.

Without the continued, unwavering support of my family, I wouldn't be doing this. Thank you to my parents for supporting me over the years – especially my mum, who might just be my biggest fan. Thank you to my amazing brothers, not just for their support, but for their friendship. I couldn't have asked for better brothers, or better best friends. Thank you to my wonderful gran, for showing me love and support that I didn't know possible, and thank you to my amazing dogs – my dogs are everything.

Finally, thank you to my incredible mister. He's the reason my world goes round. He's the reason I do everything I do. If I make him half as happy as he makes me, I know I'm doing something right. It's scary, to learn to rely on someone as much as I rely on him, but I couldn't be in safer, more loving hands.

If you liked Love and Lies at the *Village Christmas Shop*, turn the page for an extract from Portia MacIntosh's laugh-out-loud romance *Summer Secrets at the Apple Blossom Deli*…

Chapter 1

Today is the first day of the rest of my life. Well, that's what the dog-eared copy of *The Guide to New Beginnings* currently poking out of my handbag on the front seat has been trying to convince me.

The last month has been a bit of a blur. It feels like just yesterday I was sitting at my desk, mindlessly yet happily going through the motions when one of my bosses perched on the corner of my desk, offered me a new job in a different location and, before I knew what I was doing, I said yes. A more exciting role in the company and a pay increase appealed, of course, but more than anything it was the chance take my 8-year-old son out of life in inner-city London and raise him in a cute little coastal village up north. I've been worrying about a few things recently and getting out of the city seemed like the best solution – the only solution, really.

I was born and raised in Croydon, only moving closer to central London as I got older. My son Frankie has never known anything other than life in central London, living in a small flat, catching the tube to school every day. This isn't the life I want for him though. I want him to grow up in a small town, in a close community. Somewhere with scenery and fields with real grass, away from the pollution and commuting to school on busy trains, overflowing with unfriendly people.

I love my city and I'm proud of my roots, but after living here for all of my thirty-one years on this planet so far, now just feels like the right time to leave and try somewhere new.

I've always liked the idea of a fresh start. When I was much younger I would look forward to New Year's Eve because to me, starting a new year felt like starting a new chapter of my life. I used to start each year with a brand-new notebook, a diary of my thoughts. It's been a long time since I did that though, what with taking on more and more work as the years have ticked away – and being a single mum doesn't exactly allow for much free time. That's all going to change now though.

As well as the self-help book I've been reading to help me prepare, I also have a new Moleskine notebook ready for me to document my journey in just like I used to. I might not have my usual backdrop of fireworks and 'Auld Lang Syne' to thrust me into my new beginning, but as the journey up north progresses, the concrete jungle we're so used to has slowly but surely transitioned to fields of green and wide open space, and it is exactly the breath of fresh air I've been gasping for.

I'm too busy taking in the scenery to remember to change gear at a junction so the car stalls, giving us a jolt strong enough to wake Frankie up.

'Mum,' he whines sleepily.

I glance at him in my rear-view mirror and watch him rub his tired eyes.

'Sorry, kiddo,' I say. 'Your mum isn't used to driving a manual.'

Frankie doesn't need me to tell him that; this isn't the first time I've messed up with the gears today. Well, living in the city centre, I've never needed a car, so I haven't driven one in years. The only car I have driven occasionally – my mum's – is an automatic. Still, it was so nice of my bosses to give me a company branded VW Beetle to drive up here in and use as a run-around, even if it is an offensive shade of lime green. They've also rented us a cottage that looked positively picturesque in the photos they showed me. It feels weird, moving here without having visited, but everything happened so quickly. I'm sure there was time to do things properly, to come and scope the place out and make sure it was everything I hoped it would be, but I just really wanted to get out of town so that Frankie could start the new school year with everyone else – well, that's what I told them, at least.

'Are we there yet?' Frankie asks for the first time. I'm proud of him, for being so well behaved. Most kids would go bananas during a long car journey but my boy has only started to grow impatient in the last thirty minutes.

'We are,' I tell him excitedly, although I can't help but notice that he doesn't seem as pumped as I am. 'You excited?'

'I guess,' he replies. 'It's gonna be weird.'

'It's gonna be *amazing*,' I remind him. 'I know you'll miss your school and your friends, but you're going to make new friends, you're going to go to a much better school. We're going to live in a big house and there will be fields where you can play, and we can walk to the beach – every day, if you'd like.'

'There's no McDonald's,' he tells me in a smart tone, as though he's sure I already knew that. In truth, I did already know that there wasn't going to be a McDonald's nearby, and that we were going to have to travel thirty miles to get my son a fix of his favourite chicken nuggets. Apparently, no matter how hard I try, I just can't make them as 'good' as McDonald's can.

'There is a McDonald's just a short drive away,' I tell him. It might not be the same as London, where there's a Maccies on every corner, but it's going to be fine. 'You're going to have everything you had in London, plus more.'

'Sam said he's been before to visit his nan and granddad, and he said it was boring,' Frankie informs me.

'Where?' I ask curiously, although I'm pretty sure his fourth favourite friend from school isn't the right person to be taking this kind of advice from.

'The north,' he replies.

I can't help but laugh.

'The north is pretty big, kiddo. And maybe it was boring because he was visiting his grandparents' house – grandparents are boring.'

'Viv isn't boring,' Frankie insists.

'No, she certainly isn't,' I reply.

My mum, Vivien, isn't at all grandma-ish – she won't even let Frankie call her Gran, she says she looks too young, and, in her defence, she does. She's always been conscious of showing her age, insisting I call her Viv instead of Mum. She puts her all into being a cool grandparent and, to be fair, she's great at it. She was a cool mum too, much to my embarrassment. It's going to be weird, not being just a short train ride away from her.

After driving through nothing but green fields and dry stone walls for a while, Marram Bay is suddenly visible in the distance.

There are two ways we can go; one of them seems the right way, but the satnav insists we go the other, so I stick to what the map tells me and head for the town centre.

'We're here, kiddo,' I announce.

'It looks boring,' Frankie says with a sigh.

At the start of the trip he seemed excited. In fact, I think we spent the first hour of the journey singing along to the radio.

To try and distract my son, I flick the radio back on.

'...and I'm sure you'll all be pleased to hear that Rufus the Labrador is safely back at home now. And that completes today's breaking news,' a voice on the radio says. I make eye contact with Frankie in my rear-view mirror. He looks just as confused as I do.

'We'll be finishing the show earlier today, to join in with the festivities on the front. Tune in tomorrow to hear all about it. Ta-ra.'

'So I'm guessing that's the local radio station,' I laugh. 'Wanna go check out the festivities?'

Frankie sighs.

'OK.'

Marram Bay is such a beautiful town. It's small – even smaller than I expected. The town is cute, like something fresh out of a romantic movie – with ivy creeping up the walls and around the sweet little windows of the houses sitting at the top of perfectly tended gardens. Few houses look the same here, which I like. Everywhere has so much individuality and character.

It takes us no time to go from green, open space, to farmhouses, to cottages, and finally to the seafront with its cute, quirky little shops.

'Erm...' I can't help but say, catching sight of the bizarre festivities on the seafront.

'Where are we?' Frankie asks.

'*When* are we?' I laugh to myself.

Upon closer inspection the town doesn't just look old-fashioned – it looks like the setting for a Second World War book. The windows are covered with white tape, everyone is dressed in out-of-date clothing and the place is overrun with soldiers and army vehicles.

As we crawl along the road running alongside the seafront, we catch the attention of a woman in her late thirties. She's wearing a blue and white polka dot tea dress teamed with navy gloves, complemented by her brown hair that is neatly pinned into victory rolls. I stop the car at the side of the road, just as our eyes meet.

'Are we in the past?' Frankie asks.

Of course, I know that we're not – that we couldn't possibly be, unless we've wandered into some sort of *Goodnight Sweetheart* portal – but I don't really have an answer for him.

I smile at the pinup girl at the side of the road, only for her to cock her head in puzzlement. Why is *she* confused? I'm the one suddenly in the past. She calls over her friends – a land girl and an apparent member of the WRAF – who join her in staring over at us, chatting amongst themselves.

'Maybe we should go,' I say, but as I go to drive away, I – of course – stall my car again. Come to think of it, the lime-green, company-branded Beetle is probably the reason everyone is staring at us.

After another judder, it occurs to me that my loud (both in volume and colour), German car is probably ruining the war-era aesthetic of the festivities.

'Ship, ship, ship,' I say repeatedly, until I finally get the car moving and drive off.

'Swears!' Frankie chastises me.

'I said "ship",' I point out. 'Remind me who is the kid and who is the mum?'

'I could ask you the same thing,' he replies.

Frankie is smart for an 8-year-old, however, as a by-product of this intellect, he thinks he is much smarter than he is. I know that I should probably be the one keeping Frankie in check but he's no bother at all…which is probably why he ends up keeping me in check instead.

'Let's go see the house,' I say cheerily. 'We'll meet the locals some other time.'

Like, I don't know, maybe this decade instead.

After spending the past few weeks – and a chunk of our journey here – trying to convince my son that we would be moving somewhere wonderful, I've driven him straight into some kind of weird place that seems to be literally stuck in the past. But in two minutes we'll be at the beautifully titled Apple Blossom Cottage.

I glance quickly between my satnav and the road until we approach our destination. I spot the cottage of my dreams, hiding away behind a wall of leafy trees. Through the green leaves, the stone bungalow almost looks like part of the landscape. I'm so used to living in London, surrounded by either ugly old office blocks or new, ultra-modern, sky-grazing skyscrapers. Outside the garden walls, Apple Blossom Cottage is enclosed by nothing but fields – this change of scenery is exactly what I need.

It's a small, but gorgeous little cottage, just perfect for the two of us. The stone walls are covered with all different kinds of climbing plants, from ivy to roses, giving it a uniquely colourful beauty that I haven't seen before. The white-framed windows are small, peeping out from behind the plants. The frames look like perhaps they need replacing – not that I'm an expert, they just look a little tired. Then again, I imagine that's what you'd think if you looked at me at the moment, courtesy of the bout of stress I'm suffering. I'm hoping that as soon as we get our things moved in, I can finally let go of my stress and relax into country life.

The place reminds me so much of a smaller version of Kate Winslet's cottage from *The Holiday* (only with a far superior garden), and while I'd always thought of myself as more of a Cameron Diaz type, I feel like this is the place for me.

I step out of the car and take a photo on my phone. I want to remember my first glimpse of our new home for the rest of my life. I don't just feel like I've arrived – *I've arrived*. I'm here, outside this perfect house, in a gorgeous small coastal town, about to start my dream job with my healthy, intelligent son by my side. Maybe it is possible to have it all…at least, that's what *How to Have It All*, another of my hastily bought self-help books, has been trying to tell me. Packing up and starting your life again is a big deal, so I wanted to do some reading, make sure I was prepared for anything and everything. This job is so important to me, but Frankie is even more important. I just want to be a good mum – preferably one of those ones you see on Instagram with an adorable baby in one arm, and a wooden spoon in the other, standing in their immaculate kitchen (bigger than all the rooms in my London flat added together), posing in a way that makes them look like a Victoria's Secret model.

My proportions are more Victoria sponge cake, than Victoria's Secret model. Sure, we're a society who celebrates the 'dad bod' (Leonardo DiCaprio is like a fine wine, only growing more devastatingly gorgeous by the moment) but they won't be putting my 'mum bod' on any catwalks in barely there underwear anytime soon. But each stretchmark and varicose vein maps the journey I went on to come back with my son, and I'd take that over a Victoria's Secret model body any day – even if it would significantly increase my chances with the aforementioned Mr DiCaprio.

I chase my son, who is currently part-boy, part-aeroplane, in the back garden.

'Wow.' My jaw drops.

It is suddenly apparent where Apple Blossom Cottage gets its name from: the army of apple trees surrounding the garden, and the apple blossom plants scattered amongst the greenery and brightly coloured flowers, that I'm not even going to pretend I can identify. I don't know much about apple trees, but I'm guessing early September is when these beauties are at their best, because there are apples everywhere.

Frankie runs over to me with an apple in each hand.

'Can we eat them?' he asks.

'We have to wash them first, but yes,' I reply, delighted that my chicken nugget-craving son is suddenly thrilled at the thought of an endless supply of apples. 'We could even bake an apple pie, would you like that?'

Frankie nods.

'Better than the ones at McDonald's,' I tell him, instantly regretting mentioning the 'M' word, but it doesn't seem to bother him. Baking is not something that I'm good at, but I'm sure it still counts if we buy readymade pastry and simply assemble the pie, right?

I stroll over to the large pond at the end of the garden and lean over, looking at my reflection in the water. Maybe I can earn strong, single-woman, pie-baking, yummy-mummy status here – wouldn't that be nice?

'Can I unlock the door?' Frankie asks excitedly.

'Carefully,' I tell him, handing him the keys from my bag. 'I'll be right behind you.'

Inside my bag, in the hidden pocket usually reserved for 'women's things' and the rape alarm I always felt an uneasy need to keep on me at all times in central London, the corner of a postcard pokes out. I quickly push it back inside and zip it up. I'll worry about that later.

Frankie flies off towards the front door excitedly as I try to keep up with him in my heels. I'm just walking around the corner when I hear his voice.

'Er...Mum,' he shouts, and I don't like the sound of it at all.

Dear Reader,

Thank you so much for taking the time to read this book – we hope you enjoyed it! If you did, we'd be so appreciative if you left a review.

Here at HQ Digital we are dedicated to publishing fiction that will keep you turning the pages into the early hours. We publish a variety of genres, from heartwarming romance, to thrilling crime and sweeping historical fiction.

To find out more about our books, enter competitions and discover exclusive content, please join our community of readers by following us at:

🐦 *@HQDigitalUK*

f *facebook.com/HQDigitalUK*

Are you a budding writer? We're also looking for authors to join the HQ Digital family! Please submit your manuscript to:

HQDigital@harpercollins.co.uk.

Hope to hear from you soon!